Don't Shoot The Messenger Bag

by

Wendy Kendall

In Purse-Suit Mystery

Cover Art by *Teddi Black*

The Wild Rose Press, Inc.
PO Box 708
Adams Basin, NY 14410-0708
Visit us at www.thewildrosepress.com

Publishing History
First Edition, 2026
Trade Paperback Print ISBN
Digital ISBN

In Purse-Suit Mystery
Published in the United States of America

Dedication

To my dear parents John & Pam Kendall

To my dear sons Alex and Brad

Chapter One

"Tonight's the night to risk it. The New Year's Eve will keep the cops busy." His words came with wisps of breath hanging on the crisp, cold air. The clear night sky enticed him.

He went on with his familiar lecture, "No ridiculous law restricting flight to daylight hours should be enforced, especially in Seattle's dead of winter."

"I know." Amber sighed and pulled her long, thick brown hair back over her shoulders. "Darkness dominates sixteen hours out of twenty-four."

Thankful for the day off from work at the Purse-onality Museum gift shop, Amber had enjoyed a fun evening watching fireworks. She'd dressed in her customary tight-fitting jeans, tucked into her fluffy white, high ankle boots. Her lacy, baby blue blouse, her favorite color, stood out above the zipper of her winter jacket that casually fitted to her waist.

Nicky wore his ever present souvenir jacket from the aeronautics museum, adding warmth to his sweatshirt and jeans. He made an obvious move to check on Gladys across the street. Her house sat dark and silent. No sign of the old busybody sitting vigilant at her living room window, so no concern she'd shout complaints at him or call the police. Nicky prepared to launch off the balcony. He'd wanted to be a pilot ever since he could remember. Piloting his drone drew him closer to a someday dream. Time for a reconnaissance night flight.

Amber grinned, as she sensed Nicky's excitement when the drone rose. The flashing red and green lights against the starry background intensified. He maneuvered the drone away from the house, dodged trees, and avoided the beach. She suspected he wanted to protect the coveted new camera from an accidental dive into the water.

He steered toward the top of the street. Over the hill he'd be into the college campus, but he slowed it over the field instead. The drone's LED lights floated over the ground. Nicky concentrated on the live feed. Amber peered over his shoulder, impressed by the screen's clarity.

Amber jumped when a low voice boomed from the balcony threshold, "So, Nicky Mercurio celebrates New Year's with his joystick."

Nicky's hold slipped. He adjusted the drone's altitude and laughed. "Jealous?"

"Not tonight. Everyone's partying down at the fire pit on the beach. I came back for a thicker jacket." William waved at Amber. "Hey, Amber, I saw your man Michael in the kitchen. He says yes for the beach party, if you want to go. Interested?"

"Oh yeah."

"Nicky, how about you?"

"I'm good." Nicky grinned. "I'm getting in flying time while no one's around."

"Cool." William leaned on the balcony rail and scanned the sky. "I don't see it."

Nicky pointed up the hill. "In the field. I saw something on the other side of that tree in the south corner of the lot."

William paused. "Now I see the lights. Got the new camera working?"

Amber nodded. "With a video sharp and clear as cut glass."

Nicky clicked through some options on the controller's settings tab. "I'm switching to the new infrared."

William laughed. "Sounds like geek time."

"Check out this close up." Nicky showed William the screen.

"Shoes? What's next to them?" He pointed at the screen. "Can you zoom in?"

Nicky pulled the controller back again. "I'll fly lower around the tree for a better angle."

William squinted. "That's a dude."

Nicky went wide eyed. "He's totally face down and passed out."

Amber studied the screen. "Is he hurt? Should we go help him?"

William sighed. "He'll wake up with a hangover, sorry he partied."

Nicky flipped a switch and brought the drone lower. "My thermal readout shows cold."

"I told you, man. It's freezing tonight." William zipped up his jacket.

Nicky groaned. "No, the guy's body temperature. He only registers 91 degrees."

Amber gasped. "What?"

William checked the readout. "That's not normal."

Nicky frowned. "Either my new thermal camera is broken, or the guy's in big trouble."

William's grip on the railing tightened as he peered through the darkness. "Or he's dead."

Chapter Two

"Warm enough?" Jason wrapped an arm around Katherine.

"Snuggled beside you? Of course." She'd thrown caution to the wind, choosing fashion over warmth. At dinner Jason's lingering gaze communicated appreciation for her flirty strapless dress and most romantic perfume. Now she stood outside in the middle of the winter's night, shivering with excitement in her trendsetting coat. Handsome cop, and he's off duty on a holiday. Amazing.

She waved the small bouquet of delicate flowers. "I love these. Thank you. You called them snowdrops?"

He gave her a playful kiss. "Even though they grow in winter, it took a little detective work to find some around here. They're a gift of hope, new beginnings, and the promise of meaningful time together."

She leaned closer against him. "I love your hobby of flowerful meanings, and I admire your detective work to find such a romantic New Year's Eve gift."

Jason cut a suave silhouette. Fitted new jeans, beige button-down shirt, and brown blazer under his black overcoat. He stood squarely in dark brown dress shoes. With a playful maneuver in her sparkling black heels, Katherine brushed the top of her foot down the back of Jason's leg. New Year's Eve comes only once a year, and a provocative midnight kiss lay ahead.

What a holiday miracle to be with Jason tonight. How he'd dodged patrol duty remained a mystery she could happily live with. The hazards of dating a cop include a lack of special occasion availability. She put her arm around his back and felt the discreetly hidden belt bag containing a department gun, badge, and phone. Hopefully the new year begins with firework bangs, not an alert blasting from Jason's phone.

From behind the iconic Space Needle landmark, over five hundred drones dramatically rose together in multiple, precise lines creating a formation of mechanical birds worthy of a Hitchcock movie. Ten, fifteen, now more long lines of them sparkled their colored lights in the sky. Speakers strategically placed throughout the famous Seattle Center came to life with a brassy jazz rhythm improvisation. The music swelled. The crowd poised in silence for the first time tonight, watching. Suddenly the drones broke from their lines, swirled into chaos, and shut off their lights.

Katherine joined in the delighted applause and cheers when the flock turned their lights back on to suddenly reveal their new formation, creating a picture of Saturn with its rings. Then more drone planets joined Saturn and surrounded the Space Needle. The music changed to "The Planets" classical music, and the crowd cheered.

Fireworks exploded onto the scene. The noise, the drama, and the colors sparked Katherine's imagination for an adventurous year ahead. Boom! A series of exploding flashes brightened the sky.

On tiptoe so Jason could hear her better, Katherine spoke over the noise, "Fabulous. Don't you love it?" It hadn't been easy to convince Jason to come to the Space

Needle celebration and face downtown crowds.

"What a great time together." He gave her an affectionate squeeze.

Minutes to midnight and kiss-ready, Katherine threw her arms around Jason. He immediately responded, and she warmed all over with their spontaneous kiss. An explosive series above them rocked her a bit off balance, and Jason's embrace grew stronger, pulling her closer as he lifted her off her feet. When they slowly parted, fireworks once above the structure now burst from the Space Needle. Explosions climbed one by one in sequence from the bottom of the Needle to the top, each one second apart until the ultimate midnight explosion off the top. The traditional new year's song sounded. Jason passionately kissed her again.

He brushed back a lock of her auburn hair. "Happy New Year to us." She waited with anticipation as he leaned in again. A group of preteens waving sparklers danced into them, bumping them apart.

Katherine and Jason laughed. Parents rushed over and apologized. Katherine shook her head. "No apologies. Happy New Year!" Jason took her hand.

Gasps from the crowd punctuated the cold winter air with puffs of breath. A spectacular frenzy of fireworks astounded the crowd. The show built to its finale. The drones re-formed their original straight lines and slowly descended to land out of sight. A musty cloud blanketed the Needle, and all explosions stopped.

Bright plaza lights beamed on, encouraging the crowd to disperse. Katherine squinted. She stretched and scanned the horizon. Toward the top of the stairs to one of the park's exits a familiar figure stood out in the crowd. Tomás? She struggled to see his wife, Donna.

Jason wrapped an arm back around her waist. "And so, this year begins with a bang and a lot of smoke. I know where there's a cozy fireplace built for two. Ready to go?" Katherine squeezed him tight in agreement.

Their fingers entwined as they moved to the exit opposite where she'd possibly seen Tomás. They walked in a romantic haze.

"I thought we might see trouble." He pointed to the street gridlock and groaned at the long lines of cars. Nothing but bright red taillights and intersection signals in all directions.

Standing on the sidewalk by their three-story parking garage, Katherine groaned. "Too bad we got here late and parked at the top. We're stuck behind a long line going nowhere." She shifted from one foot to the other in the cold.

Jason checked up and down the street. "Sweetheart, how about we relax at McGinnis Pub until it all clears out, and then we'll sail out of here. Come on." He gently pulled her arm.

Enthusiasm renewed, she gave a joyful little hop. "I'm with you."

The charming pub provided a welcome hideout. They grabbed a table next to the roaring fireplace. Katherine put her drooping flowers on the table in a plastic cup of water. She basked in the glow of the flames reflected in Jason's eyes, as they sat close and enjoyed each other's company. Jason leaned back. "Not the fireplace I had in mind, but it'll have to do."

She ordered a mellow latte to match the tone of Jason's voice as he whispered softly in her ear. Jason drank hot chocolate. The place filled quickly. The happy and hopeful mood showed in strangers' laughter, energy, and wishes for a great year ahead. As table space ran out, they invited another couple to share their table.

Periodically Jason, Katherine, and others checked if traffic had unsnarled. As hours passed, moods deteriorated. Staff tired. Management stopped taking orders but generously allowed customers to remain inside for a while. The late, but inevitable closing came without warning. Katherine grabbed her cup of flowers, and they joined other stragglers on the street and headed back to the parking garage, where it appeared no cars had moved. Katherine refastened the top two buttons on her coat.

Climbing the stairs to the top floor, Katherine stood and caught her breath. A van parked with doors wide open, blasted music, and hosted people wrapped in blankets sitting outside on folding chairs. Others huddled in their cars, a few with motors idling. Some drivers paced. Some argued with each other. Jason led her toward the pickup truck. She stopped by a burly man who stared over the side railing with longing at the street below.

Katherine peered down too. "You've been here since the fireworks ended?"

He grunted. "No one's gone anywhere. Traffic's totally blocked."

Katherine's voice trembled. "Not any better?"

He hesitated, as if debating candor over optimism. "Another twenty minutes and we'll be out of here?" His tentative tone undermined the encouraging words.

Jason sighed. Katherine searched for a reassuring response, "Not much longer then…"

He gritted his teeth. "I've got three kids in the back

of my car and a tired wife. I better get back over there."

Katherine gave the man some mint candies the pub had given out. "For your kids."

They wished each other a fast exit. Walking away, Jason said, "I don't know about twenty minutes. I can't believe Seattle's finest haven't jumped in directing traffic."

"Seattle's finest? Do I hear sarcasm?"

"I'm simply pointing out, somebody dropped the ball on a predictable dilemma." Jason sighed again. "If a certain someone hadn't been concerned over messy hair and possibly tearing her dress on the motorcycle, we'd have been out of here hours ago."

She protested, "Who could have foreseen this?"

He unlocked the truck. "Let's sit inside for twenty minutes…or more."

Jason checked his phone. "Once we're out of here, the freeway to Bayside shows clear."

The partiers' music blared. More drivers joined those arguing, and the shouting escalated. Katherine wondered when fists would fly. The twenty-more-minutes-man leaned face down on his arms over the steering wheel. Her heart went out to the weary young couple in the sedan beside her window appeasing their crying baby. All parking spaces remained full, and more vehicles stalled bumper-to-bumper in the driving lanes. Her phone showed twenty minutes after three. Would they get home by the time the late winter sun rose?

"Jason, whenever things go wrong people say, 'Why doesn't someone do something about this?' Well, I'm someone."

He leaned back against the headrest with eyes closed. "You are someone."

Katherine checked her bouquet in the cup holder, grabbed her purse, and opened her door. She moved quickly across the lot and down to the second floor. She stood in the middle of the lane behind a car inching forward. She held up one hand to stop it and give the other driver space to back up. Two young boys stared through the rear window teary eyed, mouths wide open.

Now she saw the flaw in the garage system. Those parked on the lower floors could only exit by driving all the way up to the top floor and then back down the only exit route. Drivers didn't take turns moving, instead they blocked each other.

It took a few minutes, but with Katherine's guidance the cars on that second floor moved. She made her way back toward the top floor. Directing in earnest, Katherine found herself turning one way, then suddenly around the other way. Her purse swung wildly at times. Its golden glitter glistened in the garage lights. Slowly, the parade of vehicles moved again. Katherine blushed as drivers and passengers shouted appreciation for her efforts.

She slowed in her walk up the final ramp to the top floor. Frowning, Jason stood at the side railing. He held the phone tight and spoke in a measured tone.

As he glanced her way, his discouraged scowl stood in clear contrast to her proud smile of accomplishment. He mouthed the words, "Seattle Police."

She resumed traffic enforcement nearby. When he clicked off the phone she said, "Cavalry on the way?"

"Who knows, ma'am. They insist they're in charge of the big city and don't need advice from a lowly Bayside officer. I'm supposed to stick to my turf." He put the phone in his pocket.

Katherine motioned the twenty-more-minutes man

forward. He rolled down his window. "Bless you."

She had Jason's full attention now. Determined to impress, Katherine held up a hand and stepped forward with authority to stop the sports car with the racing engine. She jumped at hearing the vehicle's horn, followed by loud shouts and cursing. Katherine emphasized her command by pumping her hand in the air a couple of times. That brought more horn blasts. The impaired driver inched forward, alternating between brake and tapping the gas pedal. Katherine refused to move. The engine reverberations echoed. Katherine felt a steel grip on her arms as Jason jerked her out of the lane and into a tight embrace.

The car roared straight into the family car and pushed it into the car ahead of it. Children screamed in sync with shouting adults. Jason and Katherine rushed forward to check for injuries. Fortunately, everyone had their seatbelts on and remained fine.

The man who had blessed her for motioning him ahead had a few choice words for her now, as he struggled to open the car door. The drunk race car driver walked up and gruffly pushed her aside.

"Hey! Stop right there." Jason paused quieting the kids and held up his badge. The two drivers ignored him and exchanged blows. Katherine slinked out of their way, as more frustrated men joined the argument.

Sirens sounded. Three Seattle motorcycle cops arrived. Two went to work breaking up the fight. One called for backup and said to no one in particular, "We're getting complaints about someone stopping cars and causing traffic problems."

Before Katherine could say a word, Jason pulled her with determination in the opposite direction. More cops arrived, and they directed traffic around the accident.

Katherine massaged her bruised ego. "Well, I tried solving the problem."

In a mocking tone, Jason slowly repeated her invitation to him last week. "Let's go to the Space Needle. We'll have fun. We'll party. There's no rain forecast."

She had to defend herself. "Someone needed to do something. I'm someone…"

She turned to face him, then laughed at his broad grin. He said, "You are someone." He held her tight against him.

His phone alert vibrated against her heart. In one smooth move Jason shielded the screen, read the message, then handed her the keys. "I'll meet you at the truck." With a brief kiss on the lips, he walked away before she could see the message or say a word.

She turned the ignition key and then the heater to on, then settled into the passenger seat. Across the lot, Jason had interrupted one of the Seattle cops, flashed his badge, then his phone, and then pointed in her direction. The cop nodded. Jason hurried back.

Motorcycle lights glared and sirens turned on as cops cleared a path for them. Jason put the truck in gear. "I'll drop you at your place. I have to go on duty." He remained tight-lipped, while maneuvering past the other vehicles. Some people gestured and shouted at her, as they drove down the ramp to the floor below.

As he gripped the steering wheel, Katherine reached out to hold Jason's hand, then stopped herself. He'd entered the police world. Would secrets always come between them when duty called? She stared at Jason's phone lying face down between them.

Chapter Three

It had been a long night in the city and a long sleep in New Year's morning felt great. Katherine woke to the sight of her lovely snowdrops bouquet on her bedside table. Mindful of Jason's warning that the flowers are toxic to pets, she'd kept her bedroom door closed preventing Purrada from wandering in for a cat to Kat snuggle. She did not want to risk her cute stray, but she wanted to enjoy her gift.

The seductive scent of roasted coffee coaxed Katherine from her private living space over the Purse Museum. She dressed, curious why her Museum's Clutch Cafe opened on the holiday. She laughed as she brushed her hair. That name perfectly captured Pam Watson's sense of humor as she'd proclaimed, "Baysiders view an empty latte cup as a clutch situation." A funny testimonial to her dear grandmother's own eternal search for her next pot of tea.

Katherine's mind shifted to last night's sudden phone alert. She checked online news and found a brief report about a dead man found in a field, details to follow. That must be where Jason rushed after their quick good night at her door. No news from him either, not that she expected he'd text her.

The cat skidded into the hall, stopping at Katherine's feet. An indignant, high-pitched yowl announced her pampered pet's demand for attention. Their eyes met, and Purrada uttered a regal meow. Katherine picked her up and scratched that favorite spot behind the ears. "Scared of your own shadow?"

Katherine caught another whiff of coffee, and the sound of the steamer mixed with laughter. The cat jumped to the floor and trotted away, no doubt in search of a secluded corner within the rambling home and exhibits. Katherine scolded, "Relax for the holiday, Purrada. No guests for you to jump out and scare from one of your hiding spots."

Once downstairs, Katherine pulled her sweater tight and stopped at the thermostat. The digital outside temperature showed below freezing. She shook her fist at the display then took a deep breath. Threatening the messenger won't stop winter. She sighed and turned up the heat.

Right now, she could be on a Southern California beach, basking in sunny warmth and her fashion business. She'd made the choice to spend family holidays in Washington, the state of drizzle. She lingered and leaned against the wall remembering December's treasured memories with her grandparents, her sons, her family. Nothing could compete with those good times. The holidays had ignited heartwarming sparks with Jason too.

She anticipated a busy new year ahead designing new fashion and expanding her Bayside Purse Museum. Thank goodness Moonjava stepped in as barista at the @Clutch Café when the job fell vacant. It would be a challenge to replace her. Moonjava energized everyone daily with more than specialty brews. MJ shared mystical steam, recommended yoga poses, and offered unique meditations. Customers appreciated her. She wished her Moonjava mother behind the bar could be a permanent solution. Katherine knew long term and MJ fit together like delicate, beaded straps on a backpack, a novel idea sure to end in spilled hopes. She pulled out her phone and moved barista interviews up in priority on her to-do list.

As Katherine cut through the Purse Museum exhibits, she straightened the Coming Soon sign for the new 1960's Women's Exhibit. Designing this attraction with MJ had been a lot of fun. They made a good mother/daughter team, on their rare collaborations. An uncommon mother, they'd shared some best times together.

When they'd both rushed back to Bayside last year to help Gran, the pull of family had been strong. Then the crisis passed, and hippie MJ strained against the suggestion of roots. MJ left herself a quick exit route, as she had her whole life. She signed a month-to-month lease on an apartment away from the family home.

Abrupt endings had littered Katherine's childhood. MJ didn't like goodbyes when she quietly skipped away. Someone else always delivered MJ's bad news to Katherine. Childhood longing still hit square in Katherine's heart when thoughts surfaced of MJ's many disappearances. How she'd longed for her mother, never knowing when MJ would return. Katherine had learned to mask her impatience for her mother's eventual surprise welcome home. Pure happiness together, and then the cycle inevitably continued.

Katherine shook off the somber emotions. She and MJ shared great times now, and she'd been lucky to grow up with her loving grandparents. They'd given her all their love, encouraged her own taste for tea, and passion for designing purses.

She paused at the Hattie Carnegie purse display. What luck to obtain these rare 1940's era bags. This determined lady inspired herself to think big, when she adopted the last name of the richest person in America. It gave Katherine goosebumps to be surrounded by exhibits of women's accomplishments throughout the decades.

At the cafe threshold, a deep voice in reggae rhythm floated through the open door. Katherine paused. MJ had a guest? The intimate tone kept Katherine out of sight in the hall, where she couldn't help overhearing.

"My dear Moonjava. I've seen too many moonless nights. Oh you're a rhapsody reflecting the light of harmony in the universe."

Katherine leaned closer as MJ spoke. "David Sure. In my tranquil times I feel the rumblings of the earth's pulse, and you are part of it. I breathe in deep, absorb your essence, and bask in our memories. You felt me in the universe."

Katherine wished for invisibility so she could peer around the doorway or boldly step inside without detection. Movement flickered in the glass of the open door opposite her, a reflection of two figures inside.

The taller, broader shape stepped up to the MJ outline. That deep, musical voice resumed. "I always feel you. You've dwelt within my universe such a long time, and you will always. I never don't feel you." The two melted into one embrace.

MJ spoke softly, "We're in sync."

He echoed, "We are."

Katherine stood mesmerized. Who is this guy? Intriguing to catch a living, breathing MJ secret.

Katherine risked a glimpse around the corner. The Tiffany lamps dangling over the bar framed the two of them in a warm glow. Their intimate silhouette behind them on the wall's burnt sienna tones.

Katherine leaned in. The couple drew apart as the man's rich baritone resumed. "Your arms around me are medicine."

"Katherine, happy new year." Amber's unexpected greeting roared through the hall. Katherine lost her balance and stumbled into the doorway.

Despite her clumsy entrance, Katherine took the opportunity to examine the man. He wore jeans with an open denim jacket over a black t-shirt embellished with a gold lion's head and the words 'one love' in green. Gray dreadlocks hung around his broad shoulders. A large, well-used burlap sack slumped on the floor.

Amber stepped past Katherine into the cafe. "Hi MJ. The universe enters a new year." Katherine's cheeks heated as she followed Amber.

MJ motioned to the man. "The Gregorian calendar has surprised me with a gift. My friend, David Sure arrived in Bayside."

"I'm Amber. I work the gift shop when the Museum's open. Are you on vacation?"

David inclined toward her with a broad smile. "Cool runnings to you, Amber. I'm here to explore for as long as feels right."

"I'm Katherine." She stepped forward and offered a handshake.

"Aw, Moonjava family. I see her in you." He reached forward and folded both hands around hers, connecting eye to eye as he gave her a warm smile. "Nice to meet."

17

David released her hand and continued, "The nature and consciousness of the Pacific called to me some time ago. I've wandered forests and mountains happily and found myself drawn to the waters of Bayside."

MJ moved closer, with a concentrated stare and her lips a tight line. "Amber, your aura appears troubled. I see a lemon yellow color, as if you're fearing a loss. How can I soothe you?"

"There's craziness near my dorm." Amber fidgeted with her cell phone, then showed a screen shot. Several police cars and an ambulance in a field. "Michael texted a video."

As Amber enlarged the video, Moonjava commented, "Amber I'm glad you and Michael are dating again."

The brief video showed a paramedic closing the ambulance doors. Katherine recognized Jason in the background talking with two other officers. Hobbs sat at attention at the end of the leash. The ambulance slowly drove out of the lot and the video stopped.

Moonjava slowly shook her head. "Disturbing."

Katherine frowned when she recognized the location. "That field's on the same street as William's and Christopher's rental."

David asked Moonjava, "Who?"

"My grandsons. They're both in college. Michael is one of their housemates."

Amber put her phone in her crossbody. "Michael said the man's dead. He's a chemistry professor at the college. I've heard of him because he has…I mean had…a bad rep for harassing girl students."

Katherine's pulse pounded in her ears. "William works for Professor Nathan Randall."

Katherine grabbed her phone and clicked on her son's number. "I need to call them." She walked toward the window with the view of the bleak patio, all tables and chairs put away until spring. No answer. She left a breathless message, "Please call me." She followed that with a text on her group chat with William and Christopher.

As she clicked send Amber said, "Michael would have told me if anything had gone wrong at the house."

A hand brushed across Katherine's taut shoulder blades. MJ's soothing tone followed, "Don't overreact. He's fine."

Katherine clicked on Christopher's number. As it rang, Katherine turned back to the bar. Everyone stared at her. "Christopher, please call me back and let me know you're all right. I heard about the trouble on your street last night. I can't reach William either. Are you both all right? I heard about the trouble with Professor Randall. Please, one of you call me."

MJ clasped her hands together. "We'll send hopeful vibes for William, for Christopher, the family of the man in the field, for all of Bayside. You'll hear from your boys soon."

Katherine's grip tightened on her phone. "Yes."

MJ wrapped an arm around Katherine's shoulders and guided her toward the bar. "Let me create heartfelt lattes to soothe everyone."

Katherine willed her phone to vibrate. Where are they? She could find more news online. She quickly texted Jason asking him for information. He knew where her boys lived. How dare he get an alert last night on their street and not tell her. She took a deep breath.

A loud blast of steam behind the bar, and the rich

aroma of espresso drew Katherine's attention to wisps of steam rising lazily from an abandoned cup full of cooling espresso on the counter. Moonjava confessed long ago, she could never resist "the burst of awakening from the depths of my soul when I'm immersed in an espresso." David's appearance had miraculously separated MJ from her espresso. Who is this guy?

MJ washed her hands at the sink. "What do you have going on today, Amber?"

"Lunch at Julia's." She sat on one of the stools at the counter.

David joined MJ at the machine. "Let's steam the place up." He studied the ingredients on the shelves and chose three, then reached for one more. "We'll top these off with the love of lavender."

Katherine's interest grew when Amber asked, "MJ, where did you two meet?"

MJ lined up the to-go cups on the counter. "Remembering our times together brings pure joy. That beach in Florida when the pelicans took flight, how they skimmed the water."

David breathed in the lavender and lingered with a faraway, wistful stare. "A beautiful spot. Do you remember the street party in Miami?"

"I never danced or sang so much in my life. How about that march on Washington? We closed down the streets and made people listen. Then we wandered off together and recited poetry." MJ reminisced.

David still stared into space. "Spring then and the pink of those cherry blossoms in your hair drew me to you. The gentle fragrance lingered."

MJ warmed the pitcher. "How bewitching visiting DC in springtime."

Katherine couldn't relate their timeline to her childhood years, although she tried. "So, you've known each other for a long time?"

David focused on Moonjava. "I measure relations by intensity, not time."

"And you came here to fine MJ?" Katherine said.

David chuckled. Katherine felt her shoulders relax with his kind demeanor and engaging grin. "MJ as a name makes me laugh. I know her as The Moon. Yes, as I wandered the coast vibrations drew me north. I remembered The Moon talked about Bayside, and I thought I'd see it for myself. I camped in the chill and the peace of the beach shelter last night. At sunrise, I searched for the light of The Moon and found her."

MJ tapped him on the shoulder and pointed. "Can you grab the milk for me?"

He stooped to open the small fridge under the bar and took out the carton. "You know almond milk would be better, mixed with vanilla to turn the sharp to silk. Your friends and customers would like that change in your creations."

MJ took the carton from him and poured into the pitcher to steam for the tea. "I'll get some tomorrow and experiment."

He stood beside her. "I have some other ideas you might like too. You know you can decaffeinate naturally using Swiss water, for better health."

Amber spoke up, "We'll appreciate the caffeine today. Julia and I both stayed up late for New Year's Eve. We promised to help Julia's mom today with some of her house projects. I guess she's been stressed. We want to give her some time to relax."

"The holidays can be difficult," Katherine muttered.

"I'll make a relaxing latte for Donna to enjoy while watching you girls work. What about her dad? He'd want one too." MJ grabbed two more cups.

Katherine asked, "I saw Tomás at the Space Needle last night, but never saw Julia or Donna."

MJ paused. "You saw Tomás in that Seattle Center crowd?"

"You couldn't have. Julia's dad's out of town." Amber reached out to put the lid on each cup as David filled them with a tea latte that gave off sweet herbal steam. "They called him to consult on some emergency operation in Denver. He had to drop everything and go there. Her mom didn't celebrate last night. Julia said her mom hasn't acted normal for a while. She's driving Julia crazy."

"Tension between high school seniors and their mothers remains pretty common." Katherine thought of her own sons' teen years.

She glanced at MJ, who put a cardboard holder for the to-go cups on the counter. "Take a deep breath everyone. Bitterness belongs in the coffee grinds, not in the heart. Amber, share that meditation with Julia. It may help her feel kinder to her mother."

As directed, Amber took a deep breath and released it. She stood up and reached to pay for the drinks, but Katherine put her hand out to stop her. "Oh no you don't. These are on the house, a gift for the new year. Wish Donna and Julia a happy holiday from me."

"Thank you." Amber gave her a hug.

After Amber left, David made a concoction from mysterious tea leaves and herbs out of three small jars in the burlap sack.

MJ sat with Katherine. "I miss your high energy.

How late did you stay out?"

"Very. The drones amazed everyone. The crowd had fun, until we all got stuck in traffic for hours."

"Stuck for hours? Exaggeration?"

"No. Everyone wanted to leave at once and got in each other's way."

MJ laughed. "You'd have a long walk from downtown. Or did you call a ride share?"

Katherine shook her head. "I got up and did something about it. I directed traffic and sent everyone moving home."

"Personal action is admirable but be careful you're not hanging around Jason too much. That sounds like a cop thing to do. You should come out with me, and protest something. Demonstrations give a person a healthy perspective."

"I could direct traffic around you protesters. I have a real talent for telling drivers where to go." Katherine laughed.

David set the herbal concoction to steep in hot water. "You ladies are in for a treat that will set a beautiful tone for the rest of your day."

The flourishing swirls of dark orange and yellow grew in the glass pitcher and mesmerized Katherine. When he filled the cups, she sensed an exotic floral scent, beautiful like jasmine perfume. "I smell spring. What is it?"

He pointed to each of the jars in turn. "A green tea with leaves encouraging blood flow, all good for the heart. My creation sprinkles the green with rose petals and a crush of strawberry."

MJ sipped. "A gentle and soft creation."

Katherine hesitated, then she brought the cup to her

lips. The warm, sweet liquid created a surprising and joyful taste. Her expression relaxed. "Delicious."

Replacing the lid on each jar, David explained, "The blend and the temperature make or break tea. No way should you overheat a green tea."

Katherine folded both hands around the warm cup and savored the jasmine scent, while her curiosity about David simmered. Her phone buzzed, and its screen lit up with a text from Jason.

Chapter Four

Amber parked her compact car at Julia's house. Carefully balancing the tray of drinks in both hands, she walked up the driveway. The herbal scent that had tempted her while driving now danced on steam vapors drifting in the winter's breeze. Her hands trembled a little in the cold. She'd left the dorm in a hurry and forgot her mittens.

All the curtains at Julia's two story house hung closed. The poinsettias by the door and the colorful lights flickering on the front yard fir tree brightened the gray day. Amber skipped the front door. Over the years of their high school friendship, the kitchen's back door remained her familiar, inviting entrance. Her phone vibrated with an incoming text. Then another. A trio of crows on top of the neighbor's fence took off fast. Amber uttered a soothing coo. A red faced woman in the yard next door stomped forward, raised a rifle, and pointed it above Amber. An explosive bang pierced the holiday calm and Amber screamed. Another shot, then another at the birds in flight.

Fumbling David Sure's drinks, spilling some but saving any from falling to the ground, Amber twisted around in a circle. Confused, she turned back toward her car, then toward the house again. She thought to dive onto the ground, then saw Julia waving like a maniac from the door and shouting, "Over here, quick."

Amber rushed inside the kitchen, plopped the lattes on the counter and screamed while Julia shouted at the neighbor, "Leave the birds alone." And slammed the door.

"Why is your neighbor shooting at me?" Amber wrapped her arms around her friend in a hug.

"She's psycho. She's shooting everything, all weekend."

"Terrifying."

Donna walked into the room at a fast pace that matched the serious jogging pants and top she wore. "Oh Amber, thank God you're all right. Stay away from the windows, girls." Donna quickly guided the two of them across the room.

Amber bent low as she walked with Donna. Julia turned back and grabbed the lattes. "I'm embarrassed telling people to duck and cover when you come over."

Donna frantically searched around and grabbed a purse off a chair. "Julia please call 911. I can't find my phone. I can't find anything in my new bag,"

Julia slipped the strap of an identical purse off the back of one of the chairs at the table. "Mom you've got my bag again. Here's yours." They switched, and Donna grabbed her phone.

"Hello, 911." Donna raised her voice as shots echoed again from outside. "Yes, my neighbor is shooting a gun again. A friend came over, lucky she got in the house without being injured. Yes, I called you yesterday too, and the day before. And check your records from last month." Amber took a deep breath as Donna paused, then spoke again. "No, I don't see her now, but I still hear shots off and on." Donna walked into the living room.

"Thanks for the drinks." Julia grabbed two drinks and disappeared under the table. Amber felt another text vibration but ignored it and followed Julia. The pet spaniel already cowered there. The girls leaned with their backs against the wall, and Amber cuddled the dog. "Poor Perro. He's trembling."

Julia fingered her handbag and crossed her eyes. "I could get a different shoulder strap, so she can tell the difference. I don't need her searching through my bag."

Amber said, "Katherine sold them to her. I had to leave early that day for an exam. I can trade that one for a different strap."

"A Christmas gift, as if matching bags make us cool. She even clipped a daisy charm on the strap for both hers and mine to match."

Amber fingered the ornament. "Her favorite flower. Cute. Your mom loves flowers."

"She still treats me like a kid with mother and daughter stuff. A ridiculous, monster size bag."

Amber glanced at her wristlet. "They're called messenger bags. They're meant to carry a lot of stuff, even packages."

Julia shook her head. "I bet only old ladies like my mom buy these suitcases."

Amber suggested, "You can carry your school stuff in it, so you don't hurt your mom's feelings."

"I guess." Julia held it up. "It could work for books and a laptop."

Another shot echoed. "Can it stop a bullet?"

Perro let out a whine, and Amber hugged him a little closer. "What a crazy neighbor."

"Hear that siren?" Julia lowered the bag onto her lap. Her shoulders visibly relaxed. She gave her pullover sweater a tug over her jeans. When Amber peeked out, red and blue pulses reflected against the windowpane lighting the many flowering African violet plants scattered across the sill. Her phone vibrated again.

Julia sipped her drink. "Tastes great, and hot, smells good too like a lot of spices."

Amber lifted her cup, as if in a toast. "Caffeinated. I need that after New Year's Eve. I celebrated all night."

"With Michael?"

Amber's broad smile answered that question. "Lots of fun with Michael and friends to end the year." Amber took a long drink of her latte, then gave Perro more attention.

"So, you two are back together."

"So far so good. What did you do last night?"

"I wanted to be out with Kevin, but I got stuck here with Mom. She doesn't like him, and she gets between us."

"She's still getting between you two? You're like Romeo and Juliet."

"Kevin raged about it last night. He said some things that upset her more, and I'm stuck in the middle. I mean, I'm mad too, but I love my mom."

"It'll get better when your dad comes home."

"He's back tomorrow but that won't fix anything. She decided not to like my boyfriend and won't even listen. She's got some mess at work too. She's taking all her problems out on Dad and me. Anyway, I texted Kevin, and tonight we'll plan something different."

"What happens tonight?"

Julia leaned closer and whispered. "He's sneaking in so we can be together."

"Why don't you let things cool off, then talk with

her?"

She sighed. "I don't know how she found out, or who told her, but she found out Kevin has a record. She forbids me to see him alone. Can you believe it?"

Amber thought of when she'd visited Michael in jail. "What did he do?"

Julia paused as if listening. Footsteps? She lowered her voice again, "Who cares what he did. She overreacts to everything. I heard her argue with Dad on the phone. They're fighting. She's got some disagreement with her boss too. She's taking all that out on me. She's ruining my life. She needs to get her act together."

Julia stopped talking. Even in the shadows beneath the table, the scarlet of her face and determined squint of her eyes burned. Amber knew that expression. All through high school impulsive Julia excelled as a good friend but also a certified drama queen. They disagreed sometimes, but their deep friendship never faltered even after Amber moved to college during Julia's high school senior year.

Donna approached the table, her running shoes clearly visible. Amber's vibrating phone tempted, but she ignored it again. Why so many texts all at the same time?

Donna raised her voice, "Julia? Amber? The police stopped Sophie."

Perro trotted out first. Amber crawled behind him, followed by Julia who hooked her bag on the back of the chair again. Donna sat down. She smoothed the sunflower patterned tablecloth and leaned over to scratch the dog behind an ear. Amber moved the remaining latte. "Do you want me to reheat it in the microwave?"

"Amber, how nice. Thank you. Sophie's very upset.

Even with the police there, she's yelling. I'm sure I'm not the only neighbor who complained, but she's shouting threats at me. Anyway, the police stopped her." Donna hung her bag on the back of her chair.

Julia crossed her arms. "I hope they take away her gun."

Donna sighed. "This time they're taking her away."

Julia jumped up. "What? Come on Amber."

Julia ran out the door despite Donna's objection. Amber hesitated, then followed.

The neighbor stood in handcuffs with two officers, one talking directly to the woman and the other speaking into his radio. One held the woman's gun. A pair of crows gazed down from the nearby fir tree. The woman stared daggers at Julia from the foot of the driveway and spit out a threat, "Your mother will regret this when I'm out."

The cop moved her into the back of the patrol car. Amber's cell phone vibrated, and tones rang out. She checked the screen. "Michael's calling."

Julia showed her the picture she took of the neighbor in the police car. "I've seen enough. I'll be in the kitchen when you're done."

Amber clicked on the call as she walked back into the warm living room. She may want to linger on the phone. "Hi, Michael. What's up?"

"Hey beautiful, can't wait to see you later."

Amber sighed. "You called to tell me that? You're romantic."

"I called to change plans."

Amber shifted her weight onto her other foot, then sat on the couch. "Oh."

"I still want to get together. Not here at the house,

too intense since Nicky found the dead guy."

"Why?"

Michael groaned. "The cops are crawling all over the place. They're questioning Nicky and Will at the station. I know what that's like. Bad."

Surprised, Amber became concerned. "We came to the house last night too, but we didn't do anything wrong. None of us did."

"The cops are asking all of us what we did and where last night." Michael reassured her, "I didn't mention you."

Amber frowned. "The police should leave Will and Nicky alone and focus on the professor."

"Nicky told them he cut across the field to get home and found the guy. The cop came back later and said a neighbor complained about his drone launch."

"Oh man."

"Yeah, so now Nicky's in trouble for what he said and for droning at night. I'm betting on that snitch across the street. She doesn't have enough in her life."

"Why question William? What are the cops thinking?"

"You know how suspicious cops are. Their radar went up when Will told them he worked for the guy."

Amber shook her head. I bet they find out the professor had a heart attack, and they'll owe Nicky and William apologies."

"That's not all. They've got a patrol car parked on the street here, like they're watching us. I need to get out of here before they're after me. Let's meet at the Campus Coffee House and figure things out from there."

"I'm at Julia's. I'll text you when I leave. I wonder if Candace knows."

"Candace who?"

"Remember I told you how Randall upset her. How he came on to her? She dropped his class."

"Oh yeah. Hey, I'll see you later, babe. I can't wait."

"See, you are romantic." Amber clicked off. The patrol car had driven the neighbor away. Busy day for Bayside police.

In the kitchen, Donna and Julia frowned at each other.

"Are you all right?" Donna stood up and motioned to Amber. "Come sit down."

Amber sat. "What a bizarre day. Michael's roommates found one of the college professor's dead. William works for him. Professor Randall. I mean. William worked for him."

Donna swallowed hard. "The chemistry professor?" She froze in place. "Dead?"

"Yeah, in a field by the campus, and by the roomies' house. Sounds intense with the cops investigating everyone."

"I know Professor Randall." Donna's voice broke.

Julia leaned toward Amber. "The creepy science teacher you said came on to girls who have to take his class as a prerequisite for the major?"

The vase with the arrangement of roses in the center of the table wobbled, as Donna leaned on the table and stood again. "Dead? It hasn't been on the news.."

Julia said, "Don't worry, Mom."

Donna paced toward the door, then back to the table. "Girls, I have to go out." She grabbed a purse and turned to leave.

"Mom wait, you have my purse again."

"Sorry. Why do I keep doing that?"

"Fifty-fifty chance and you keep getting it wrong."

"I won't be gone long." Donna rushed out the door.

Amber felt the twinge of a headache. "I'll text Katherine. She might find out something from Jason. A perk of dating a cop should be answers to questions."

"What's wrong with my mom? Why would she know a jerk like that guy?"

"She must not know about how he treats women students. Do you still want to surprise your mom with some chores done?"

"Yeah, that might get her off my back."

They worked together for a couple of hours. Sitting back at the kitchen table, Julia sighed. "Thanks for helping me. The place sparkles with clean. My mom can calm down now, especially with crazy Sophie locked up."

Amber put her coat on. "We did a great job."

Julia smiled. "Go see Michael. Enjoy."

Amber gave her a hug. "Talk to your mom tonight. Convince her to let Kevin come over."

Julia gave an exaggerated pout.

Amber giggled. "Oh, don't get like that. You don't want everyone to get madder. Go out and pretend you accidentally met him. Then enjoy a night out. Don't sneak him in—"

"She's so preoccupied with all her problems, she'll never even know he's here. It'll all work out."

Chapter Five

Bayside's wintry sheen wrapped around Katherine's office den, but her attention focused on her phone. She frowned as she wrote her sons yet another group text. It spanned the length of a couple of screens. She'd added snippets of beautiful memories from their childhood and her pride as their mother. She'd ended it with a heartfelt plea to contact her soon. Her finger hovered. Too long? She clicked. As she waited for a response, she debated driving to their place.

In typical William fashion, when she finally heard back he texted a brief reply.

I'm okay.

Katherine took that as an invitation to call him right away. No answer. Then her phone swooshed with a text from him.

Can't talk now.

Katherine gazed out on her yard and the space with the Brenda Dirling Memorial garden. Struck down in the prime of life, Brenda had accomplished so much in her time. Yet she always had time for fun, always ready for the beach, loved to tease, and always supportive of her friends. Katherine still woke up some nights in a sweat, tormented with the guilt of her innocent mistakes that may have given the killer their opportunity to strike at Brenda.

At least there would be justice for Brenda in the

future, with that rotten killer in jail waiting for trial. Who would ever have thought that a fashion purse designer could confront a killer. With the memory, a deep chill ran through her and then a surge of adrenaline in the pit of her stomach over the search for clues and the thrill of that chase. She shifted position, attempting to get comfortable.

The movement disturbed her meowser, Purrada. The cat rolled on her side and stretched out full length. Katherine warmed her fingers massaging the depths of luxurious, thick, black fur. Purrada closed her eyes and leaned into each touch with an upturned nose and catatonic face. The long tail twitched. Did she remember her stray, scrawny, back-alley days? No trace now of that forlorn creature peeking through hopeful, adopt-me eyes from under the porch. That whiskered rascal stole Katherine's heart.

She scratched behind Purrada's ear, thought of the morning text from Jason, and reconciled herself to the challenges of dating an ever vigilant patrol cop. She leaned back in her chair and checked her phone again. No text back from Jason. No information on the dead man in the field. Judiciously tight-lipped, or doesn't he know anything yet? He never even mentioned William being involved. Her gaze lingered over the phone image of Jason kneeling, arm around trusted partner Hobbs. The text faded and went to black.

A breeze stirred ripples in the pond. Birds flitted to her grandmother's feeders and squirrels scavenged underneath for stray seeds. Under the deep, dark seamless cloud cover, the shining headlights on an empty transit bus lit the street. It traveled Main Street west to the Bay. The drizzle extended forever, giving the afternoon a dusky tinge. The big leaves of the rhododendrons drooped in the garden with the accumulated rain. Some of the branches parted now from the bushes hiding her driveway. A large animal bounded forward followed by a tall man dressed in dark, layered clothes, a gun hanging from the belt. The man moved a hand near his gun, and the dog trotted beside him. The stomp of feet on the porch put Purrada on the alert. Jason in person, peered through the glass of her French doors.

He confronted her with luscious chocolate brown eyes. The cold red tinge in his cheeks deepened. He opened the door and rushed in, the cold breeze rustling papers on her desk.

Purrada arched her back and hissed pointedly at the dog as he crossed the threshold. Jason shut the door. The dog promptly indulged in a long shake from snout to tip of the tail, leaving a wet and muddy mess. Purrada jumped up twice her height and dashed away. Her long black tail curved around the corner wall as she vanished into the large closet full of the final summer fashion designs. Hobbs yawned.

Jason struggled to take off his boots. Katherine ran to the hall closet for one of the dog towels and handed it to Jason. "Thanks." He wiped the dog, and then the floor. Jason shifted all attention to Katherine. "You're a beautiful sight for a tired man, or am I hallucinating?"

Katherine straightened her long sleeved sweater and knit top. A sunny beach landscape embroidered in the woolen pattern, the tropical colors and flair contrasted to her plain black leggings and to the freezing weather outside. "A hallucination? That depends. What do you see?"

He stepped toward her. "A most alluring vision."

A nice, romantic tone from Jason. The room's temperature jumped up a few degrees. "You enjoyed your New Year's Eve, did you?"

He put an arm around her, then pulled her into a tender hug. "The first part of it, filled with the heat, sight, and excitement of you."

Some sparks lit a flame, after all. She felt a shadow of whisker against her cheek and whispered, "A new year brings new possibilities."

"How about a toast to that?"

A thud, followed by a crash and a growl pulled them apart. Hobbs sprawled across the floor. A fast glimpse of a tail belied Purrada dashing back into the closet. The animals had knocked over the tall table lamp. It fell on one of Katherine's demonstration purses, bursting apart a seam.

"Oh no." Katherine let go of Jason and put her hands on her hips.

"Hobbs, kommen." The dog went to Jason's side and sat down. "Okay, Hobbs."

Jason's German commands when on the job with Hobbs no longer felt out of place, as they once had to Katherine. Jason gave reassuring pats that Hobbs soaked up. She opened the top desk drawer and held up the treat tin. She gave Hobbs a biscuit. He helped her pick up the lamp, right the table, and she gently piled up the purse pieces. "Back to the designing board."

"I'm sorry, Katherine. An accident."

"No worries. This work-in-progress has a ways to go. I'll take Hobbs' critique under advisement."

The dog lay down by the closet door. Jason signaled for him to move away from there, then Jason gave into gravity. With a sigh, he sank into the cushion on the bay window seat behind her desk. He leaned against the pane, closed his eyes and rubbed his forehead with a deliberate movement.

Her heart skipped a beat. Although tired, Jason had come to see her. "You've had a tough time."

He grinned. "All part of the job. They wanted a K-9, and we're it for regional support."

"No wonder you're exhausted. What did you find out?"

He slowly closed his eyes again. "You know I can't say anything about an open case."

Katherine contemplated what that meant. "So, it qualifies as an open case?" She paused. "I know you can't talk about work with anyone outside the department, but you can talk with me. I have a track record analyzing clues."

He frowned. He reached for her hand and pulled her onto the seat next to him. He softly held her hand. She waited for him to tell her more. Jason remained silent.

She prompted him, "Should the community be concerned for their safety? What about my sons? I heard the police questioned William."

"The residents are cautioned, but probably an isolated case. I can't tell you more than that." He paused. "Have you heard from William today?"

"He said he's fine. He's fine, right?"

Jason continued with a concerned tone. "The department must question people with ties to the case. He's one of the people who found the man, and there's a link between them."

Katherine nodded. "He worked for Professor Randall as his assistant."

"So, you know. Since William worked for him and

found him…" Jason paused. "Don't get upset, but I heard from dispatch that an officer picked him up for further questioning."

Katherine froze. She jerked away and grabbed her phone off the desk. "They're questioning him at the station? Why didn't you tell me? I have to go."

Jason stood and grabbed her hand again. "Wait. You can't help him. He'll be fine."

"I have to go. I'm not staying here knowing he's being questioned at the station."

"They're asking him questions as a witness, not a suspect. You won't be able to see him until he's through. He may already be done."

"Of course he's not a suspect. What are you talking about? I have to go." She scanned the room for her purse.

Jason went to the door for his boots. "I'll drive you."

"I can drive. You're tired." Purse in hand she turned to go. "My coat's by the back door."

He snapped his fingers at Hobbs and followed her. "We'll find out together what's happening at the station."

Katherine stopped before pulling her coat off the hook and gave him a grateful hug. "Thank you." They shared a brief, sweet kiss. Katherine stepped back. "Not an accident then, the dead man?"

Jason helped with her coat. "The medical report isn't in. The evidence hasn't been analyzed. No signs of a struggle."

Katherine couldn't move.

Jason put a hand on each of her arms. "William will be okay."

Katherine wiped away a tear. She jerked open the door. "I'll make sure of that."

Outside he stopped her. "Give me your keys. You need to keep your doors locked, especially until we know more." He turned the key to lock the bolt. "No need to tempt fate while we have an unsolved mystery." He signaled Hobbs.

They walked along the path to the car as Katherine vowed, "Yet. We haven't solved the mystery yet, but we will."

Chapter Six

Amber paused outside, staring at Julia's closed door. Should she stay and convince Julia to rethink a late night rendezvous with her new boyfriend? No. Why would Julia listen to her anyway? She'd met Kevin a couple of times and liked him. He had a sense of humor, Julia boasted about the intensity of his blue eyes, the way he'd put an arm around her so tenderly despite a muscular build. He had a record. Julia had never mentioned that before.

Another buzz from her phone. She pulled it out as she walked to her car. A message from Michael.

—See you on campus—

Tempting to call and hear Michael's always energetic, deep voice sink in and tickle her romantic imagination. Her thumb hovered over the call button. No, not now. She reached for her car keys. She'd stop by the dorms and see Candace first. She may need a friend.

A car engine revved on the road a few houses away. The reflection of the magenta light on the dashboard identified it as a ride share. The older model, dark blue four-door sedan turned off the road too fast to recognize the driver. Kevin drove ride share. If he's driving, wouldn't he stop in and see Julia?

Amber drove to the corner and turned left too. She kept an eye out for the ride share, but it had disappeared.

No delays along the deserted streets of Bayside, as

residents recovered from the holiday. Amber turned into the parking lot shared by four dorms and a couple of faculty buildings. A small crowd gathered outside her dorm. She recognized several people, including her roommate Trish. Surprised to see a news camera there, and an interviewer at work. Amber recognized Katherine's friend Rob.

Trish ran over and hugged her. "Hi, Roomie. I'm so glad to see you. I still don't know everything that happened, except Professor Randall's dead."

Amber nodded. "They found him in a field near Michael's house."

Trish frowned. "The professor's conscience could have caught up to him for all the girls he's harassed, and he killed himself." Her mouth dropped open as she gasped, "Or, one of the girls he tormented could have killed him."

Amber put her hand on Trish's shoulder. "Don't let your imagination get carried away. No one said murder. Have you seen Candace?" Amber took a deep breath.

Trish raised her eyebrows to emphasize. "I haven't seen her."

"Let's go check her room. If she's not there, then I'll text her."

"You don't think she…"

"I thought she'd want friends around."

Rob and a film crew blocked the path. As Amber and Trish approached, he signaled for the light and camera to go back on. They quickly moved aside to stay out of the shot.

"Rob Tomlinson, I'm here for Western Washington Online News. I'm live here at Bayside college campus where they've lost of one of the faculty. Professor

Randall, a chemistry professor, found deceased in an abandoned field blocks from here, where he'd taught for the past five years. The cause of death has not yet been determined. I'm here with a student from one of the professor's classes, Raymond Stokely."

With a dramatic turn, Rob brought Raymond into camera view. "You're a sophomore and one of Professor Randall's students. How are you today?"

Rob tilted the microphone closer to the student, who didn't hesitate, "I'm in shock. I never knew anyone found dead somewhere before. I took a couple of classes from him."

Rob asked, "Did you enjoy his classes?"

"I'm a chem major. I know my stuff, but I worked hard in those classes. We all did. After class he told jokes and stuff, pretty funny guy. He'd hang around with lots of us students."

"You'll miss him?"

"Whatever happened, I'm sorry. We'll drink one for him at happy hour. If they replace him with an easier Prof, that's cool." Raymond stepped toward the camera lens. "Can I say hi to my girlfriend, Jana?"

"Thanks Raymond." Rob swung around in the other direction.

Amber grabbed Trish's arm, and they retreated further. Rob tracked a young woman bundled in a ski jacket and jeans, holding her backpack over one shoulder. She walked with her face staring straight down at her feet.

One hand instinctively covered Amber's mouth as she pointed at the girl. Trish said, "Candace, stop! You're walking straight into him."

Rob smiled to the camera. "Hello. Excuse me,

miss."

Candace bumped into him. "Who are you?" She stared at the microphone.

Rob stood a little taller. "I'm Rob Tomlinson, Western Washington Online News discussing the death of Professor Randall. Did you know him?"

She stared, tears in her eyes.

Rob motioned subtly to the camera assistant. "You knew him pretty well."

At that statement Candace took a step back and glared at the reporter. "What do you mean by that? I took one class, but I had to quit it. I...I almost quit school because of him."

Candace moved to avoid Rob. He countered her move. "So, you dropped out of one of Professor Randall's classes? What about his death today?"

Candace zigzagged to get past the persistent reporter who blurted out another question. "Have you talked to the professor recently?"

Candace came to a full stop, and with her face red she pushed her hands forward, palms out toward the interviewer, as if to push him away. "Please, let me go by. I don't want to talk to you."

Amber rushed up to her friend. "Leave her alone. Can't you see she's upset."

Amber and Trish each took one of Candace's hands and guided her between them toward the dorm. As the camera lingered on the three of them, the reporter shouted, "Did either of you know Professor Randall?"

Amber put her arm over her friend's shoulders. "Are you okay, Candace?"

"I'm not answering any more questions," She squinted fiercely back at Rob as he cornered another student, "especially on the news. I hate the professor. I'm glad he's dead." Candace quickened her pace.

Amber kept up. "Let me help." She tried pulling Candace into a hug. "Take a deep breath."

With tears in her eyes, Candace gently pushed her back. "I'm outta here." She darted away.

Trish caught up and shouted, "Don't go. We can all hang out."

Candace never turned back.

Trish gave up the chase. "We'll never catch that track star."

Amber sighed and faced her roommate. "She's so angry."

Trish shook her head slowly. "At least she'll never have to worry he'll touch her again."

As winter's early dusk fell, Amber's energy dimmed. A promising holiday had evaporated into a sorrowful, long day.

"I'm meeting Michael. I need to go up and take a shower." She felt her phone vibrate. "A text from Katherine. She might have news from Jason."

Trish pocketed her phone. "Work? Isn't the shop closed for New Year's?"

Amber nodded while she read. "Katherine's dating a cop. She found out the police took William and Nicky in for questioning. She's freaking. She's on her way to the station. Michael told me the cops took them in, like they're criminals or something."

Trish's jaw dropped. "They're being questioned? For what?" She wrinkled her forehead. "Wait. Do the cops think your friends killed him, or something?"

Amber shook her head. "Don't get crazy."

Trish gasped. "If he chased after the wrong girl,

someone could have reported him for harassment. Or if he got scared about what could happen, and suicide became his only way out of it. Or instead of reporting it the girl killed him? Or the College found out about what he's done and fired him, and he couldn't take it and killed himself."

Amber put her hand on her friend's shoulder. "Slow your roll, Trish. Katherine didn't say any of that."

Another text grabbed her attention, and Amber clicked on it. A selfie popped on the screen. Julia modeled a big smile and a sparkling, red, short dress. Her winter coat lay on the bed behind her.

Kev didn't want to sneak in. So, I'll go out and surprise him, in my new year's dress.

No one said anything about a murderer, but still, not a good night for Julia to wander around town. Instead of texting back, Amber called. No answer.

Chapter Seven

At the police station, Jason swung open the staff door. The dark of winter surrendered to bright lights and heat. Katherine stepped onto the linoleum entry. Across from her, framed pictures of retired officers covered the wall. Behind a plastic sliding window, a cop stopped her work at a computer screen and greeted them. "Can I help you?"

Jason walked in with Hobbs. "Hi Sheila. Where can I find the detective on the Randall case?"

"Hi, Jason. In Room B with a witness."

"Thanks."

Sheila ignored Katherine. "Jason, while you're here, I have a problem on your morning report to go over with you."

"Okay. I'll be right back. Katherine, I'll show you where you can wait for William." He indicated a hallway to the left.

She followed him. "Wait for him? I need to see him."

After turning a couple of corners and moving past the restrooms, the hall opened up into a space filled with a few chairs. The Bayside Police Department logo loomed above them on the wall.

She frowned. "Where's William?"

He pointed to the two doors a little further ahead. "He's in room B."

She frowned and walked around Hobbs to get to the doors. "Katherine, stop. They're not letting you in. Wait here, and I'll find out the latest. Sit down, and as soon as he comes out you'll see him."

Jason told her about William and how to find him. She'd listen to Jason, for now.

He smiled. "I'll do a quick fix on that report, check in on William's status, and be right back." The dog followed him. Jason used a hand signal, and Hobbs sat on the floor next to Katherine's chair. "Mind keeping Hobbs company?"

"Sure." She scratched the dog under the chin, the way he loved it. He leaned in against her knee, keeping an intent eye on his partner. After Jason disappeared around the corner, the dog tensed. His gaze never wavered.

Silence held her in its spell, and petting the dog helped calm her. Katherine's mind filled with images of William growing through the years, such an independent spirit, never ending science experiments, those silly jokes and pranks he delighted in. One of the doors opened, and she leaped to her feet. A uniformed cop spoke on her radio, "Will do." She escorted a teenage girl who wore a sports shirt emblazoned with a logo from the college women's track and field.

Katherine sank back in her folding chair, wrapping her fingers tight around the seat.

The girl stopped the cop and pointed at the restroom door. The cop nodded. "I need to report. Stay here, and I'll be right back to walk you out." The teenager walked inside, tears down her face and a trembling lip.

As the cop disappeared around the corner, Katherine wondered how much longer Jason would take. She stood and paced back and forth. Hobbs watched her. The first time she passed the bathroom door she paused, curious. Her next pass confirmed it. She heard crying. Poor girl. The door opened, and the young woman peeked out with her red eyes brimming.

Katherine reached into the tote she'd grabbed in her rush. She pulled out a small packet of tissues. "My name's Katherine Watson. I'm so sorry you're upset. Come and sit down."

"I'm Candace."

"Are you a student at the college? I'm here waiting for my son, William."

"Will Watson? I know him. He helped me. He's here?" The girl sat gingerly, eyeing Hobbs.

Katherine smiled. "Don't worry about Hobbs. He's a friend." She pointed. "William's in that room. What's upset you?"

"Did William tell you a professor's dead?"

"Yes."

Candace dried her tears with a tissue. "I filed a complaint against the professor. When Will found out he helped me. The cop asked me all kinds of questions about my complaint. I wanted to run out of here, away from them." Candace blotted more tears with a tissue, then stared at her knees.

"All a terrible misunderstanding, I'm sure. William worked for him, so they brought him in too." Katherine's lips tensed.

"What a mean professor. He treated girl students wrong. I told the college about it so they'd stop him."

"I'm so sorry."

"Your son helped me drop the class and got me into another prerequisite instead. He's a good guy."

Katherine smiled. "I'm sure the police understood you had no information about the professor's death. They'll leave you alone now."

Candace leaned against the back of her chair. After a pause she spoke in such a low tone Katherine had to lean forward to hear. "I saw him that night. On my way to the bus, I cut across the parking lot. That's when it happened." Her eyes got wide. "I heard him on his phone. I ducked behind one of the cars."

"He saw you?"

She slowly nodded. "He did. I accidentally dropped my key ring with my bus pass on it. I grabbed it, terrified he'd heard it."

Katherine put her hand on Hobbs back and felt his muscles tense. "I can imagine."

Candace went on, "He strutted around showing off a tuxedo under his unbuttoned coat. He said into the phone that he'd be home an hour before the party. My prayers got answered when he got in the car and drove away."

Her breathing came in spurts now. Katherine put her hand over the girl's shaking fingers. "Let's both take a deep breath." After a couple of exaggerated inhales and exhales, Katherine asked, "You told the police all this?"

A daze came over the girl's eyes. "They kept asking questions and saying nothing. Like they blame me for something. Like I did something wrong, and they want me to tell them about it. I didn't do anything wrong. The professor did. I got so mad in there, then I couldn't stop crying." She hiccupped. "I can't help it that he died. I wanted him to leave me alone."

Hobbs jumped up in place and stood at attention, as Jason turned the corner. Behind them a door flew open.

Katherine leaped to her feet when a middle aged man in a button down shirt and slacks stepped out of the room.

William followed. "You're done, right? I'm headed home, or I'm calling a lawyer."

"I've got your statement. You're free to go."

Katherine couldn't keep silent. "Of course he's free to go."

The detective lowered his chin and stared over his glasses at her.

Jason positioned himself between them, Hobbs at attention. "I told the desk I'd take it from here and make sure the witnesses get home." The other cop walked past.

"Mom, what are you doing here? Candace, they questioned you too?"

She sniffled, brushing a tissue under her eye. He softened his voice. "Candace, take it easy. No worries."

Jason said, "Let's get everyone home."

William crossed arms over his chest and stared at Jason. "I'm not leaving until Nicky gets released."

Jason's eyebrows arched. "He's downstairs, in the jail."

Outrage infused William's outburst. "Jail? Show me where, or I'll find it on my own."

Hobbs stood on alert next to Jason. Katherine joined her son. "The jail?"

Jason motioned with both hands to quiet down. "He's in the jail room, not a cell. We're a small town station. You and Candace occupied our only two rooms. They're talking, getting a statement."

Katherine muttered, "That's intimidating."

Jason motioned to Hobbs. "Let's go see Sheila and get an update so all three of you witnesses can go home."

William rushed to follow right behind him and

Hobbs. Pulling another tissue out, Candace followed, and Katherine brought up the rear of the procession. Nicky had made it to Sheila before them. A uniformed officer stood next to Nicky while Sheila handed him his wallet, phone, key ring, and drone.

When he saw Will, Nicky's scowl softened for an instant. "Dude. You're still here?"

"No way I'd leave without you. They took your stuff?" William's mouth stuck open.

"You don't know the half of it." Nicky gave a sideways glance at the cop next to him.

The man held a clipboard up to him. "Sign here for receipt of your belongings."

Nicky put the clipboard on the counter and delicately balanced the drone in one hand while he signed with the other. He put the pen down and gestured to William, "I'm outta here."

William nodded. "Candace, you want a ride to the dorm?"

She agreed. "Thanks."

Katherine cleared her throat. "William, we can drive you all."

"No, Mom, I drove my car here. I'm fine. Really. I'll stop over and see you tomorrow."

Nicky kept a tight grip on the drone and shoved a shoulder against the door. "Dude, wait 'til you hear this."

William held the door open for Candace. "Michael texted they're at the Campus Coffeehouse."

The trio disappeared into the dark, as the door slammed shut.

Chapter Eight

Jason yawned again as he parked in Katherine's driveway. The motion lights popped on. With an instinctive reaction, he scanned the area. Katherine took his hand. "Thanks for driving me to see William. Already a tiring new year for you, including an extra shift." They shared a good night kiss. Katherine lingered, and Jason pulled her to him for another.

Katherine leaned in and bumped against a switch on the panel between the seats. The computer popped on, lighting the screen under the windshield, and playing an audio. Jason quickly switched it off.

Katherine smiled. "What romantic background music you have, witness statements uniquely designed for a moment such as this."

Jason slowly brushed a lock of hair back from her face and grinned. "I'd say that playlist is suspect. Can you hear those bullfrogs from your Brenda garden? They create a more enticing rhythm and blues background."

Hobbs sat up in the back and moaned a loud yawn, the rear view mirror reflecting a dog mouth stretched wide. Jason laughed with Katherine, then spoke to the mirror "Okay, pawtner, rest time is coming." He turned back to Katherine. "Apparently the universe conspires against us and pushes for a brief good night."

"You've been around MJ too long." She grabbed the door handle and paused. "Nothing more for William, right? You know he didn't do anything wrong."

"Hey, don't worry all night about your son in routine witness questioning."

She frowned. "He worked for the guy and found his body. Coincidences happen. Police know that, right?"

Jason gave her little reassurance. "Any insights William gives the detectives speed up the investigation."

She groaned. "I don't like seeing William there." She frowned. "And Candace cried when she talked to me. And why drag Nicky into the jail cells."

"Not in the cell, in the jail room. I didn't have anything to do with that." He sighed. "My responsibility stopped with the four-legged evidence searching, and of course the never ending paperwork." Jason grinned at Hobbs. "You always leave that part to me." Hobbs yawned.

Katherine took a moment to calm her rising anger. "You're right. You didn't even have to tell me about William, let alone drive me to see him." Katherine wrapped her arms around Jason. "Thank you for taking me to jail tonight."

"Anytime." They sealed the sentiment with a kiss.

Reluctant to leave, Katherine opened the door. With a tug on her shoulder bag, Jason added, "When you get inside, be sure you lock the door."

"I will. Good night." He waited for her to walk in her house. She crossed the threshold and blew a kiss. He waved and drove away.

She walked through to her office and sank into her chair with a deep breath. Thankful to see William tonight, she remained disappointed by how he left. She reached for her phone, then stopped. She'd call him tomorrow morning.

The detailed sketches she had for her new line held no allure tonight. The energy to resume work had vanished. Instead, she scanned local news. The professor played a starring role in online comments. Accusations about extracurricular activities dominated the remarks. The focused attention mimicked a new, spring bag going viral. Not notable yesterday but today capturing everyone's interest. Katherine indulged in a luxurious stretch and remembered her signature Sensational Saunter shoulder bag getting the benefits of a viral premier last year. Purrada opened her eyes, but didn't move an inch from her contented snooze sprawled along the desk.

Time to raid the pantry for a hot chocolate. Yawning, Katherine wandered into the kitchen. She turned on the light over the stove and picked up the kettle. The window over the sink brightened as the motion detector yard lights flashed on. Some water spilled. Leaning into the window, she didn't see a person or a car. She put the kettle on the counter when the back door opened and shut. No rattle of the key in the sticky latch. After Jason's last words, how had she missed locking it?

She turned to face the doorway into the mud room, wondering who would appear around the corner. She mentally noted the knife drawer and inched closer to it, in case.

Footsteps, and then a familiar voice. "Katherine? Are you here?"

Katherine's tensed muscles relaxed. "MJ, glad to see you." She glanced beyond her. "Your friend David here too?

"He fell asleep at my place. I came from your

grandmother's. Thought I'd stop by and see you." She took off her scarf and unzipped her jacket.

"Hang on a minute." Katherine walked into the mud room and locked the back door. Promise to Jason fulfilled. "How about a hot chocolate? That's what I'm up to."

"Sounds good, then tell me your news."

"You first. Are you happy to see David?" Katherine spooned cocoa into two large mugs while the water heated on the stove. She focused her eyes intently on the mugs as she stopped herself from asking if her mother had plans of traveling with her friend.

"David exemplifies the exuberance of joy. I'm saturated with the fun of being in his company once again."

"You make it sound like you got caught in a downpour without an umbrella."

"How did you like him, and the drinks he makes?"

Katherine surprised herself to admit, "I liked him, and the drinks are good. I like the variety of spices. You two make a great team." MJ's smile prompted a familiar lump in Katherine's throat.

MJ hugged her. "He harbors a love for creating and cooking. He knows no bounds." She pointed to the table. "Have a seat and let me finish these drinks."

Grateful for the break, MJ concocted savory mochas and Katherine debated whether to update her about her grandson. Knowing MJ's views about the cops, she decided against it.

They chatted until MJ served the drinks and sat with her hands wrapped around her steaming mug. "David wants to come by and talk with you tomorrow."

Katherine gulped as she struggled with the sip she'd

taken. "With me? Tomorrow might be a little busy."

"I told him how I'm filling in at Clutch. He asked about joining me in serving the public. You know, he has a food workers license."

"He has a license."

"He suggested we'd make a great team for your cafe, for a while at least."

Katherine held her mug in thought. A reprieve from finding a more permanent barista? A valid license makes a talk with him worthwhile. "I'll stick close to the Purse Museum as it opens post holidays tomorrow. I'm seeing William whenever he stops by, otherwise, happy to chat with David."

MJ slapped a hand on the table. "Good. David's a soul mate. I treasure him. He likes you. He likes the Museum's stories of women's history. I gave him a tour."

Katherine finished her drink. "Did he preview your new exhibit?"

MJ got a faraway glint in her eye. "Oh yes, the Sixties Exhibit triggered so many moving memories for him. A true revelation."

"We've got to finish it, and the party planning. We're mired in the pit of January now, but the beginning of your February love month lays on the horizon. We have lots of details left."

"We'll embrace time, and it will become our friend."

Katherine sighed. "Right."

"I'd like to see William and give him my wishes for the new year. Will you see Christopher tomorrow too?"

"I hope so." Katherine hesitated, then plunged forward, "The police have asked William, and drone flyer Nicky too, about anything they witnessed."

"I'm sorry to hear of someone suffering. I hope he died peacefully. Did William see him before he died?"

Katherine leaned forward and stared at her hands wrapped around her empty mug on the table. "No. William explained exactly that to the detectives, I'm sure."

MJ lowered her voice, "How brief a life, and all the other people we touch within our own. Accepting another person's death incites a struggle against destiny. Poor man, and poor William and Nick."

Katherine tapped a finger gently against her mug. "I've been reading about Randall online. Some people think he committed suicide because the college found out he's been coming on to some of the girl students. Some of the news reporters are talking about that."

MJ finished her drink. "Did William know about the accusations?"

"I met one of those students tonight at the police station. The police questioned her too."

"What do the cops want to know?"

"I don't know what they're after. Jason calls it routine questioning. All three of them went home. William didn't want to talk to me at the station. That's why he's coming over tomorrow."

MJ went wide eyed. "Smart man to keep quiet around the cops. Jason took part in it? You'll be facing a conflict of interest there."

Katherine resisted a rise in battle over MJ's accusation. MJ had such trouble seeing past the uniform. Purrada strolled across to the mud room, no doubt to check her dish for treats. "No, that's not it. William left to meet friends at the Campus Coffeehouse."

MJ purred almost as smoothly as Purrada, "It'd be fun to be a fly on the wall there."

Chapter Nine

After they grabbed their mobile orders, Michael led Amber to a table. She peered through the crowd and cocked her head to the side, her dark brown hair wrapped in a long ponytail. "There's a smaller table over by the window."

"The guys are on their way over to tell us what happened with the cops."

Amber sat down. "I can't believe the professor's dead, and Nicky found him."

Michael pulled a chair next to her. "And William works for the guy. I mean worked." He stared at her with those soulful blue eyes. "Life's getting good. I don't want to deal with the cops."

She leaned her shoulder against him. "It can't. Nicky and William didn't do anything wrong. So creepy not knowing what happened to the prof. You know, Julia's mom said she knew him, like a friend or something."

"Well, Bayside can feel small. Sometimes too small. Everyone knows everyone."

Amber thought a moment. "True, but even Julia didn't know how they knew each other. When I told them he died, Donna seemed so upset and left the house in a hurry."

"What's it to her?"

"I have no idea. I told you he kept coming on to

Candace."

"Candace, that track star? He sounds like a jerk, and now he's messing with my life."

"Julia's been fighting with her mom a lot, especially over her new boyfriend. She's tired of her mom stressing over everything."

Michael looked at the door, then back at Amber. "She'll get over it."

"Her mom messed up Julia's New Year's Eve date with Kevin."

"Her boyfriend? Her mom's got problems about them dating?" Michael took a long drink.

"They made a date tonight to make up for it, and her mom stopped it again. They had a big fight. Julia called, hysterical. I would have gone back over, but Julia didn't even want to see me. She's never been so mad at her mom."

Michael put an arm around Amber, drawing her close. "Let's talk about us."

"Oh us? We had a great holiday fireworks count down together." Amber relaxed and put her hand on his knee.

Michael grinned. "Oh yeah. I like being with you." He pressed against her and whispered, "I know a place for you and me…"

Her dreamy stare became focused as the door banged shut. "They're here." Michael kept an arm around her.

Nicky wore the aeronautical museum jacket, as usual. He led the way to the counter for their orders and reached for his. Jaw tight and brisk, William snatched his order. Michael waved them over. They zigzagged through the crowded room.

"Hey, Michael, Amber." William settled in. "What a day."

"And night." Nicky took a big bite out of his sandwich.

Michael sat up straighter and kept his voice low. "What happened with the cops?"

William answered. "First they separated us. No idea where they're taking Nicky. I'm like, what's the deal here? No answer. They shove me in a dark, little room and ask questions. They don't like the answers, then they ask more."

Christopher walked in. He saw them immediately and walked over. He slapped his brother on the shoulder. "Glad to see you."

"Yeah, glad I'm out of there."

Christopher pulled over a chair and nodded at Nicky. "You okay too?"

He answered with half a grin and a wave of a sandwich. "I'm good now. I needed to eat."

Michael leaned toward William. "So? What did the cops want to know?"

"First, he reads me my rights. Then, straight into my job for the prof. What did I do? How long did I work there? Why did I choose to work for Randall? I didn't say much. Another cop steps in. He says he understands, like a friend. He says he feels bad about what happened to my boss, must have been a shock. He assures me I'm safe, if I want to talk about it. I didn't say anything."

Christopher frowned, obviously concerned. "You might need a lawyer."

William paused in thought. "I hope not. They asked if I hung out with Professor Randall at bars. They wanted me to give a list of friends he'd hang out with, especially girlfriends. The cop goes on and on about the girls."

Amber flinched. "I thought they wanted to hear how you found the body."

"Then the cop did something meant to bug me." William leaned back and drank his latte.

Christopher urged him on. "What?"

"He showed me evidence." William watched Nicky wolfing down the last of the sandwich. "Stuff we saw in the field."

Christopher prompted him again. "Like what?"

"Randall's id badge, key card, a plastic wine glass, and work phone. The cop wanted to know the password for the phone. I know it, but I didn't say anything. They can talk to the college. They'll need a warrant or something legal first."

Michael bumped fists with him. "Cool."

William watched the steam rise from the mug, then broke the deep silence. "So, where's Randall's personal phone?"

Nicky said, "Must not have had it on him."

William answered, "When he didn't carry it he kept it hidden, no idea where." William spoke directly to Amber, "Your friend Candace got questioned too."

Amber frowned. "Where is she now?"

William answered, "At the dorm. She wouldn't come here."

Nicky wiped his hands with his napkin. "She freaked. She called her mom from the car. We dropped her at the dorm."

Michael gestured at Nicky. "What about you? Did they come down hard about night droning?"

Nicky grunted. "They led with that. I had to listen to threats of fines and tickets and confiscating my drone.

63

As if. I didn't say anything. They worked the bad cop thing. A couple of times, I thought they wanted to throw me in a cell."

Michael visibly cringed. He groaned and hunched over, with glassy eyes and a cold stare. "I've been there man, not good." Amber guessed his thoughts had filled with his ordeal last fall, abandoned behind bars at that same jail.

Amber trembled remembering what she and Michael had endured. Under the table she took his hand. He stirred again at her touch. "You never want to hear that cell door close on you."

Nicky frowned. "Sorry, didn't mean to bring up bad memories."

"Cool. I don't let it get to me."

Amber added, "We've both moved on."

William nibbled a sandwich and asked Nicky. "So, they talked about the drone then? I mean, you didn't even know the guy."

Nicky spoke directly to William. "When they got off the whole drone thing, they talked about you knowing him. They made me feel like they wanted me to say you killed him. Of course, I didn't."

William went pale and put the remains of the sandwich on the napkin. "Me? Insane."

Christopher had gone as pale as his brother. "A set up? You should lawyer up, in case they want to frame you."

Nicky added, "William and the rest of us may have a problem too. They knew all the names of us at the house, and they talked about everyone."

Michael gestured toward Christopher. "About us?"

William added, "Michael, you had a snack in the

kitchen when we found him, and Amber saw the screen."

Nicky leaned forward. "We didn't tell them about you two, but I wanted to warn everyone. They're fishing for something. Like a cop wants to make a big name for himself. He kept talking to me about drug dealing, like he's sure I deal through our house."

Michael sighed, "Drugs? Oh, great." Amber gave his hand a squeeze, but he didn't act like he felt it at all.

Nicky sighed. "It might get dicey, until the cops figure it out."

William groaned. "Or we prove there's nothing going on."

Christopher took out his phone. "When I left to come here, I got to the stop at the end of our street and there's a cop car in my mirror. I'm thinking, aren't they done with that field yet? Here's our outside camera now." He showed them the screen and a police car parked across from their house.

William groaned. "They're at our house? Are they raiding it?"

Christopher put the phone down. "The alarm's still on. They're waiting."

Nicky leaned back. "I'm staying here for a while."

Michael slammed a fist on the table. "I'm outta here." He stood up.

Nicky said, "Chill, Michael. Together we'll beat them. You're not alone."

Michael reached for Amber's hand. "I need some air. I'll text you guys later. I'm staying away from the house until we all go."

William reached out with a fist bump. "Check the group text."

A full round of fist bumps followed.

Chapter Ten

Few guests stopped by the Museum on its first day after the holidays, but the Clutch Cafe enjoyed a rush of activity. As late afternoon approached, tables emptied. MJ and David cleaned up the bar. MJ dressed in jeans, her t-shirt emanating every color imaginable. Katherine recognized it as one of MJ's favorites, tie dyed personally to emit only good vibrations. It positively pulsed with enthusiasm. David's baggy, flowing beige shirt draped almost mid thighs over his jeans. The open collar framed a necklace made of shimmering seashells.

Katherine sipped an herbal mocha at the counter and silently celebrated her decision to engage David as barista. Not the barista she'd envisioned. Setting new sights can bring better results.

Katherine wrapped her hands around the mug and savored David's delicious liquid sensation, as she relaxed after a busy design day. Birds in the backyard flitted around her grandmother's feeders, enjoying their dinner before the early darkness of the season descended. Purrada sat by the window, also keeping a keen eye on the feathered activity.

MJ stepped around the bar and tapped Katherine on the shoulder. "I had a flash of insight into what's missing in the essence of the '60's exhibit. I want to make some changes. Care to join me?"

"Your broad smile tells me you're inspired. Go

ahead. I'll join you in a bit. I want to catch Amber before she heads home."

William's brief phone call had reassured her, but it had been a disappointment not to see him today. No more demands for him to appear at the police department, Katherine gave another sigh of relief. Of course, today would be hectic for William. The first day back at classes, and what about his job? William's safety, that's all that mattered. She could wait another day to see him. She slipped her phone out of her wristlet and checked her to-do list. She had plenty to keep her busy in the meantime.

Through the deep winter day, Katherine had adjusted the thermostat higher several times, making a cozy haven at the Museum. Now she considered lowering the heat. She braced herself against a sudden chill at the thought. First she'd have to add layers to her fitted, festive winter pullover sweater and her lined, navy blue stretch pants.

She walked into the gift shop. Katherine marveled at how Amber stayed warm in a short sleeved knit top that barely hit the top of her jeans. Katherine leaned against the gift shop wall by the new window display, and they chatted about inventory. Amber pushed her hip against the large storage drawer built in under the counter, and it rolled closed.

Katherine mentally ticked off the last of her thoughts on inventory. "Don't forget to follow up on the macrame shoulder bags order. We need those stocked by the end of the month. I predict sales will surge during the Peace and Love music concert on Valentine's Day."

Amber nodded. "Do you want me to order more of the leather ones with the fringe hanging from the bottom too?"

Katherine paused. "Yes, let's add ten more. Good idea."

Amber spoke while she keyed on the electronic order pad. "Moonjava's excited for the opening. She said she wants people to come together over the 1960's spirit and feel the vibes."

"The new exhibit has been a 'love-in' for her, whatever that is." Katherine laughed.

Amber asked, "What about her daily meditation for the opening?"

"She'll say something groovy." Katherine said. "My imagination runs wild with possibilities." Purrada's loud purr got Katherine's attention. The cat had sneaked inside and sprawled in the middle of the window display. Katherine straightened one of the wallets her pet had batted away.

Amber closed another cabinet. "All done. Hopefully things will be chill at the dorm tonight."

Katherine decided to mention her friend, the Pulitzer-Prize-wishing local journalist Rob. Although his columns could be sensational, she respected the way he stuck to the facts, not to mention a tenacity to stay on a story. "Rob's morning column speculates a drug overdose killed the professor. The investigators will be long gone by now. Thank goodness they'll leave William alone."

"Last night he said the Prof never used drugs."

Katherine crossed her arms. "Why would he go use drugs in a field in the middle of winter? I mean, he has an office, a house, why some arbitrary field off campus?"

"He could watch the fireworks from there."

"By himself? William said he's married." Katherine

shrugged and purposely faced out the window as she asked, "How about Michael? Did you see him at the coffee house last night?"

Amber cleared her throat and spoke without hesitation. "Yes, We left early. He doesn't want anything more to do with the police."

"I can imagine." Katherine put her hands on her hips and squinted to focus on the scene out the window.

In the wintry mix of rain and snow, a red splash of color came into distinct view under the streetlight. A young woman wearing a bright red coat charged full force along the sidewalk and through the gate straight toward them. Over her left shoulder hung a large, red messenger bag, but Katherine focused with concern on the frenzied swinging of her black gloved hands. Below her right hand, a blue wristlet bounced with wild abandon. Katherine pursed her lips, as she hoped it remained secure and zipped. If not, a phone, or cash, or the little bag itself could go flying.

Katherine leaned forward. "Someone's headed this way in a hurry."

A jump onto the porch steps, then the door burst open. Purrada yowled, leaped out of the window and scurried for cover. Katherine tensed as the cat raced away, but then Purrada stopped in the hallway. The kitty sat in a sudden picture of total nonchalance, licking a paw and then gliding it over her ear.

The young woman stopped to catch her breath in the open doorway. In one move she dropped the messenger bag, pulled off her hat, and swept her long black hair behind her shoulder. Amber rushed forward. "Julia, what's wrong?"

Katherine recognized Amber's friend Julia Ruiz.

She often stopped by, and Katherine related her own passion for purses with Julia's love of music. Well-mannered Julia had never been a person to shout and bang her way anywhere, until now.

Julia stared at Amber and thrust her hands forward. Her cell phone balanced on her glove as Julia announced, "She's disappeared."

Amber stared wide eyed. "Who?"

Julia raised her voice, "I mean vanished. No one's seen her. I can't get in touch with her. No one's heard from her all day."

Amber hesitated. "Who are you talking about?"

Julia held her phone higher. "My mom. She's not answering texts or calls. She's never done that. And I talked to Sarah too—"

Katherine asked, "Who's Sarah?"

Julia's words spilled out faster. "She drives Mom's carpool. Sarah said mom missed today's ride. And Brittany said she never showed up at work. Why won't she answer my texts? She always does."

Amber frowned. "Did you talk to your dad?"

"He hasn't heard from her either but said not to worry. How can I not worry? He won't be back until tonight. What if the flight gets delayed?"

"Not home? I could have sworn I saw him…" Katherine wondered who she saw at the fireworks?

Amber interrupted, "Remember? He's been out of town on a medical consult."

Julia turned her head with tears brimming. Katherine gently pushed the door closed and patted Julia on her arm. "Let's not jump to conclusions. We'll help you find your mom. Let's sit down and talk it through." Katherine wished Julia's cell phone would beep with a text from Donna, but in the meantime she wanted to reassure the girl. "How about something warm to drink in the café? We'll sit and figure it all out."

Julia paused before a shaky reply, "I should call 911."

Amber gave her friend a hug. Katherine offered a steady smile of encouragement. "If we need help, we can call from the cafe. Let's figure it out together."

Julia's tense expression eased, although she continued her tight grip on the silent phone.

"Good. I'll go ahead, and you two join me when you're ready." Katherine locked the outside door and put the closed sign in the window.

Purrada brushed against her leg. The sly cat had quietly returned. Katherine picked her up and walked out to the hall. When she turned back, the girls whispered to each other. Worry lines on their youthful faces stood out like the wrinkles on a couple of purses stored for years in the back of a closet. Immediately Katherine's concern grew.

Determined to reassure, Katherine said, "We'll find your mom. Come into the cafe. I'll have a nice hot drink ready for each of you, and we'll figure it all out."

As Katherine entered the cafe MJ announced to her, "Good news tonight. My exhibit changes truly engage viewers and defy the passage of time. The universe awaits the optimal vibration waves for you to breath it all in."

"I'll can't wait to breath it in soon. In the meantime, a bump in the road. Amber's friend has a problem and needs a solution."

"Oh?" MJ paused.

Katherine's grandmother sat front and center in the

cafe, surrounded by her group of dear friends who had earned the affectionate title, The Ladies of the Round Table. Each of the seniors lingered over a teacup. Katherine gave her gran a kiss on the cheek and a hug. "Nice to see you all here." The ladies greeted with festive replies. Only a couple of other customers lingered in the place. David served them at the counter.

Winifred answered immediately, "So good to hear you, dear. You're a warm, dulcet sound on a wintry day." Ever vigilant, caregiver Amanda monitored Winifred's blind return of her cup to the saucer.

Judy and Liz stopped examining a map spread out on the table. Those two seniors remained determined and delighted to keep up their travels and see the world. Had they been talking about their last trip, or their next one?

Margaret held up her hand in a wave. Her ever-present, always full book bag hung on the back of her chair. She may have stopped at the library. She earned her reputation as their best customer and volunteer. "Katherine, I've got a book recommendation for you. Any news from your friend Anthony? How is research for the newest mystery book coming along? The new plot sounded so good, but I haven't seen him in town lately."

Peggy grinned. "That Anthony, he's a thriller, and I don't mean only his books."

Margaret groaned. "Peggy, you're at least two generations too old for him." Peggy laughed.

Pam hugged her granddaughter with a loving smile. "We couldn't wait for our weekly dinner at Al's to cheers to the new year…"

Judy chimed in, "We agreed to delicious fun at the Clutch Cafe."

The Ladies murmured their agreement as Pam continued, "So we came here for a teatime toast instead."

Katherine smiled. "How do you like our new barista?"

Peggy leaned back in her chair next to Pam and clapped her hands together. "Your Clutch Cafe is great, and the new barista creates bliss."

A hum of approval circled the table. Pam said, "Moonjava's friend David treated us to a delicious new tea blend."

"High praise from an English Breakfast Tea devotee." Katherine teased.

From behind the bar, David broke his intent stare with a couple of blinks. "You ladies are most gracious. Would you prefer another round of tea, or a latte?"

Peggy leaned forward with a tentative expression and suggested to Katherine's grandmother, "Pam, a latte. That sounds nice. Something different."

Pam shook her head. "If a latte had been better for teatime, we English would have invented it long ago. But you have one Peggy if you feel the need. Or any of you. David knows what he's doing behind that bar. You can't go wrong with any choice."

Peggy grinned at David, casting lavish, twinkling eyes and eyebrows raised.

"I'm happy to create you a fresh vanilla coconut latte, Peggy. The vanilla will be most calming, and at the same time it helps protect your beating heart. The heavenly allure of fresh coconut heals the soul. Can I interest anyone else?"

Unanimous around the table and Pam relented too. "I can't resist."

Peggy leaned forward and added in a loud whisper,

"Don't you love that accent?"

Katherine seized the pause to alert the Ladies, "I'm letting you know, Amber and her friend Julia are on their way in. Julia's having some trouble. She's upset."

Pam smiled. "We'll all help her." No time to respond, as Amber guided her friend through the doorway.

Pam greeted with a wave. "Girls, join us. David you're such a dear, can you please make two more lattes? Julia, tell us how we can help." Pam offered up the cookie plate.

Julia's bottom lip trembled as she took off her gloves and coat, put her red bag on the floor by a chair, and sat next to Amber. "My mom's missing. I'm worried."

A series of sighs followed and wrinkled brows deepened. Pam patted Julia's hand. David served drinks, gave MJ her fresh espresso, and poured more hot water in the teapot while Amber explained. Julia sniffled into a napkin. David busied himself behind the bar.

Katherine shifted in her chair. "Julia, what do you know about your mother's morning? Can we retrace her steps from the last time you saw her."

"Totally strange. Why wouldn't she go to work today?" Julia tensed. Her eyes widened as she stared at Katherine.

Amber brightened. "You said she had an important meeting."

Julia shook her head. "Brittany said she had to cover for her at a big meeting because she never showed up."

Pam asked, "Brittany?"

"She's my mom's assistant."

Katherine attempted a comforting answer. "Your

74

mom may have suddenly remembered an appointment, or a friend may have needed her for an emergency, so many innocent events may have caused this. Did you see her before she left the house today?"

Julia focused on the question. Purrada strolled by rubbing against Katherine's leg and posed by Julia with an expectant expression.

Scratching Purrada gently behind the ear, Julia's answer came with hesitation and great emotion, "The last time I saw Mom...in our kitchen...we had a quick breakfast...she got ready for work...I had an early class today...she took out a roast to thaw...for dinner...to celebrate...Dad's home tonight for his birthday..." Julia reached toward her phone on the table.

Pam leaned forward. "All right, dear. We'll all think positive thoughts for your mom."

Julia glanced from her phone to Pam. "For breakfast I drank a protein shake. My mom said she had to leave early. She said she had a big meeting early today and wanted to go over her information before she caught her ride."

Katherine nodded. "So far it sounds like a normal day for a busy lady."

Julia cleared her throat. "I only saw her for a minute." Julia glanced at Amber before continuing. "A quick goodbye and see you tonight. She acted kind of worried, or nervous or something." Julia leaned into Amber and muttered so Katherine could hardly hear her add, "Or still mad at me."

Intent on each word, Katherine pressed her finger lightly on her lips, debating whether to pursue that sentiment. "It sounds like her work meeting preoccupied her thoughts. Did she remember to take her purse with her? In her rush, she could have forgotten it and her phone. So, she missed all your calls and texts."

Julia's wiped away a tear, and her face reddened. "She got a call as she left. She answered it, grabbed her bag and left. When I got to school, I realized she took the wrong bag. She took my bag, and I have hers." Julia frowned and strained lifting up the messenger bag with both hands. "What a hassle for me. I called Mom when I figured out I had the wrong bag. No answer, all day."

Katherine grew pensive. "Funny she didn't notice the switched bags. Do you know anything else about her morning?"

"No. She always parks in the same place on Maple, by 84th to catch her van pool. I didn't check to see if her car's there. I could do that. She walks that trail that ends at the Park and Ride. I called Sarah. She said Mom didn't go with them today. She got a text from Mom to go ahead without her." Julia's shoulders sagged and her whole being sank in her chair.

Pam asked, "Who's Sarah? Did I miss something?"

Katherine said, "Did you say she drives your mom's van pool?"

Julia answered in a low voice. "Yes. She said Mom texted she forgot her badge, and not to wait. Did she get in an accident?" Julia teared up.

Amber said, "She could have gone home to get her badge and switch bags but left her phone then by accident?"

Julia shook her head. "No."

Katherine's stomach churned. "Your mom wouldn't have parked in the lot instead of the street? Such cold and wet weather today, and early in the morning with the dark, would she take that trail? I'm pretty sure the trail you're talking about has no lighting. The lot would be safer." Katherine regretted speaking her mind as Julia's eyes brimmed with tears.

"I don't know. She always parked there. We never thought of it as dangerous."

MJ calmly interceded, "Sounds like she had no concerns about her commute routine."

Katherine battled her racing pulse. "Of course, you're right. We need to find the car and go from there."

Julia said, "I went home, before I came here. There's no car in the driveway, and there's no one there. A thawed roast sits in the sink and birthday candles on the counter. She planned to pick up a cake for Dad at the bakery on her way home."

Julia's cell phone lit up with music. The caller id showed "Dad." Julia lurched forward and answered with tears streaming down her face. "Dad. Did you hear from her?"

Chapter Eleven

For privacy on her call, Katherine motioned for Julia to follow her through the kitchen and into her office. After grabbing her purse, Katherine hurried out and closed the door. She glanced at the polka dot satchel in her hand with disappointment. How inappropriate for her next steps, but Julia's needs came first over taking time to review her purse choice. Besides she wanted to get out and back before the storm forecast for tonight. Anyway, no fashion critics stalked the Bayside van pool lot. At least, none with a column, podcast, or show.

A heavy, ominous quiet surprised Katherine when she entered the café. Amber paced alongside the barista bar, Purrada peeked out from around the corner of the abandoned messenger bag, swiping at Amber's foot every time she stepped by. Peggy grabbed her latte and held it close, as Amber's animated arms swung precariously close. Gran, never known for holding back, stopped on the brink of a comment and shifted in her chair. Amanda whispered to Winifred who sipped her drink. Judy and Liz had folded up their map. Margaret slipped her book back in the bag and sat with hands folded, seeming to be in deep contemplation. The relaxed group Katherine had left minutes ago had changed.

Registering the sudden chill, she glanced at the door to the patio. Closed. The chill came from the vibrations, as MJ would say. The ominous change hovered like a snowpack teetering on the brink, before a trigger released an avalanche.

MJ gazed out the window at the horizon, apparently in meditation. "When today's mantra came to me, I quieted my own concerns. Now I see it becoming real." She had the room's attention, and she turned to them. "Erica Jong gives us today's thought—'Advice is what we ask for when we already know the answer but wish we didn't.' " She raised her eyebrows. "Dangerous vibes surround us. Time to raise alarms."

Katherine sat at the table realizing MJ had now put the trigger to an emotional avalanche in play, so she tried applying some avalanche control. "Julia isn't asking for advice, like Erica indicates. She's asking for action. There's no evidence of disaster yet. Let's not get crazy."

MJ shook her head. "We may not know what's happened, but we know something's wrong. I have a foreboding."

Katherine held her hand up. "Well, I'm going to act and see where Donna parked her car. If you can meditate on anywhere Donna might have gone and you get an answer, let me know."

"I'll expand my contemplation." MJ grabbed a pen and paper and stood in deep thought. David leaned forward against the bar and stared as if in a trance.

Katherine moved to stop Amber's pacing marathon. "Julia's in my office." Katherine made eye contact with each of the Ladies of the Round Table. "It would be best if she can stay here until I get back so she can calm down. I hope to be back with good news soon."

The ladies voiced their agreement. Amber nodded. "I'll put an alert out on social media. There's a missing person hashtag on the county page."

Gran spoke up. "Not yet dear. Let's wait to hear what Julia tells us from her call with her father. We need the earl. That will help keep everyone calm."

David asked, "The earl?"

Peggy laughed. "She means a pot of Earl Grey tea, her solution to all life's troubles."

Pam nodded. "Tried and true."

Katherine turned back to Amber. "Can you text me with whatever information Julia tells you from her dad? I want to know right away."

Her gran crossed the floor to make the tea. Katherine glimpsed Peggy with her full attention on the hallway and fluttering her eyelashes, then she raised her hand in a slight wave, and the tone of her voice sweetened, "Hello Anthony. You're the breath of fresh air we're needing. Donna Ruiz has gone missing. You're a mystery author. What should we do?"

Anthony bowed slightly. "Peggy, lovely as ever."

The key ring that Katherine had been pulling out of her purse slipped and dropped to the floor with a loud clang. She put the purse on the table, but before she could stoop to find the keys on the floor, Anthony Marconi swept in with one smooth move and retrieved the ring. He held it out to her.

With an unexpected giggle that felt so unlike her mood Katherine took the keys. "Thanks, Anthony." She hoped he didn't see the sudden heat in her cheeks. Why does he have an emotional effect on her?

He winked and greeted the others, "Hello, charming Ladies of the Round Table. Glad to see you keeping warm on a January day."

The tension in the room eased and the ladies happily greeted their friend. Margaret blushed. "Anthony, how goes your new book?"

"My dear, thank you for asking. Tonight's writing will be another long session. I hoped to sneak in here before closing for a spectacular latte to keep up my energy. The wonderful flavor and caffeine will be perfect to help me finish these next, critical scenes. I may ask you to preview some pages if you're willing."

Margaret raised her mug in a toast. "I'd be delighted. Here's to your evening of mystery."

David playfully juggled a couple of stainless steel canisters. "Let me conjure a mix to inspire creative magic instead of simply wakefulness."

MJ stood up. "Anthony, meet David, a friend of mine and Clutch Cafe's new barista."

"David, nice to meet you. A taste of creativity would be welcome. Thank you" He turned to Peggy. "What did you say about Donna?"

Peggy gestured for Anthony to sit next to her at the table. "Julia came here, in a terrible drama. She can't find her mom anywhere."

Anthony sat down. "Julia's here?"

Katherine answered. "Yes, she's in my office on a phone call with her father. She can't get in touch with her mom."

Anthony sat back. "Oh, that's why you said Donna's missing? I had lunch with her Friday."

Peggy fingered her latte cup. "You took her to lunch?"

"Donna's been kind, helping me with medical facts for my plotting, because the crime takes place at a medical facility. I hope everything's all right."

Katherine picked up her purse. "I'm investigating."

Anthony stood up. "Donna's a friend. Let me help."

Katherine paused, interested. "Are you sure you have time?"

Over the sound of the steam spurt David announced, "Ready for ya, Anthony."

"My car's parked out front, and I'm happy to drive on these slick streets so you don't have to. Hang on a minute." He walked to the counter and paid.

David handed over the latte. "Savor it, man."

"Thanks."

Moonjava's eyes widened. "Be careful. There's a storm on the horizon. I feel the tremors of it in our universe, and I'm not talking about the weather."

Anthony paused. "You're a weathervane to the temperature of our souls, Moonjava. We'll be wary, and we'll find Donna." He tried the drink, paused in consideration, and gave David a thumbs up. "I like it. Thanks again. So, Katherine, where are we headed?" They left the cafe to a chorus of good luck wishes.

Katherine filled him in on the destination as she grabbed a jacket, then reconsidered and put on what she called her arctic coat. She pulled the double lined winter gloves out of the pockets and slid them on as they walked outside.

She snuggled into the luxury leather seat of Anthony's Maserati, glad to leave her classic Mustang out of the ice and safely in the garage. She took off a glove and slid her hand back and forth along the seat enjoying the buttery softness that reminded her of one of her own favorite designs, that lambskin flap over clutch. That bag had earned its name—Sultry. On such a cold night, she appreciated the electric heat from the car seat, a real bun warmer.

In the winter dusk, Anthony did not give in to the

sports car's bait to accelerate. Anthony drove with unusual caution. They crept through the streets. Katherine tapped her fingers on the door's arm rest. She directed him to where Donna left her car every day, but he seemed to know already. How well did he know Donna? He'd never spoken about their friendship.

They rounded the corner by the park, and the car headlights revealed a green Toyota Corolla. Anthony parked in front of it, next to the trailhead of the dark path into the trees. It led over the hill to the ride lot. Twelve hours ago, Donna arrived. That's winter in the Pacific Northwest, dark going and also coming home after a day's work.

Katherine jumped out of the car before Anthony had the engine off. He pointed to the license. "That's her car all right. See, her personalized plate with DR D R on it? She always liked that her initials match her title."

Katherine held her breath as she peered through a window. No one inside. She sighed and her shoulders relaxed. Katherine tried the doors on her side, and found them locked. Across the top of the car, she saw Anthony do the same, then shake his head.

She grabbed her phone from the front pocket of her purse. "My cell has a flashlight on it."

"Good idea." Anthony pulled a phone out of his pocket. Katherine scanned the front passenger window and across the interior. Anthony bent next to her and did the same. Anthony's warm breath blew against her cheek and steamed the glass. The front seat, the steering wheel, dashboard, seats, floor, nothing out of place.

Katherine pointed and tapped on the glass. "There's her work badge hanging from the rear view mirror, Northwest Medical Research Labs. She never took it."

Anthony frowned. "The badge has the NRML logo. Nothing seems to be out of the ordinary. She could have gone to work without it and still hasn't returned."

"She never came back from wherever she went." Katherine explained that Donna never showed up at work that day, despite an urgent meeting. She played her flashlight along the interior. "Anthony, do you see that?" She trained the light directly on the side edge of the car seat where it curved up slightly. "There's a stain on the side of the seat."

Anthony pressed closer. "Who knows how long that's been there. It could be coffee, or anything."

Katherine shuddered. "It could be blood."

Chapter Twelve

Katherine's phone screen lit up the early evening dusk, and Amber's frustration simmered in the message.

—*Her dad is clueless. Julia in panic. Taking her home. Wait 4 U there*—

Katherine responded by clicking on a heart. She updated Anthony. "Tomás didn't have any answers for Julia. Amber's taking her home and will stay until we get there."

Anthony shook his head. "Poor kid."

"We should contact the police. I can call Jason without making it official and see what he says."

A scowl passed over Anthony's face as he answered, "While you're calling, I'll knock on a couple of these houses and see if anyone saw Donna."

He crossed the street and approached the closest house. Lights went on, and a face in the front window disappeared behind a sudden movement of curtains. How long have they been watching? Curious neighbors wondering why they peered into the car? Or another motive? She shivered a little despite the arctic coat and pulled up favorites on her phone. She clicked on Jason's grinning face with the shining eyes.

He answered right away. "Hi there. You've been on my mind."

At the sound of his deep, romantic tone, an unexpected rush of affection filled her heart. Katherine wished they had time for sentiment now. "Jason, hi. I need your help."

In an instant his voice turned urgent. "What's wrong? Where are you?" Katherine pictured those wrinkles deepening between his eyebrows, as they did whenever Jason showed concern.

Her stream of consciousness jumped the banks as it poured out in a surging flood. "I'm standing next to Donna's abandoned car in the cold at dusk, and no one can find her. She never showed up at work today. You don't know Amber's friend Julia, but she hasn't heard from her mom, that's Donna. No responses from her calls and texts. At first I thought Julia overreacted, but we haven't been able to find her mom anywhere, and now I'm next to her car and there's blood stains. I'll search the area, but I want to make an official missing person report through you."

His voice softened, "You worried me for a minute. I'm glad you're not in any trouble."

Katherine took a breath, and as she released it her shoulders and stomach immediately loosened their tight grips. She rubbed a finger across her forehead. She took another deep breath.

Jason's official voice rang in her ear. "Are you sure they're blood stains?" Katherine stifled a groan as he continued, "Is Donna's daughter there with you? Make sure you're in a safe place."

"Julia's at the cafe with Amber and MJ, but they're headed over to Julia's house. I'm at the park by the Bayside transit center. Donna parked her car here on the street. I'll investigate the park trail. I might find her there."

"I'm coming with Hobbs. He can pick up a scent.

Don't investigate without me, and don't touch anything."

Katherine caught a guilty lump in her throat. What had she and Anthony touched on the car in their haste? She gave Jason the address of the house across the street. Anthony stood in deep conversation with a woman at the door.

"I'm on my way. I know there's no point in asking you to go home and let me call you later. Instead, I'm asking you to go sit in your car and wait for me."

"I'll see you when you get here. Thank you. Please hurry." Katherine clicked off the call.

A car drove past, and she moved out of the street. She stepped toward Anthony's car, but a glance toward the darkening path through the woods beckoned. She continued with her original plan. Her boots crunched up the gray gravel path and she moved along without hesitation. No time to wait. Donna might be lying somewhere injured, waiting for rescue.

Before disappearing into the trees, she glanced back at Anthony. An animated homeowner in furry red slippers, pajama pants showing beneath a thick blue robe spoke to him. He stepped back a little as her hand pointed at the park in an erratic gesture. She appeared ready early for a long winter's nap. She opened the door wider, and a man stood behind her. They motioned for Anthony to come inside and closed the door behind him. They must have seen something and have a story to tell.

Katherine shook her phone to turn on the flashlight. She slipped through the edge of the tree line of firs, mixed with tall, wild bushes that never lost their leaves to the seasons. She slipped along on the bigger, slick stones, struggling in her boots made for fashion, not traction. She ventured on, calling out Donna's name over and over.

The short hike to the crest revealed an overlook above the transit center. A bus released its passengers. Bundled commuters, puffs of breath visible, trudged toward cars in the adjacent lot. It all seemed so normal. How could such a mundane site be shrouded in mystery? Coughing close by caught her attention, and a man rounded the bend. He put a handkerchief up to his face as he passed. A line of people followed him, wearing heavy coats and some scarves, carrying briefcases, totes, and some wearing backpacks. Katherine smiled as they passed and received weary expressions in return. She asked if anyone knew Donna, or had seen a woman today, around age fifty carrying a red messenger bag.

One young man with a beard stopped, as others passed by shaking their heads. "This morning when I turned down the hill I noticed a flash of red off the path, up against the bottom of a tree. I got here late for my bus, so I rushed by. That bright red stood out. It showed over that way. I don't see it now." He pointed, and Katherine thanked him.

He turned back with a brief wave and continued down the trail to home. "Hope you find what you lost." The crunch of the gravel faded, as the parade disappeared. Alone again, Katherine put renewed pep in her steps, moving in the direction he'd indicated.

The evening darkened when she stepped off the path and proceeded deep into the silent trees. With every step, her beloved boots sank into the damp ground. She checked them in her light. "The mud will ruin these gems." Reluctant to trudge farther, she pointed her shining cell phone along the ground and into the distance. Nothing red. Nothing suspicious.

"Donna? Donna?" Her hesitant calls scared a squirrel up a tree. From a deemed safe distance, tail quivering, the animal scolded her with a clicking diatribe before running out on a branch and jumping away. A bunny crouching by the foot of the tree froze. Bayside bunnies set up residence for years now in neighborhoods. So cute. She crouched over with one hand on her knees, moving her light to the side. The animal slowly hopped away.

Katherine debated whether to further sacrifice her boots to the mud or continue to the transit center. Neither option appealed, but concern for Donna and a demanding curiosity moved her forward. That man had seen red. She moved with care around the mud, but avoiding it proved ineffective, like hoping to save money by closing her purse after already pulling the wallet out.

Bird tracks on the ground surrounded some scattered trash. From observing her gran's bird feeder antics and her local bird watching companions, Katherine guessed the tracks came from scavenger crows. She focused in closer. Empty cookie wrappers and a pretzel bag. Something laminated, a picture of Julia next to her full name. Katherine gently picked it up.

One of the bushes shook. Katherine straightened immediately. There's no wind. An animal? She traced the perimeter with her light. A wide indentation swept through the muck by one of the trees. No wheel marks, something dragged? Her thumb and finger tightened on the school ID.

Another bush shook, closer to her. Not a rabbit. A bigger animal? Or a person?

Pushing optimism, Katherine called out, "Donna? Donna?" Silence now. Katherine played her light along the leaves. "Donna?"

The light gleamed on a root, monopolizing her attention. A chain, and a pendant? And boot prints. She wouldn't let this discovery get away. She moved toward the mystery item, talking as she did, "Donna? Whoever you are, the police are here. They're right behind me. They're coming here to find you." She reached down and disentangled a necklace, with a broken chain. A short, loud groan rumbled from the other side of the bushes.

"Donna? Are you hurt?"

Staring into darkness gained her no answers. Had she scared an animal? A two-legged one?

She checked the time on her phone. Jason must be here by now. She felt again in her pocket the smooth ID as she deposited the jewelry there too. She kept a watch on where the mysterious sounds had occurred, while she stepped forward. In an instant her heel caught on the uneven ground, and she went down. Now the mud she'd regretted on her boots became the least of her mess. She struggled to stand and move. Her pristine purse lay clasp down in a puddle. She reached for it, then flinched when she heard the discreet crunch of gravel and something on the trail coming her way.

Chapter Thirteen

A light bounced in and out of the bushes. She panicked to her left, then her right seeking a hiding spot. Which direction promised safety, and a discreet observation point?

"Katherine? Katherine."

A cough, then a powerful beam held her in its grasp. Frozen in place like one of the startled bunnies, she heard a familiar voice, "There you are. I figured you wouldn't wait by the car, unless you parked it here in the woods?"

Katherine didn't know whether she should feel relief, or irritation at the sarcasm. Behind her, Jason's powerful flashlight lit up the whole area. Still nothing to see in the bushes. She decided on relief.

Jason laughed and helped her stand up. "You're taking a natural mud bath for a new fashion trend?"

She made a feeble attempt to wipe away the mess on her coat, managing to smear it deeper. "Despite your one-star attempt at humor, I'm glad to see you."

"Ouch. A designer and a critic. I think you're the one who needs to clean up their act. I'm glad to find you anyway. Why are we in the middle of the forest, when you're worried about a car?"

She pulled her bag off the ground and smeared a streak of mud through it. "First I want to show you something else. Right over there."

Jason shook his head. "You may have to run that bag

through the washing machine before you hit the runway."

She reduced her voice to a whisper, "I heard something hiding in those bushes. I don't see Donna. I called and she didn't answer me. I have no idea what made the noise."

She barely heard his response, but she couldn't mistake the sudden serious tone. "Wait here." He walked with caution, leaving one hand on the holstered gun. He motioned back at her several times to stay put. Katherine pulled her wet coat tighter, with furtive glances in every direction.

Jason shook foliage. He stopped and listened. He retraced his steps and whispered, "It might have been an animal you heard. I'm not seeing anything. I'm on duty in an hour. If there's anything suspicious about Donna's vehicle, I'll come back here and do some tracking with Hobbs."

"I found this on the ground. Jewelry." She pulled the necklace out. In Jason's bright light some stone chips shimmered. A flower design and along the bottom the name Julia. From top to bottom the name Donna. The two names intersected at the "a." "See, Donna came through here. How could she break her necklace?"

"She lost it on the way to the bus?"

"She took a van pool. It has both their names, but it must be Donna's. I guess it could be Julia's, but why would Julia be here?"

"I may want to let Hobbs out for tracking. I want to examine Donna's car. Can I take that? It may have her scent for Hobbs."

Katherine reluctantly held it out. Jason carefully took out an evidence bag, and she dropped it inside. He pocketed it. "In case she's a missing person."

"Yes, missing."

They walked to the street. Hobbs' sudden bark echoed. Muscles bulged, as Jason raised an arm and signaled the dog to quiet. She admired his stance in the streetlight. Her gaze locked on him with admiration and a moment of allure, until the weight of her muddy pant leg registered again, and a chill vibrated through her. What a mess, and the heel on one of her pathetic boots, gone.

Jason grunted. "That her car?"

Katherine pointed. He flooded it with the spotlight he used when he pulled a driver over at night.

Transferring the muddy, polka dot purse into her other hand, she hurried forward. Jason shook his head. "You should have waited for me here. Where's your car?"

"I needed to do a preliminary once over, or whatever you cops call it. Now that you've got it all lit up, come see the inside. I saw blood."

"Maybe blood. You don't know."

"Alleged blood." She motioned at the window. "The glove compartment's open. How did that stuff get on the floor? Nothing fell on the floor before. What happened?"

She stared at Jason, who watched her. "You're sure what you saw?"

"Yes. I saw blood on the front seat. I would have noticed this. Oh my gosh, the visors. They're down."

"Are you…"

"Yes, positive. Besides why would she use visors before sunrise?"

Jason stepped around the car. "No evidence of a break in, so only someone with the keys has been in it.

You're telling me I'm here because of a messy parked car at the end of the workday, and a lost necklace?"

Katherine scowled and pulled her coat tighter. "I told you, Donna never showed up at work. She's late getting home for her husband's birthday celebration with the family. She hasn't responded to her daughter's calls or texts all day."

"Now I'm wondering, why am I talking with you and not Donna's family. How are you getting pulled into this? And where's your car?"

Across the street a front door opened, and Anthony thanked some people. Jason watched him cross the street. "You're not here alone."

"He gave me a ride because he wanted to help."

"Uh huh."

Jason stared at Anthony as the trio met up. Anthony waved in greeting. "Jason, good to see you. We need police help here."

"Uh huh."

Katherine implored him, "Anthony, please tell Jason if anything is different about the car now."

"Why? Did you see Donna?"

Jason motioned before Anthony took a step. "Please don't touch anything, in case it turns into a crime scene."

Anthony put hands on knees and leaned into the passenger window. "Your light shines stronger than what we used, but I don't remember anything on the floor, or the glove compartment open."

"See? And check the windshield. The visors are down now."

Anthony straightened with a puzzled frown. "That's odd. I don't remember about the visors, but the lanyard with her badge has disappeared from the mirror."

Katherine stopped in her tracks. "It is. Jason we both saw her badge. Someone has been here in the last few minutes. They could see us right now."

Anthony scanned the neighborhood. "Donna's here?"

Jason walked around the car. "Let me make a more detailed inspection."

Anthony and Katherine moved onto the grass. She stood vigilant as Jason examined what he could see of the inside of the car, and then the outside in slow, methodical movement. He noticeably lingered over the stain she'd pointed out. Anthony watched with interest, deeply concerned for a dear friend? Or learning as an author from an expert how a cop surveys a crime scene? She focused back on Jason's actions. After circling the car two more times, kneeling down to inspect tires and bumpers, he stopped again by the driver's door.

Anthony blew on his hands. "I spoke to the woman in that house. She gets home from her night shift before 6:00 a.m. She unwinds a little after work, eats a snack, and she sits in her living room watching the world go by, as she said."

"Any chance she saw Donna park her car?" Katherine listened with enthusiasm, and Anthony had Jason's attention too.

"She said this car parks here every weekday. Then she complained at great length about the inadequacies of commuter parking. Anyway, she said the car parked there early this morning, before she got home from work. She didn't see anyone around the car, but she slept most of the day. I showed her a picture on my phone of Donna. She said she might recognize Donna from seeing her on other days. Not sure. Right before she went to bed a maintenance truck came out of the park."

Jason asked, "Maintenance?"

"A white pickup, like a Parks Department truck, with branches covering the back drove out and over the curb to get back on the street."

"Not much to go on." Katherine calmed her bubbling frustration.

Anthony shrugged. "I knocked on a few more doors. A couple of them, no answer. One other, a man said yes he sees people, women and men walking up to the trail. Most light their way with flashlights that early in the morning. He didn't notice anything unusual with today's early morning commuters."

"Commuter traffic and a white truck." Jason focused again on the car's interior.

Jason reached for the police radio on the shoulder of the vest. "Dispatch, Holmes."

No static disrupted the reply. "Dispatch, go ahead."

Jason gave the location. "Missing person's abandoned car. I'm investigating with Hobbs. Will report anything found."

"Roger. Sending backup. Over."

Jason clicked the radio off, and Katherine nodded at him. "You're filing an official missing person's report then?"

Jason nodded. "Yes. Time to track with Hobbs. Why don't you …" Jason glanced at Anthony. "Why don't you both go over to Donna's house and help Julia. I'll call you later when I have news." Jason hand signaled the squad car. Hobbs' face dominated the windshield, staring at his partner's every move.

Anthony lifted each foot in turn and sighed. "Sounds like we're getting the brush off."

Katherine stood her ground and reached into her pocket. "Jason, I found something else in the woods. Julia's school ID laying on the ground." Jason carefully held the card by its edges and examined it. He put it in an evidence bag. With an on-duty, official firmness in his eyes, Jason clicked the switch on the vest, and Hobbs rushed out as the car door opened. The K-9 raced to him and sat attentive for any command. Katherine knew to let a working dog alone.

Jason pocketed the evidence. "Did Julia come here today, for her mom?"

"She never said she did, but Donna accidentally had Julia's purse. What if Donna's hurt up there on the trail? We need to help you find her." Katherine crossed her arms with impatience, as Jason took time to check the equipment and secure Hobbs' dog vest.

Anthony shook his head. "If she came back to the car now to get her badge, why wouldn't she go ahead and drive home? Unless someone else came here."

Jason attached the dog's leash. "Someone else may have keys to the car now."

Hobbs gave a short, loud whine. Katherine encouraged him to begin work. "Good dog, Hobbs. Let's find Donna."

Jason gave the dog a hand command, then addressed both Katherine and Anthony, "If you won't go, then you should both stay here, Don't touch anything. Wait for the backup team."

Katherine shook her head. "I need to show you what I found. You need me there."

Anthony took a step forward. "Me too. Donna's more than a friend. She's important." Anthony spoke to Katherine, "I want to see all you found."

Katherine felt a jolt at that declaration. Did Anthony share more than a book with Donna? Whether he did shouldn't make any difference to her. Jason gave a quick, subtle hand gesture directed at the dog. Hobbs immediately faced Anthony and barked vigorously and without stop. At the outburst, Anthony took a quick step back.

Jason faced Hobbs. "Beruhigen." Katherine recognized the German command, as the dog immediately stopped.

Jason glanced at Anthony. "Good idea to keep back when he's on the job."

"Sorry. I didn't know …"

Katherine heard Jason's familiar phrase muttered, as he turned back to Hobbs, "Braver Hund." Good dog? Katherine stifled a groan. Jason's sense of humor needed work.

"I'll see if Hobbs can get a scent."

Regretting once again her fall in the mud and the resulting chill through her arctic coat and thick wool gloves, Katherine stood next to Anthony on the sidewalk and debated asking him more about the work with Donna. Anthony plunged his hands deep in his jacket pockets. His shoulders drew up and then relaxed as he sighed a visible puff of breath. Jason led the dog through a painstaking, slow walk around the car. Wherever Jason stopped and pointed, the dog sniffed deeply.

"Darn the rain and slush, washing away any trace of scents." Anthony walked around in a tight circle, then stopped and studied the dog's movements again.

Pleased to share her recently acquired knowledge Katherine explained, "Actually the wet surfaces help with tracking. People shed dead skin cells all the time, and those cells float on top of water. Seattle rain gives a police dog advantages."

"I hope he takes advantage soon then."

Katherine couldn't resist showing off. "Light rain brings best results, so the cells stay in place. A downpour can be too much, and if a wind kicks in the cells will scatter all over."

Jason had the dog next to the driver's door. He took out the necklace. He crouched to Hobbs' level and offered Hobbs that scent.

Anthony pointed. "That dog's onto something."

Hobbs sniffed the ground next to the car, then Jason offered him the necklace again. The command for the dog to sit came sharp, as Jason pocketed the evidence bag again. Then Jason gave a thumbs up to them. "If you insist on coming, stay at least 10 feet behind me and follow any instructions I tell you." He grinned and said, "Voran."

Hobbs trotted along the sidewalk, with Jason keeping pace. They headed to the path through the park.

Anthony shrugged. "Voran? I guess that means 'move it.' Let's go."

When the group crossed the tree line into darkness, Jason used a flashlight, and the beam sliced through the night. Hobbs made smooth, determined moves straight up the path, without hesitation.

Over the crest, nose straight down, Hobbs circled the area faster and faster. He moved in one direction then reversed and circled again.

Anthony tapped Katherine on the shoulder. "He's lost the scent."

Right then the dog zig-zagged away from the path, and the transit center. The human parade followed as best they could in the underbrush. Katherine tripped over the uneven ground. Anthony helped her. "We need to keep up."

Katherine grabbed her muddied handbag and wished for her styled backpack, or even a hands free crossbody. Jason made an abrupt move away from where she'd searched earlier. Oh no, Hobbs must be on the wrong track.

When they caught up to him, Jason stood transfixed. Hobbs sat alert at his side, snout pointed at something next to a tree. Katherine stepped forward. "What do you see?"

"Stay back, Katherine. This may be a crime scene."

Katherine walked closer and squinted to see. "Why?"

Jason swung an arm out to stop her. "A phone on the ground, see it?"

"Right there? Oh yes, it fell screen down." Katherine gasped. "The phone cover decoration is all daisies."

Jason pointed. "And you see the name engraved on it? Your friend, Donna Ruiz." He gestured to the left toward the ground a few feet farther. "A scarf, with what may be blood stains. I'm suddenly uneasy about her disappearance."

Anthony groaned, "Oh no."

A short blast of static, followed by a woman's voice. "Backup arrived on site."

"Tell them to set up a perimeter around the car, license DRDR. I'm in the woods next to it."

"Roger."

"We need forensics out here."

"Roger."

Jason signed off. "I still need legal permission for inside the car."

Katherine reached for her phone. "I'll text Amber to see if Julia can call her dad."

Anthony clicked his cell phone. "I'll call Tomás and ask him to drive here after he lands, or can he give permission over the phone? No need to upset Julia more."

"That would be helpful. Thanks." Jason took pictures.

"Tomás? Anthony here…What? Wait, don't hang up. The police…Here, talk to Katherine"

Wrinkles appeared on Anthony's forehead as he handed the phone to her. "Tomás? Katherine here. Hello?"

"I'm here. Don't put him back on the line. Where's Julia?"

"She's all right but anxious to see you."

"Where? I'll go to her now."

"Your plane landed early? Tomás, we're with the police at Donna's car near the transit center. The police need permission to search the car."

"The police? What's happened to Donna? Where are you? Are you where she usually parks?"

"Yes."

"I'll be there right away. Get rid of Anthony. He better not be there when I get there." The call cut off.

Katherine handed the phone back to a grim-faced Anthony. "What did you do to upset him?"

Sirens pierced the air, then stopped. Anthony silently pocketed the phone. In the distance, red and blue lights continued to pulse.

Jason herded them back in the direction they'd

come. "Let's get back out to the street."

As they emerged from the trees, Jason walked straight to the officers. Another car turned the corner and parked across the street. The profile of a stocky man pulsed in the red and blue police lights. He wore a long, thick coat and a grim frown. Anthony grabbed Katherine's hand and moved to the sidewalk. "There's Tomás."

While crossing the street, Tomás spoke in a loud voice, "Where's Donna?"

Katherine shook her head. The man's ragged edges showed through the sunken eyes, beard stubble, and unkempt hair. He stepped over the curb and Anthony answered, "We can't find her."

Tomás pointed at Anthony and growled, "You should leave."

Jason's professional voice broke in, "Mr. Ruiz? Sir, I'm Officer Jason Holmes with Bayside Police. I spoke to you on the phone. Any word from your wife?"

"I haven't been able to reach her. My daughter can't reach her either. No one has seen her since early morning."

Jason pointed behind him. "Is this her car?"

"Yes."

"With your permission, we'd like to check inside for any indication where your wife is."

Jason's eyebrows raised briefly as Tomás pointed a key chain at the vehicle and pressed. The double beep punctured the evening's silence. It became a prelude to Katherine's sudden phone tone.

Katherine answered Amber's incoming call. "Amber?"

"We're at Julia's. We're scared. Can you help?"

Katherine's wide eyes met Jason's glance. She clicked the speaker on. "You're at Julia's, and there's a problem?"

"We're standing in the living room in the middle of a total mess. Someone broke in through the kitchen door. They trashed the house."

Tomás shouted, "What?"

Jason interrupted. "Amber, no. Both of you, get out of that house right now, Lock yourselves in your car. I'm sending an officer over to do a safety sweep." Katherine gave him a startled expression. He added, "We want to clear the premises of anyone still there."

"Someone here? Julia, we have to go…" Amber hung up.

Tomás shook his fist. "My wife…missing, my daughter…terrified, my house…broken into. What next?"

Chapter Fourteen

Jason signed off from dispatch. He spoke to Tomás, "Officers are headed to your house."

"I need to be with my daughter. Do whatever you need to with the car to find my wife."

Jason gestured to an officer close by. "Tomás, this is Officer Roy Jacobs, meet Tomás Ruiz. Escort Mr. Ruiz home, and keep him informed of developments here."

Katherine wanted to stay for the car search, but she also needed to check on the girls at the break-in. She put a decisive hand on Tomás' arm. "I'll drive over too. I can help."

Tomás turned and sprinted to the car, followed by the officer.

Anthony put an arm on Katherine's shoulder. "I'll drive you."

At Donna's house, Amber's car stood bookended by patrol cars at the curb. Anthony parked behind Tomás' car in the driveway. Katherine's vision blurred as tears welled up over the touching father and daughter reunion on the front lawn.

Anthony left the key in the ignition. "I'm not sure I should get out."

"After that phone call, better not to push it. Do you want to go, and I'll fill you in later?"

Anthony took a deep breath. "I'll stay for a while.

I'll stay in the background."

Amber tapped on the window. Anthony rolled it down, as Katherine got out and walked around the car to hear Amber's update. "Julia came home to a mess. They still haven't said when we can go back in. What happened at her mom's car?"

Anthony pointed. "The cops are coming out now."

Two officers walked straight to Tomás and engaged him in deep conversation.

Katherine stepped forward. "Let's join them."

As the trio approached, the officer glanced their way but never paused the conversation. "We're still taking pictures and dusting for fingerprints. Don't know if we'll get any. We've cleared the living room if you want to come inside. Can you indicate to us anything missing?"

Tomás stepped forward. "Yes, I want to go in."

Julia put her hand in his. "Me too."

The officer moved toward the house, followed by the group. Another officer appeared at the front door. "No prints so far, sir. We're wrapping up soon."

A dark chill dominated the interior, despite the hum of the heater. Katherine switched on another lamp. Anthony stood in the back corner of the room, out of the way. Amber put her phone in her pocket as father and daughter walked into the middle of the living room. He glared through squinting eyes. Julia sobbed, and his expression softened as he hugged her. Couch cushions tossed on the floor, shelves emptied, a colored glass candle vase had fallen to the floor and broken in countless pieces, and the candle had been stepped on and crunched in the middle of it. Side table drawers pulled all the way out lay abandoned on the floor, their contents scattered.

Katherine heard a faint, terrified whimpering. Behind the couch she found poor Perro. She picked him up and soothed him.

The officer paused at the stairs. "One room upstairs appears to be an office, got ransacked, and the primary bedroom too. The rest of the rooms appeared untouched, except the kitchen door got forced open. Potentially how they got in."

Tomás stood silent. Tense. Katherine motioned at the couch. "You said you're done in here?" She straightened the cushions and gently guided Julia to sit with her and the dog.

The officer prepared to take notes. "Your wife hasn't been heard from in over twelve hours? You've been out of town. And your daughter?"

Tomás focused on his girl. "Julia."

"I'm sorry to press you, but I have a few questions to help investigate the case."

"Which case?" Katherine knew the significance of naming something a case. "The break in? Or Donna's disappearance?"

Ignoring her distraction, the officer continued, "Sir, when did you last contact your wife?"

"We talked on the phone New Year's Eve night."

"Not since then?"

"Yes." The following silence fell heavy.

The officer resumed, "How did that conversation go? How did she sound? What kind of mood…"

"We had a happy conversation."

"About what?"

He hesitated, folded his arms across his chest. "We remembered the loving new year celebrations we've shared, and our hopes for another bright year ahead. I wanted to come home early, but I couldn't. I had commitments."

The officer leaned in. "You had a work problem?"

"No work problem. I'd been asked as a consultant."

The officer shifted his weight from one foot to the other. "And your wife? Under stress at home, or in her work?"

Julia and Amber exchanged a fearful glance.. The officer remained preoccupied with Tomás, who flashed a momentary tight jawed defiance. A thin veneer of calm masked all emotion, Tomás continued. "Donna has a stressful job, but she's handled that for years. She reviews pharmaceutical test results before drugs are placed into the market. I don't know a lot about her current assignments." He stared at the floor a moment, then raised his voice, "We share a beautiful marriage and family, and no one can say otherwise."

The officer made a brief note on the screen device. "And Julia, you started the day here with your mom? Did you see her before she left for work?"

"Yes."

The officer encouraged a more complete answer. "What did you talk about?"

"She didn't say much." Amber grabbed a box of tissues and handed them to Julia.

The officer frowned. "I'm sorry my questions are upsetting, but your answers may help us find your mom. Did she say anything about stopping somewhere before work? Or meeting anyone on the way to the van pool?"

"I don't remember, but most days she stops at the coffee house between here and the transit center for a latte."

The officer made another note.

Julia blurted out, "I don't know why she isn't texting or calling me. She always answers me." Julia eyes met Amber's again, as she sat on the edge of her chair.

"If either of you think of anything else while I'm here, please let me know." The officer gave each of them a card. "Or later, you can contact me directly at that number. The back of the card shows the number for the department."

Katherine took Julia's hand. "Officer, does the break-in have something to do with Donna's disappearance?"

"We keep all options open as we investigate. It may be an unrelated robbery. I'd like you to walk through sir, make a list of anything missing."

Tomás plowed through the piles in the room, picking where to step as best he could. He put his hands on his hips. "The TV, the stereo, they left all the big items. Oh, the desk top computer drive is gone. It stands behind that screen."

The officer took a picture of the screen and made a note. He pointed to the officer still in the doorway. "Confirm the photographer got it too."

"Yes, sir."

"Mr. Ruiz, I'd like you to view the rooms upstairs to see what's missing too."

Tomás gave Julia a hug. "Be right back."

Intrigued and tempted to tag along, Katherine resisted and stayed in the living room. As they left the room, Amber stood up. "How about some water?"

Something about the intensity of Julia's demeanor aroused Katherine's curiosity. Julia slowly stood up. "I'll go in the kitchen with you. I left my phone on the counter."

As the girls walked out of the room, the edge of a cell phone stuck out of the top of Julia's jeans. Katherine left Perro on the couch and moved closer to the kitchen doorway. Anthony paced back and forth, along the front window.

Katherine strained to hear Amber. "You should tell them about your fight with your mom. He needs to know everything."

"Shhh. Bringing all that up about Kevin won't help them find Mom."

Amber spoke again, slowly. "She's been upset. The police need to know."

Julia's voice peaked on the verge of hysterics. "Now I wish instead of fighting about Kevin, I should have made her tell me what upset her. It all became about me and Kevin. Amber, the last time I saw my mom I treated her so bad."

A trio of loud knocks on the front door got Perro barking. She and Anthony exchanged glances. The door slowly opened. A shout intruded, "Hello. We're here to console, to help…"

From the room behind her, Julia's voice tentative, then stronger, "Who? Who's there?"

"Hello? Anyone?" A man's shiny and large sized oxford shoe, perfectly clean despite the weather, crossed the threshold. His fitted black business pants matched the expensive overcoat with the deep pockets. The gray streaks in his short hair and wrinkles indicated middle or more age and portrayed a distinguished air that complemented an overall physically fit stance. He certainly played more than golf. When he knocked again, the lamplight sparkled on an oversize diamond embedded in a wedding ring. He smiled with perfectly aligned, bright white teeth. "Oh, hello. I'm Stephen. I work with Donna. My wife and I grew concerned. Have you heard anything from her?"

"That's Mom's boss." Could he also hear Julia through the wall?

Katherine stepped away from the wall. "Hello, we're friends of the family. I'm Katherine, and let me introduce Anthony." He mumbled a greeting.

Stephen spoke again, "Nice to meet you both. What have you heard from Donna?"

Katherine answered, "I'm afraid we still haven't heard anything."

A striking woman entwined her arm in Stephen's. Her makeup accented her dazzling green eyes that darted around the room, and around Katherine, taking in every detail. Blonde locks fell loose from her up-do hairstyle and framed her face, a flawless complexion, and shiny lipsticked red lips pursed to speak. The older woman's evident fight against aging showed head to foot, in her healthy figure and even muscular demeanor. A daring purse choice of suede in the wet winter hung from a thin shoulder strap. Katherine recognized the designer instantly and knew he'd never approve his work of art exposed to today's risky weather. A miracle no visible marks showed in the leather from the winter rains. The woman's knee-length, cream colored fashion coat hung beautifully and perfectly clean except for a small mud splotch on the left side on the hemline. The spot appeared as a recent stain, no doubt the coat would soon get a trip to the cleaners. Her ankle height designer boots could also use some tender loving cleaning. Matching gloves hid any jewelry.

The man moved forward as she closed the door.

"I'm sorry. Shocking news. She will turn up. I'm sure. I wanted to give my consolations in person. I mean, Cleo and I, of course." He patted her arm.

Cleo gazed around the room. "Such terrible trouble here. What happened?"

Katherine shrugged her shoulders. "No one knows. Donna's daughter discovered the break in. The police are upstairs now with Tomás."

Cleo gave a small gasp. "How terrifying for her, in addition to worries about her mother. I hope she's all right."

With Amber's encouragement, Julia stepped into the room. Perro trotted over and sat next to her. "I'm okay."

Stephen extended a hand. "Julia, we're so sorry about what's happened. We'll help however we can."

Cleo added, "Think of us as family to help support you and ease your troubles. We want you reunited with your mother." Cleo's soothing, almost lyrical tone matched her concerned expression. "I'm certain Donna will be found safe and soon."

At the sound of footsteps Katherine pointed to the stairs. "You may be able to help the detective. He had some questions about Donna's work."

Stephen straightened his posture. "Of course." He left Cleo at the door and met the police officer at the bottom step. Holding out a hand he introduced himself. "Hello, I'm Stephen Rider, Donna's boss at NRML Pharmaceutical Company. Please let me know if there's anything you need from me or my company."

The officer shook the extended hand. "Hello, sir. When did you last see Donna Ruiz today?"

"She didn't come into the office today."

The officer gestured across the room at Cleo. Stephen said, "Let me introduce my wife Cleo. We stopped by to support the family." Cleo smiled.

The officer said, "I'm investigating the break in. Another effort deployed tracking the woman's disappearance." Julia stifled a cry, and Amber took her hand and comforted her. "The other team may want to question you about Donna Ruiz's work. Can I have your contact information?"

"Here's a couple of my business cards. Contact me as needed." Stephen handed the officer the cards and handed one to Tomás. "We don't want to get in your way now. Tomás, we'll check back with you but call me if you need anything." He crossed the room and opened the door for Cleo.

She lingered. "We'll get together and celebrate when Donna's found." Stephen waved as they disappeared into the cold and firmly shut the door.

The frowning detective turned to Tomás. "So, you don't know if someone stole that laptop, or if your wife took it with her?"

"How would I know what Donna took with her?"

Julia answered for him, "She carried everything in her big shoulder bag she got from Christmas so it might be in there." She asked Katherine, "Did you find that big bag in her car?"

Katherine said, "Julia, the messenger bags got mixed up. She took yours, remember? Did her laptop get left in her car? Officer, have you heard anything about the car search?"

"Nothing reported. Uniforms remain there. I'll make a note about a red bag and laptop."

Katherine added, "It has a big red bow on the front.

Julia, where did you leave the one you had?" Julia stared at her blankly.

The officer turned to Tomás. "We'll be on our way now. I'll file a report on the break in. If you think of anything else, you have my card so please contact me right away. And sir, don't forget to secure your kitchen door."

As the officers left, Katherine whispered to Anthony, "You've been awfully quiet."

He stood in place. "Not now, Katherine."

As the front door closed behind the last officer, Tomás guided Julia back to the couch. "I didn't say anything with the police here, but we both know who broke in here."

Amber blurted out, "Mr. Ruiz, Julia would never do something like this. She could never be that mad at her mom."

Julia blushed, and she threw an alarmed frown in Amber's direction. "Not me. Why would I mess up our home? I bet that crazy lady next door did it. She shot up the neighborhood, what would stop her from breaking in?"

Anthony nudged Katherine toward the door, but she had no intention of moving an inch.

Tomás turned his back to Amber. "No. We know who did this, and you need to tell me where I can find him. I forbid you to see him again. He acted with vengeance against your mother and me."

Julia jumped to her feet, both hands clenched. "You blame Kevin for everything. He loves me. He'd never hurt me. You hurt me by hating him."

"Julia, you're blind to him. He's wrong for you and what he does destroys our family."

"No, you're destroying our family. I can't be with you. I'm leaving." Julia stared at Amber. "Drive me?"

Julia rushed toward the door. Katherine stepped in her way and put an arm around her. "Emotions are exploding. Everyone, stay calm. The police will solve the break-in. Julia, pack a few things, and come stay with me. Amber can drive us in her car."

Tears falling, Julia ran to the stairs with Amber at her heels.

"No!" Tomás glared at Katherine.

She picked up Perro who sat whimpering again, then she stood her ground. "Tomás, please reconsider. A short cooling off time, one overnight. You'll know where to find her, a safe place. We'll reunite you both, and Donna tomorrow."

Tomás said, "No! I'll take care of my daughter." He focused on Anthony now, as if seeing him for the first time. "You, get out. You'll never see my wife again. Tell me where she is, then get out!" Tomás shouted and moved maliciously toward Anthony.

Katherine jumped in between them. "Tomás, please stop. Anthony, you better—"

"You're making a mistake." Anthony moved out the front door.

Tomás pushed Katherine aside, ran to the door and slammed it shut. Katherine stared at him, stunned.

The girls thudded down the stairs, and Katherine attempted to restore some calm. Julia carried a small backpack. Her eyes focused on the front door, she walked deliberately to Katherine. "I'm ready." Outside, Katherine heard the Maserati engine.

Tomás walked over and held Julia's hand. "I love you, Julia. You may not agree right now, but I'm your father. I'll always be your father, and I always want only what's best for you. That Kevin, he's not the best for you. He did this."

Julia snatched her hand away. "You're wrong."

Katherine hesitated. "Julia, do you have everything you need? Where's your mom's bag?"

The moaning girl broke away from her father and charged out the door. Amber followed with a hasty word to Katherine, "We left the bag at Clutch Cafe."

Katherine faced Tomás. "I'll take good care of her."

Tomás said, "It appears I have no choice. I will see her tomorrow."

Katherine gently handed him the dog. He held Perro close, but focused attention on the open front door and the girls running to Amber's car. "I know Kevin did it. He stole my daughter's heart, broke into my house, and may have hurt my wife too."

Chapter Fifteen

The four bedroom, two story dorm-like house stood like a towering bastion of liberty on the meandering residential street. The day Michael moved into the house on Grove Street, Amber christened the four housemates' oasis "All Man's Land."

Amber parked at the curb. In the driveway rested a beat up, rusted, four door car affectionately known as Michael's tank. At the top of the driveway, between the tank and the house stood a motorcycle.

They'd dropped off Katherine at the Purse Museum, after she insisted they promise to return soon. Amber turned off the engine on her coupe. Julia's lips tensed into a frown. On the edge of tears, she sniffled. "Could Nicky use his drone to find Mom?"

"We can ask."

"I'm so worried about her, and on Dad's birthday. I never even said happy birthday to him." Julia bowed her head and wiped away a tear.

Amber had second thoughts. "We don't have to go in. I can talk to Nicky about it and let you know."

Julia sat up straight and unbuckled her seat belt. "No, I want to do it. I texted Kevin so he knows where to pick me up." Julia reached for the door handle.

Smoke curled from the chimney and music pounded as they approached the front door. The door swung open. "Saw your car through the window." Michael reached forward and gave Amber a kiss. "Julia, right? Hi."

Julia managed to smile.

Michael motioned for them to come in. "Everyone's in the kitchen talking about dinner. Hungry?"

Katherine's sons stood at opposite ends of the room. Christopher studied the contents of the refrigerator, while his brother William leaned against the counter snacking on a bag of chips. Nicky took off that beloved airplane museum jacket and hung it on the back of the barstool, as he joined William at the counter. Nicky offered everyone a bottle of beer, then opened one for himself. "So, what did they say about the professor on campus today?"

Michael pulled Amber into the room and Julia followed. They greeted everyone. Michael took out a frying pan. "I made a killing at the store on fish if anybody wants some."

William groaned. "A killing? Bad taste, man."

Michael cleared his throat. "I didn't mean… sorry. I could've said that another way."

Christopher waved a hand at his brother. "No one called it murder."

William muttered, "Not yet."

Michael continued cooking. He grabbed a bag out of the refrigerator. "Anyway, there's lots of fish here, whoever wants some."

Christopher voiced interest in the fish. "I've got some spices that would go great on that fish, and a pasta with broccoli if you want." Christopher always enjoyed cooking, and he collaborated with Michael.

Nicky added, "I've got stew in the fridge to warm up." He turned again to William. "So, what happened on campus?"

William swallowed. "I bought some sourdough bread you can throw in. I put it on the counter over there. Tough first day back. Everyone's talking about Randall. Online went crazy about a drug overdose."

Christopher asked, "Did you get your stuff from Randall's office? Who's taking over his classes?"

"Security kicked me out of the office, police orders. They're investigating."

"Bad times." Nicky shook his head.

William added, "Can't believe he's dead. I have a meeting with Professor Anderson. She's taking over the classes for now."

Michael turned on the burner. "When are the cops leaving? There's a patrol car on the street again tonight."

Nicky stared at him. "I'm telling you, a car watched me leave for work today, and I saw another one drive by the transit lot." Nicky pounded a fist on the table. "Idiots think I'm dealing drugs on my way to work?"

William pushed the bag of chips away. "One followed me to class."

Nicky said, "Guys, we've got to do something about this harassment. We need a plan."

Christopher cautioned, "We can't let it turn into arrests."

Amber spoke up, "They may get too busy to keep bothering you guys. They're searching for Julia's mom." Amber rubbed her friend's back. Julia sniffled and wiped away a tear. "And Julia's house got broken into."

Michael covered the simmering frying pan. "Let us know what you need."

Julia's eyes shimmered. Amber glanced at Christopher and then William. "Julia's staying at your mom's Purse Museum for now."

Michael asked, "Any idea why your mom's missing?"

Julia shrugged her shoulder. "She won't answer her phone, never showed up at work."

Amber said, "She works at the same company as you, Nicky."

"Wait, who?"

"Julia's mom is Donna Ruiz."

Nicky almost knocked over a beer. "She's in my van pool. She works at NRML with all of us in the van. She's missing? Her assistant approved final test results on a new drug treatment today. Our whole department celebrated."

Julia wiped away a tear. "I haven't seen her in too long."

Amber suggested, "Nicky, could you run your drone around where her mom parked her car?"

"Sure, no problem."

Julia's phone buzzed. "Kevin's here." She ran out to open the door.

Michael moved the pan off the burner. "Watch out, Nicky. Now the cops will use your van pool as an excuse to question you about her too, and the professor. Harassment might get worse."

Julia returned with her friend, a pale, wiry, red-haired, and liberally freckled young man dressed in well-worn jeans and a thick crewneck sweater. Julia introduced everyone. "Kevin drives a ride share. We want to drive around some places my mom goes."

Kevin put his round lens glasses in a jeans pocket and wrapped an arm around Julia. "Whatever you want to do."

Michael said, "Eat here first if you want."

Kevin perked up at the suggestion, but Julia said, "No. let's find Mom."

He grunted. Amber stepped forward and hugged her friend, and the housemates gave her their well wishes. As they turned to leave, Nicky confirmed he'd fly the drone near the transit center.

Once they'd left William said, "Busy cops could work to our advantage. We should spread out as much as possible in a lot of directions. They can't cover everyone all the time. If I can get back into the Prof's office, I might see clues about how he overdosed, and prove we had nothing to do with it."

Christopher suggested, "If we can keep the cops busy, and you can get around that security, you might find something."

Michael served plates of fish with the stew and more. Amber thanked him and inhaled deeply the savory spices steaming up from the table. She sat down between Michael and Christopher. Her stomach rumbled. "News got out about Julia's mom, and some of her friends are organizing a community search to find her. That will keep the police busy too."

Christopher grinned at Nicky. "The cops may want you to join the search piloting your drone." After a tense moment of silence, laughter burst out around the table.

William shifted in the chair. "Hey, Amber, can you text me about that search tomorrow? While the cops are away, I might make a play to get in the office. I want to see what else the prof had in play."

Michael added, "I don't wish anything bad on Julia's mom. Hope they find her soon, but whatever gives us a break from the cops, sounds good. It feels like they'll break in any minute and accuse us of who knows what."

Chapter Sixteen

Katherine stole a glance at Anthony in the driver's seat. His grim expression and white knuckles against the steering wheel increased her own anxiety. More than twenty-four hours since Donna had disappeared, Anthony's distress continued to grow.

Amber and Julia sat in the tight quarters of the backseat. Amber gasped and pulled out her phone, quickly clicking.

Julia asked, "Did you forget something?"

Amber kept clicking. "I forgot to text Will we're headed for the search. After you left dinner last night he asked me to let him know."

Katherine turned her head to them. "William's interested?"

Amber finished her text. "Oh, all of them at the house are." She glanced at Julia, then she put her phone back in her wristlet. "Oh yeah, Nicky talked about bringing the drone." She turned to her window.

Amber seemed agitated, but the whole ride had felt uncomfortable. Tense circumstances surrounding Donna's disappearance and a definite lack of sleep all around can put people on edge. Katherine held Anthony in her peripheral vision. He appeared lost in emotion rather than intent on the road. Katherine pulled her seat belt tighter. She could feel a sway when the Maserati slid over a slick patch, then the car swerved as he took the next corner too fast.

Her hands automatically pinched the edges of her seat in a hard grip, and Katherine fought to stay centered. "Slow down, Anthony. The search teams are still getting organized. There's time for us to check in. No need to get in an accident."

He shrugged, then glanced in the rear view mirror. Katherine reached back to retrieve her purse fallen between the seats. Julia braced against her car door, and Amber frowned. Anthony straightened, easing up on the gas pedal. "It got a little icy tonight."

Amber continued questioning her friend, "Did Kevin go with you to the police station?"

Reluctant to host Julia's boyfriend at her place yesterday evening, Katherine didn't want them leaving together either, not while she remained responsible for Julia. He'd had a calming influence, yet Katherine remained unconvinced of Kevin's complete innocence in the break in. She listened to the girls intently, as Julia responded.

"He stayed with me as long as he could, but not at the station. What if my dad accuses him to the cops? I couldn't stand it. Kevin's working tonight, but he said he'd see me after the bars close."

Confused, Katherine had to ask, "The bars?"

Julia nodded. "As a ride share driver, he gets some good late-night business. Anyway, the police took me into a room and asked me a lot of questions. My dad said my mom's car got impounded at the station, but I didn't see it there."

Katherine interrupted, "You and your dad have made up? That's wonderful."

"Not exactly made up. Now we're barely talking,

instead of yelling at each other."

Amber sighed. "That's progress."

Julia pouted, and in a panic blurted, "I can still stay with you, right Katherine? I can't live with my dad, not the way he treats Kevin."

Katherine smiled. "You're always welcome."

Julia's shoulders dropped, and she wiped away a tear. "Thanks again for picking me up at the police station. I wanted to get out of there."

Anthony checked the mirror. "Happy to drive you tonight."

Katherine said, "Your dad might have more information from the police when he joins us at the search."

Amber wrapped both her hands around Julia's. "We'll find your mom."

Julia whispered, "We have to."

Katherine faced forward as the car sped up again. "We will."

The car skidded as Anthony steered it into the Transit Center. The headlights showed some groups of people scattering out of their path. Katherine and the girls lurched forward when Anthony slammed on the brakes and the car slid into a stop.

Despite her seat belt, Katherine had her hands up against the windshield. Her pulse pounded hard, and she had a lump in her throat as she heard the concern in Anthony's voice, "Sorry. Everyone all right?"

Nods all around, then Anthony opened the window and shouted apologies. Katherine could see that even in the cold, he sweated. He parked, and they all got out and walked to a spotlighted tent in the back of the lot.

The large number of volunteers impressed

Katherine. "Julia, how wonderful all these people here with so much love for your mother. You and your family are loved."

"My mom has a lot of friends."

They greeted some people in line, conversation punctuated by wisps of steam escaping from mouths. Some shifted from foot to foot, others pulled their coats tighter against the cold.

A voice from behind Katherine repeated, "Julia. Hey, Julia."

A young woman dressed in fitted, mauve ski pants with black lines down the sides and a matching ski jacket with a turtleneck underneath walked slowly and deliberately toward them. Her serious expression caused a faint worry line to form above her nose. Her dyed teal hair fell freely around her shoulders under the damp, black knit cap framing her face. Her steps deliberate, her stare focused on Julia as people moved out of her way.

Amber whispered, "Who's that?"

"Brittany."

Katherine asked, "Who?"

Julia raised her hand in a brief wave. "She's my mom's tech assistant."

She approached with a sudden stop toe to toe with Julia, who stepped back, reclaiming some personal space. Brittany spoke to her, ignoring everyone else. "Julia I'm here to help with the search. Are you all right?"

Julia slowly shook her head. "I want to find Mom."

Brittany put her hand on Julia's shoulder. "I'm worried too. I don't know why she never made it to work yesterday, of all days. I covered for her. It turned out amazing."

Katherine cleared her throat. "I'm Katherine. We're headed up to the front desk."

Brittany glanced at her and smiled broadly, then she turned her attention back to Julia. "I want to search with you. Help you through this."

Katherine turned to Anthony who faced away from them in conversation with Melanie, one of countless adoring fans. Katherine tapped him on the shoulder. "I'm taking Julia to check in with the organizers."

Anthony offered apologies to Melanie. "Let's talk again under better circumstances."

She stayed close. "I'll go with you."

Katherine excused her way through the crowd, leading their group, which now included Brittany hovering next to Julia and Amber, and Melanie who clung close to Anthony. Behind the organizers' desk stood Jason with Detective Grace. Almost cheek to cheek, they huddled over a clipboard as she pointed to information on it. Hobbs sat at Jason's feet. He gave a couple of wags of the tail, as Katherine approached. When she cleared her throat, Jason took a step back.

The detective looked up. "Hi Katherine. Are you waiting for an assignment?"

"Yes," She gestured with her mittened hand, "and Julia's here too, Donna's daughter."

Grace put her clip board on the table. "Oh, your dad's still at the station. I'll check, and let you know when he's coming. You can wait here under the canopy."

"I don't need to wait for him. I want to find my mom."

"The first volunteer groups are leaving soon." Detective Grace replied.

Brittany volunteered, "Come wait in my car, Julia.

I'll run the heater."

"No, I'll stay here." Julia and Amber moved to the other side of the table, behind the officer. Brittany followed. Julia twisted her arms in front of her stomach. Her fingers entwined tightly as she stared toward the street in silence.

Katherine's glance swept back from the trio to Jason. "Are you and Hobbs headed out?"

Hobbs stood at the sound of his name. Jason grinned and patted him on the head. "We've been out a couple of times. We had one promising hit that fizzled. We'll go back soon."

Anthony asked, "Turned up anything helpful?"

Jason said, "Officers collect anything found at the different sites, for review. When you go out in your group they'll explain it to you."

Detective Grace glanced at her laptop. "You could join the B-6 group. Type your name here please." She turned the screen to them.

Jason crinkled a skeptical eye at Katherine's high heeled boots. "The walking could get a little rough. They've got a couple of vans that will drive you out, but the fields will be muddy."

Katherine hesitated. "Fields? We're searching around the transit center."

Jason shook his head. "We extended the perimeter. We're exploring all options." He returned the tablet to a vest pocket.

Katherine leaned forward on the table. "All options?"

"I'm reporting to the van, Grace." Jason said, with an abrupt, tight-lipped exit. It didn't surprise Katherine. Either he refused to step over an official department line, or he held an unsteady foothold on buried secrets of the case. Either possibility alerted Katherine. Ominous alarms sounded in the core of her mind, as her initial worries grew.

Melanie wandered off as Anthony stepped up to the table and signed on. "Whatever helps find Donna."

Detective Grace addressed people who'd walked up behind Anthony, including Cynthia.

A polished, deep male voice, "Hello. I'm Stephen Rider. Donna worked at my company." He wore a long, black raincoat, buttoned to the top and a thick brown scarf hung around the collar. The lingering shake in his solemn tone and his concerned frown impressed Katherine. It never occurred to her that he and his wife would show up to help search. He slipped a little as he took another step forward in a pair of slick, shiny black office shoes.

Grace responded, "Yes sir. You'd like to join a search team?"

He shook his head and gestured to his fashionable wife. She stood on platform heeled knee high designer boots over fitted leggings, wide-eyed and surveying the surrounding commotion. With her sparkling gloved hands, she pulled her tailored, fur trimmed jacket closer.

"Cleo and I are concerned. We want to contribute another way."

"Oh?"

Cleo offered a brilliant smile, then turned and wandered across the canopied hub. She hovered near a trio of officers deep in conversation, including Jason and a relaxed Hobbs.

"Yes, I've paid for a service from the local shop. It includes coffee, tea, hot chocolate, and some food too, for you and the volunteers. Can they set up their truck in the lot?"

"Thank you. Refreshments will be appreciated. Can they park at this end of the lot near the canopy, so they don't block official vehicles."

"I'll let them know. Here's my card."

Grace put the card in her pocket. "Next please."

Stephen joined Cleo at the edge of the canopy. Katherine's curiosity moved her closer.

"Cleo, I'll get the truck in place, and then we'll go." He waved in the direction of the lot. A food truck moved in the direction he pointed. A quick kiss and he left.

A figure brushed past Katherine. Brittany called out, "Mr. Rider."

He stopped and smiled at her. "Good of you to be here tonight."

"Oh yes sir. Donna's more than my boss. I consider her a friend."

"I'm grateful you stepped up yesterday and presented those test results. I can't stress enough the importance of us moving forward on that drug, getting it out on the market with no more delays. We want to help the people who need it."

"Whatever's best for NRML. What else can I do for you, Mr. Rider?"

"Brittany, again there's no need for formality. Call me Stephen."

"Yes sir…Stephen."

"Excuse me, let me help get the truck into position …"

"Oh, I can help." They walked off together.

Cleo stood her ground, slowly twirling, not intent on her husband but inhaling the full surroundings. Cleo's momentary glance of recognition became Katherine's invitation to join her. "Hello again. Nice of you to volunteer refreshments."

Cleo sighed. "Least we could do." She glanced over her shoulder at the group of officers.

"There are a lot of volunteers. I'm on the next van."

"Well good, and you can warm up with coffee later."

"Do you know Donna because she worked for your husband?"

"I know all my husband's employees to varying degrees. Donna works closely with Stephen. She's a responsible professional."

The truck stood in place, already handing refreshments through the window. The driver and Stephen stood in conversation, with Brittany beside him.

Katherine tested Cleo. "Did your husband talk with the police today?"

"What?"

"When you left yesterday, I wondered if you'd be talking with the police today?"

"Yes, I think Stephen did. Things are in such turmoil at the company. Many of our employees are out here tonight."

A bus pulled in at the transit stop. Riders descended and some headed for the tent, including MJ and David. While others around them trudged forward, the two of them seemed to glide along the grounds. David took in the scene with great interest and raised a hand in greeting to some people along the way. MJ's gaze remained transfixed on the canopied area.

Cleo checked her phone. "Stephen's ready to go. Good luck tonight, Katherine."

Katherine tracked down MJ as she comforted Julia

with a prolonged hug. "My dear, I communed with the universe, and it drew me to you. All my focus, all my loving vibrations are dedicated to you and your family." Julia teared up. MJ held onto both her hands. "We're here for you."

MJ's appearance didn't surprise Katherine, but why would David join her? "You both decided to join the search?"

David put an arm around MJ's shoulders. "When a community in need calls, I answer."

MJ squeezed Julia's hands. "Of course." Brittany crowded in again next to Julia.

David turned away from the uniformed cops. "What have they found so far? Do they think someone attacked her?"

Katherine tried to hide her concern that his mind would leap to someone hurting Donna. "They're keeping quiet so far."

David said, "Not surprising." He gave a brief smile, then glanced behind him.

Anthony appeared. "They want us on the van now."

The phone in Julia's hand buzzed and lit up with a text. Katherine's hope to hear good news from Donna wavered.

Julia clicked on the screen. "My dad's on the way." Her bottom lip quivered.

MJ nodded. "We'll wait for him with you."

Brittany gazed in the distance as she added, "Of course." Katherine followed her line of sight, discovering her watching Stephen and Cleo get into their car.

Anthony gave a thumbs up, grabbed Katherine's hand and tugged. The van's engine revved on. The line of people waiting to board cheered.

MJ shared a parting thought, "The truth cannot remain hidden, when people act with courage."

At the end of the line, Katherine found Anthony's silence unsettling. She tried urging him into conversation. "Nice so many locals are volunteering, and also people from Donna's company." No response at all. "Donna's assistant seems very concerned."

That remark sparked something. "Not about her missing boss. She cares about the company." Anthony growled. "Business before compassion. Or, passion before business?"

Katherine hesitated at the van door. "Why would you…"

"Come on now, let's not waste time out here." Anthony cut in front of her and climbed into the van before she could finish her question.

Chapter Seventeen

Katherine slogged along the curb. A wet rain and snow mix swirled on strong winds and soaked her, despite a tight grip on her umbrella. For hours they'd searched a rural neighborhood bordering Bayside. Thank goodness for thick gloves and a matching knit hat pulled over her ears, not to mention the cashmere scarf tight around her neck tucked into her fitted full length coat. Knee high boots purchased for the darling fringe tie detail on the sides included a lining that warmed her legs. The heels wobbled, but Jason would never hear her admit that. The waterproof, plaid, canvas backpack left her hands free to carry her umbrella and search with her flashlight and stabilize that wobble.

She pulled off a glove and checked her cell phone. The light from the screen blazed bright. She squinted at 5:50 a.m. An involuntary shiver crept down her spine. Two full days since Donna had been heard from. The dark of night hung long and heavy in the Pacific Northwest in January. Her yearning for daylight maliciously ignored by the short, gray days and agonizingly long, pitch black nights. Katherine clicked in her password. No new messages.

She pocketed her phone and moved her flashlight beam along the uneven field and bordering shrubs, parallel to the road. Similar shafts of light jerked back and forth in a multitude of spots across surrounding lots.

The scattered beams traveled in jagged lines around intermittent houses, and interspersed fields on both sides of the roadway. She marveled that even in the miserable, dark winter people cared and acted to help. A dull whirring alerted her to a slow moving drone hovered in the sky, with its own spotlight pointed down.

The organizers assigned all volunteers a specific area to search, but Katherine had wandered a little. Anthony searched about half a block ahead of her. Shuttle vans stopped periodically to act as warming stations with water, drinks, and snacks. One drove by reminding her of Stephen's donation.

Katherine speculated why Donna would travel out here instead when she needed to get to work. What could have prevented her from attending her big meeting? No return calls to her daughter. No homecoming for her husband's return. No birthday celebration, although one had been planned. Katherine stood still, took a deep breath, and waited for inspiration. She swept her flashlight beam into the overhanging branches. Wisps of her exhaled breath danced in the air. Her thoughts turned to Jason.

Where did he end up searching tonight? He could be out here, across the field for all she knew. If he stood here with her, even in dim light he'd be able to recognize the type of tree from a glance at the branch. She remembered on their fall picnic he'd identified plants with eyes closed, from only the scent. He had many talents and strengths.

She had strengths too, including finding and noticing design details. Her business thrived on those skills. She recommitted to her search. Any detail out of place, any clue no matter how small, she would find it.

Katherine took a determined step forward and the fashionable heel of her boot sank into deep mud. She groaned as she pulled it out and examined the mess. Searching for solid footing, her tentative steps forward now sank both boots in the ooze. Her heavy sigh steamed in the air before her. These chic boots would unfortunately pay a heavy price for tonight. At least she appreciated their waterproof warmth. She scanned the ground, the shrubs, all her surroundings with renewed intensity, inching forward as she searched not only for clues but also solid footing.

"Find something?" Anthony had sneaked up on her. She straightened as he leaned in. "I saw your light slowed down."

She shook her head. "I guess discouragement affects my pace, and so does the mud." She lifted her boot and showed him the dripping sludge.

Anthony gently tapped it with his own mired shoe. "I hear that."

Katherine lowered her foot. "I ache for daylight, still some time away."

"Not too long. Nights are shorter every day since solstice."

Katherine held her umbrella closer. "Why do the police have us assigned so far from Donna's car and the transit center? Are we wasting our time here?"

Anthony cleared his throat. "Let's head back and ask some questions."

His tense tone touched Katherine to her core. On impulse she reached out and held his hand. "I don't have much farther to finish this stretch, then I'll tell them I want a new location."

"I'll walk along with you then."

"I'm fine. You deserve a break. Go warm up with a coffee, and I'll catch up to you."

Anthony smiled, a weak imitation of the usual broad, dimpled grin. He stepped a short distance away and swept the ground with a bright flashlight beam, as he resumed a search.

Katherine imagined an MJ search strategy and decided to send her thoughts out to the universe. She stood still and envisioned the messenger bag belonging to Donna. In these calm moments, she sensed a pull to move away from the rest of the searchers. She walked closer to the road, but away from the police barricade. A hint of daylight peeked over the horizon.

Why would Donna be out here on the road, about five miles from her parked car? If she needed to be here, why didn't she drive? How could Julia and her father bear waiting, praying for good news of their beloved mother and wife? Her body trembled with the intensity of the cold. The drizzle had now turned to a dusting of snow. The comforts of Beverly Hills and Rodeo drive beckoned.

Despite the temperature, Katherine stood still and focused again on Donna and her messenger bag. She moved with measured steps along the road. As daylight pushed the night aside, half buried in mud on the edge of the deep ditch that ran parallel to the road, a sparkle seemed out of place. She leaned in to examine it closer. Silver? A momentary thrill quickened her pulse.

She instinctively reached out, tossing her umbrella to the side. Glasses. Etched on the frame, a daisy. Donna's favorite flower, Katherine grabbed the glasses. One lens missing, and one arm bent. Katherine's heart raced.

With the flashlight in one hand and the glasses in the other, Katherine did a quick but careful search of that ground area. She stood up and inched forward, then doubled over as she examined the ground closely. She stood straight and stretched a little, examining the glasses again. The burden of her soaked coat and hat hung heavy.

She picked up her umbrella, fumbling a little with the glasses held in the same hand. Despite the police instruction to text them and stand in place next to any findings until an officer came, Katherine stuffed the glasses in her pocket. She took out her cell phone for a picture of the spot she'd found them. She turned on the flash and snapped a couple of shots. She checked the pictures, then decided to step back for a wider shot of the ground. When she flipped back to check that photo, she saw it. A glimmer reflected in the flash.

She almost dropped her phone as she shoved it in her pocket and pointed her flashlight at the drainage tunnel in the ditch. It stuck out from the culvert beneath the crossroad. Inside that tunnel, two hands lay visible. The camera flash had caught a diamond ring on one. She slipped into the ditch. After a momentary hesitation, she pushed herself up with trembling hands and forced herself to stomp through the slow stream of water toward a motionless body.

She called, "Donna? Donna? Can you hear me?"

No answer.

She leaned between two boulders, then moved closer and crouched down. She steeled herself, then gently rolled the body over. Donna had a plastic bag over her head. Sickened, Katherine couldn't bear looking at her as she pulled to get the bag off, with no success.

Thick, wide, red duct tape secured the plastic bag over her head. She forced her nails through and finally broke the plastic. No breathing.

Katherine reached to check for a pulse. No pulse. Katherine's stomach turned. She attempted shaking off the nausea. She choked on the lump in her throat and struggled to breathe. The bushes and wall of stones closed in on her as if defying physics. In her claustrophobic panic, she retreated into the open again. She sucked in some frantic breaths she finally calmed into some deep breathing.

Donna's body lay almost entirely hidden from anyone walking by and from drivers on the road. Besides the wedding ring, Katherine didn't see any other jewelry except an elastic bracelet looping around one wrist with a key card showing the NRML logo in one corner. The broken fingernail on her ring finger, and another. Her clothes drenched. No shoes. No bag.

Directly across the street stretched an open field with a few trees. The one opposite her had a tire swing hanging from it. She could sight her position from that, as well as the tunnel itself. She grabbed a fallen fir tree branch, and stood it upright into the ground, in case she needed to return later. She pulled out her phone to text the police, then hesitated.

Julia and Tomás and so many people who will mourn her. "Oh Donna. I'm so sorry." She stood in solemn silence, grieving the senseless loss of a beautiful life.

Footsteps encroached. "Katherine, what's up?"

She turned to Anthony. Her lip trembled as he stared hard at her, waiting. She found her voice, "I'm so sorry. Donna's dead." She motioned to the ditch.

Anthony lurched forward. "No. Not dead. Donna?" With a savage expression on his face, he moved around her. Katherine texted Jason, and then the police alert number she'd scanned on the bus. A funny buzzing sound penetrated her brain. A drone flew over her head. She couldn't tell if it belonged to the police or Nick.

Her phone chimed. An incoming call from Jason. Katherine monitored Anthony while Jason's voice came over the speaker. "Where are you? I'm coming from the volunteer van stop. I alerted the team."

"I'm halfway down the block, between the road and an open drainage ditch. I'm waving my flashlight."

"I see you. Don't touch anything."

Anthony finally blinked. He leaned over with his hands on knees..

Jason's calm voice echoed as a professional on duty. "I'm almost there."

A siren shriek shattered the dark silence. A police car hugged the middle line on the road. Tires crunched on the gravel, as it stopped on the shoulder across the street. The strobe lights flashed. An ambulance followed, and then another squad car.

Emergency lights blasted the area. Katherine squinted when the strong spotlights positioned on her. The sirens stopped. Paramedics rushed in her direction, as police pulled tarps and bags of equipment out of the trunks of their cars. Katherine froze in place. Anthony stepped back into the shadows. He reached vaguely forward, hands dangling palms up. Katherine stood in stunned silence, willing these professionals to find life, but knowing it would be a miracle. Some force punched her in the heart as they continued their vain attempts.

"Katherine, let's move back and let them work."

Jason gently touched her arm. She watched him, as he paused and took in the full scene. What revelations stood out to Jason's trained eye? He guided her to the edge of the road, then he signaled to Anthony to join them. Did she see tears on Anthony's face, or melted snowflakes, or sweat? How could he possibly be sweating on this winter morning? Other searchers approached, and a crowd gathered.

Jason waved an arm to one of the officers. "We need to set up a perimeter and pull these people away. We can take them to the buses now and take statements as needed. We need to clear the area. Do you want my help?"

"We're on it." The officer motioned to two others, and they approached the people. "Please stand back everyone."

Jason's radio broke in, "Chaos. Heads up, chaos coming."

Katherine went on immediate alert. "What happened?"

Jason grimaced. "Not chaos like you're thinking. A signal, the chief has arrived." Jason lowered his voice. "Things may take a political turn."

More cars parked, and Tomás raced out of one. His eyes fixated past Katherine to the tarp tent blocking a section of the ditch. Jason stepped in front of him and put a hand on the man's chest. "Mr. Ruiz, please wait here."

Anthony walked a few paces away, into the crowd. Tomás did not protest Jason's request. Terror etched itself across his features, raw and unfiltered, then a sickly groan. He bent over and groaned again.

A commotion and yelling from the street distracted Katherine. "Get out of the way."

Tomás straightened up and took a menacing step in that direction. "No, not him."

Jason put a firm hand on the Tomás' shoulder, and he stood in place. Kevin's red hair glowed bright in the sunrise. Julia rushed through the gap Kevin had made in the crowd. An officer stopped her. She screamed. "Mom…"

Jason allowed Tomás to push past him and run to embrace his daughter. Tomás yelled over her shoulder at Kevin. "You dare to be here, after all you've done. Your crime will not remain a secret."

The two men faced off. The crowd gasped. Some commented in low tones to each other. Julia ran to her father, "No! Papa!" He hugged her to him.

Jason and another officer focused on the family, while others on the force moved bystanders away. "Everyone, the vans are available to return to the center. Our search is over, at least for tonight. Please move back to the van pick up now. Right this way." The searchers followed directions. Katherine and Anthony didn't move.

Julia squirmed out of her father's arms. "Kevin, tell him you didn't do anything. Tell him he's wrong."

Instead, the young man fired back an accusation. "You're the one with the secret. Yesterday morning rush hour I'm on my way to pick up a ride, and who do I see? Your own daughter didn't know you'd come home. Did your wife? Here to see your wife? Here to kill her?"

"Kevin, No!" Julia stepped back. "Papa?"

With a shaking left hand, Tomás reached out to Julia. "No. How can you ask, my dear Julia. Our dear family, shattered. Julia, don't you see? He's dangerous."

Kevin planted his feet in place. "I know who I saw.

When did you come back? Tell her."

"Julia…"

"Papa? Why didn't you come home?"

"Julia honey, mi joya, not here. Not now."

"I'm not your jewel if you don't care enough to come home to me."

"Your mother…" Tomás pivoted toward the tent and tears fell down his cheeks.

Julia stood between them, on the verge of tears. A burly man approached. Katherine recognized the silhouette and purposeful walk immediately. The police chief trudged on the soaked ground directly through the taped off area, oblivious to the family drama. The officers at work stood to prevent him from disturbing potential evidence.

Jason stiffened, as the chief walked under the tape. "Holmes. Did you hear me on the radio? Expedite clearing the scene, before the press jumps in." He eyed her then, "Katherine Watson, a surprise to see you here. Don't tell me. You found her, didn't you? We'll need your statement, and then your involvement will be over. Of course, I thank you for locating the missing woman."

Katherine bristled at being dismissed. Tomás' groan, the embodiment of agony, captured the chief's attention. "I'm so sorry to meet you under these circumstances. I am Police Chief Harrison. Are you Mr. Ruiz, Donna Ruiz's husband? We will do all we can to determine what's happened."

An officer turned on a flashlight. "I'm sorry sir, can I see your identification?"

Jason spoke up. "I'll vouch for him. No need for that official check." The officer looked to the chief, who nodded.

The chief spoke quietly, "Mr. Ruiz would you come with me to the paramedics' tent for a potential identification of your missing wife?"

"Julia, mi joya, I want you to stay with Katherine. Be brave."

Katherine put her arm around Julia's shoulder. "I'm here for you."

Julia protested, "Why can't I go with you?"

"No Julia, I will go alone."

"No. I want to find my mother." Julia stamped her foot as she shouted.

Tomás went to her and held her in a tight embrace. Resting a cheek against her hair, he squeezed his eyes shut and choked out, "Your beautiful mother no longer walks with us. I feel it. Stay with Katherine." He released her.

The faintest of whispers escaped Julia's trembling lips, "Mama. Dead."

Kevin's keys jangled as he pulled them from his jeans pocket. "Julia, don't you get it? They won't let you near her."

"Stay away from my daughter, you filthy…" Jason and another officer held back Tomás.

The chief pointed at Kevin. "Young man, move away."

"I'm outta here. Julia, do you want a ride?" He received no answer before he turned and walked away.

Tomás let out a long breath. Julia clasped her hands over her heart. Tomás gazed again to the field where Donna lay and absently spoke, "I will go with you." The chief gestured for the man to walk ahead of him. Tomás never turned back. He crossed the ditch and lifted the tarp to disappear into the makeshift frame.

In the opposite direction, Kevin stopped after opening the car door. He stood still and stared down the road. Katherine wondered if he regretted what he'd said. He got in the car. Julia sprinted after him.

"Julia, no!" Katherine reached out too late. Kevin pushed the passenger door wide open. Julia jumped in. Tires spinning, they turned onto the road. As the taillights disappeared, Katherine vowed she would not let down sweet, troubled Julia again. She would be the friend Julia needed. Her father had entrusted her, and Katherine would not fail. Funny that a father so devoted to family came home two days early from a trip and didn't rush home to them.

An officer with more crime tape moved the remaining group to the side and waved a police van through. A city police bus progressed down the road. When it stopped, its doors opened, and a uniformed driver stepped out. She held a PA speaker attached to a police public address system on the bus. Her voice boomed, "All searchers, board the bus back to the transit center." She repeated the announcement several times.

Katherine walked to Anthony who stared at the remaining tarp. "I'm texting Amber. I need her to track down Julia."

A hand on her shoulder and Jason's professional voice stopped Katherine. "You can't leave yet. I need your statement. I have questions."

Chapter Eighteen

The bus filled with volunteers and pulled away from the curb. A dim illumination behind the storm clouds represented the Pacific Northwest's winter sunrise. The bus rumbled down the road, around the corner, and out of sight.

Head down, Tomás emerged from the tent, escorted by an officer. As he approached, he took out a handkerchief. "Where's my daughter?"

"I'm so sorry, Tomás. She left." Katherine answered despite the lump in her throat.

With eyes blazing, he stepped in front of her. "Left? With him? You watch over my precious Jewel and lose her?"

"I'll find her. I will find her and…"

"Empty promises."

An officer cleared his throat. "Sir, I'll drive you to the center so you can head home."

"No wife. No daughter. No home anymore. A house that's been robbed, all that remains of my happy life."

The officer indicated a patrol car. Tomás glared at Katherine, got in, and they drove away.

"We need to talk. Over there." Jason marched ahead and then held the passenger door to a car open for Katherine. Anthony stood still, staring at the tent.

Hobbs' insistent bark steamed the back window. A quick hand signal from Jason, and the dog went silent.

Katherine got as comfortable as she could in the passenger seat. The thin covering of snowflakes over the car and its windows dimmed the interior. Her skin tingled as warmth streamed out of the vents and wrapped around her. She took off her gloves and scarf for the first time in hours. She sent Anthony a quick text not to wait for her.

"Hi, Hobbs. Good boy." She pressed her hand against the metal screen between them. The dog stared at her, then moved to greet his partner. A sharp swoosh of cold invaded, as Jason gave Hobbs a treat and then sat behind the wheel. He turned up the heat and turned on the windshield wipers.

"Oh, Jason, how heart-wrenching."

"Toughest part of the job, seeing what loved ones go through. Answers bring the only peace we can offer them in their devastation. Let's get your preliminary statement, then Hobbs and I will go search for any additional evidence. The detectives take over soon. I can give you a ride home when I'm done, if you can't find another ride. You can wait in my car."

"I can help you search…"

"A police investigation has begun." He covered her hand with his. "I didn't realize you're on staff."

"As a concerned citizen, I could be helpful."

He withdrew his hand. "Your statement would be helpful." Jason turned on the recorder, identified himself and badge number, the time, date, and witness name.

"Please describe how you discovered the deceased."

With a loud sigh, Hobbs lay down. Katherine leaned back. The passenger seat felt stiff and utilitarian compared to Anthony's luxurious ride. "There's not much to tell. I walked along the ditch by the road I got assigned to. Before sunrise, I'm using my flashlight, and something sparkles. I stopped to investigate. I mean, all that mud, that trickle of water, how curious. A diamond ring stood out on her hand." Katherine took a deep breath. "The rocky ditch splashed with a stream flowing through it, behind bushes. Donna lay face down, her arms raised over her head."

Jason placed a hand back over hers, and his voice softened. "Can you describe anything else about the deceased?"

Katherine rubbed the palms of her hands along her thighs and gathered her thoughts. "A plastic bag over her head fastened hard at the neck by tape shocked me. No easy way to tear it off. I wanted to check for a pulse. With her hands bound together, I had to fidget to feel for it. I did it though. Nothing. She wore slacks, a winter coat, but then her feet…barefoot. Her feet black." Katherine held onto Jason's arm. "She didn't stumble and fall. Someone dragged her there. When they got her where they wanted, they hid her and left."

Jason paused the recording. "A description will do. We don't want a witness to draw conclusions on an investigation." He patted her leg gently. "I know. You want to help. You help if you stick to what you saw."

"I could show you better and gather more evidence at the ditch."

His finger hovered above record on the screen. "Let the officers do their job. Ready to continue with your statement?"

She nodded.

He clicked on record. "When you found the body, what did you do?"

"I called you, and I called the search line. Then

Anthony got there."

Jason interjected, "Anthony Marconi, witness interview by officer Hendrix." With raised eyebrows he motioned with the device for Katherine to continue.

"After that you officers took over."

Jason ended the recording with an official sign off. "I want to walk Hobbs around and see if he picks up a scent."

"I can help."

"You have helped. I'll get a volunteer to take you back to the center."

"If you won't let me help, I'll text someone for a ride." Katherine pouted.

"You can stay in the car until they get here. Keep the heater and the wipers on. I'll see you later." Jason put an arm around her shoulders. "Go home and take it easy. Get some sleep if you can. You've been through a shock."

Jason walked away with the dog. Katherine turned the windshield wipers on low and stared out the windshield. Jason chased away a familiar figure taking pictures and trespassing within the sphere of police spotlights. A vigorous conversation followed until another officer escorted local reporter Rob Tomlinson behind the yellow tape.

Rob shook his head, turned away from the officer, and recognized her as the wipers cleared the windshield. He pointed his camera directly at her. He waved, hurrying over. Katherine got out, curious what information he might have.

"Katherine, good to see you."

"Hi, Rob. Did you hear something on the police band?"

"Good guess, but I searched over on that hill." He pointed across the road. "Bad luck for me I didn't find her. These cops are doing their best to stomp on freedom of the press."

"Donna's dead. Be a human first and a reporter after."

Rob grinned. "I'm a professional doing my job. I heard you found her. What did you see before these cops descended? Any theories on how she died? Anything suspicious? Give me something page one worthy."

Katherine slid her chilling hands into her coat pockets. Her fingers bumped against glasses. Her eyes widened, and she gasped. She'd forgotten all about finding the glasses when she gave Jason her statement. She needed to tell him and revise her recording. Remembering her pictures stopped her cold. She'd keep copies of the pictures.

Of course, Rob continued. "Hey, Katherine, what are you thinking?"

"How would I know what belongs on page one? Yes, I'm suspicious about Donna out here in a field after being missing two days with her car parked, what three or four miles away? You don't need to hear that from me though. You're already skeptical."

"She's got a kid right? A daughter? Rough. Any theories on who killed her?"

"Who killed her? You don't know there's a killer."

"Come on, stop holding out on me."

"I see my ride coming." Hobbs kept pace with Jason's long strides.

"You're waiting for Jason? If he gives you information, text me. Come on, Katherine, let's collaborate. Free press, heart of democracy, one hand washes the other and all that." Rob turned, pointed his camera at the ditch, and filmed a video. "They're moving the body into an ambulance. Gotta get a clear shot."

The paramedics wheeled the stretcher to the back of the ambulance, the body covered. Rob rushed away, eager for a scoop that could give him a lead story. He'd learn soon enough about the plastic bag and other details from some other source. Or she might talk with him later. In the meantime, she wanted time to think, and to warm up.

She smiled at Jason as he pressed the vest button, and the back door popped open. The dog leaped in. Jason smiled back at her across the roof. They both sat in the front. Katherine fastened her seat belt. Time for true confessions and a statement revision. The ambulance dipped and weaved through the uneven field. She pulled the glasses out of her pocket.

The ambulance stopped at the edge of the road. A car passed driving the opposite direction. A blue light in the windshield, the car slowed and parked. The driver and passenger both got out. Katherine could barely stop herself from running to Julia with arms outstretched. Kevin said something, and they embraced. He watched Julia cross the street before he drove off.

Katherine leaped out of the patrol car. "Julia." Jason turned on the car's spotlight, despite the daylight.

The girl ran to her. "Can I still stay with you?"

"Of course." Katherine hugged Julia tight. Over her shoulder the silent ambulance drove to the stop sign. Katherine whispered, "For as long as you want."

Chapter Nineteen

MJ greeted Katherine and especially Julia with much sympathy, many hugs, and a touching meditation, "Let your heart speak to other's hearts."

Julia wiped her tears. "My world's collapsed."

MJ held her close. "We're here to listen Julia, for today and to help and be with you through it all."

The exhausted duo talked with MJ over hot chocolate until Julia could hardly stay awake. After she fell asleep upstairs, Katherine took the opportunity to fill MJ in on details of the search, and her suspicions.

After an accommodating pause, MJ tapped her knuckles on the table. "I had a flash of insight into the ambiance and content of the '60's exhibit. I want to make some changes. I know you're soul tired and body weary, but want to join me for a while?"

"How do you switch topics with such speed?" Katherine sat torn in two directions. She sat bone weary exhausted. On the other hand, she'd had some thoughts of her own on the exhibit. Katherine preferred to know in advance what MJ has got up her sleeve, rather than regret in hindsight. She yearned for company now too, for a mother and daughter connection. "Sure. Tell me what you have in mind."

MJ smiled with a thumbs up. "I want you to experience it. Come with me and see what I'll change. I've got a hip surprise, if it all goes how I've envisioned."

She put her fist in the air with pinky, forefinger, and thumb extended. Katherine marveled at how that familiar sign from MJ always touched her heart, love you. "Come on. While the creative spark sizzles, the brilliant women strike."

"I'm coming. I need a few minutes." MJ walked on ahead.

Bright sunshine hit the window and splashed around the exhibit room. As Katherine walked in, her shadow decorated a wall. Her head tilted from side to side. She took a couple steps back as she reconsidered the new display. She appreciated MJ's meticulous work, and her determination to finish before the Valentine opening celebration. MJ committing and seeing something through felt astonishing. That compliment may be premature. The party looms in the future. Love and flower power. MJ stood in the middle of the room. Katherine shook her head, as if anyone would call that standing. MJ bent over sideways in a pose. One hand and foot placed flat on the floor and the other hand and foot flung up in the air, as she breathed a soft, humming undertone.

Katherine crouched down to meet MJ eye to eye. "Exercise time? Do you have to do that in the exhibit room? What if a guest walks in?"

MJ rotated back on two feet and took in an audible deep breath, then let it out. "I'm feeling the room and meditating whether it reflects the history and stories we want told."

"You can't feel the room when standing on two feet? That's how our guests will see it, I hope."

"My ardha chandrasana pose brings creative thoughts, as if my namesake pose, since it loosely translates as Half Moon."

Katherine straightened up with a groan. "In that case, please, spare me the full moon pose." She blinked at MJ, and they both laughed.

Katherine pressed on. "The Jackie Kennedy exhibit sets off better now as a perfect focal point for her widely imitated fashion and style. The clean lines and simple shapes of some of her favorite designers' purses are shown off appropriately and reflect their influence. The feature article on the First Lady's personal couturier stands out too."

MJ said, "I don't agree that Mrs. Kennedy and Camelot reflect the biggest story of the decade. I lived it, and we need to emphasize the mood that saturated these years. After a decade of 1950's cinched waists, full skirts, and perfect hair and makeup, fashion traditions got broken in acts of rebellion. We need to mirror the momentous social and political changes of the decade."

After a quiet sigh, Katherine responded. "Yes, MJ, but we can't ignore the impacts on style of the White House, and Hollywood too. But you're right, purses changed a lot in the 1960s. With the women's liberation movement, they became purposeful. The Cassini quote reflects it, 'fashion anticipates'. We need to show how Camelot's style set the stage for your turmoil of change."

"The sixties awakened people's sense that they wanted change. They had to act to fix it. No one else could do it for them. While in my half-moon pose, today's meditation came to me. 'You can't reach for anything new if your hands are still full of yesterday's junk.' That sentiment describes that time and generation."

"You're telling me you can't sling a macramé

shoulder bag over your shoulder if your hands are clutching a gold plated evening bag? Contrasting the highly structured early decade against the youthful counterculture tells an important part of the story." Katherine stood frozen in place with the shock of consensus with MJ. "We agree."

MJ picked up her yoga mat. "We've made progress today, and we still have a few weeks. I'll elaborate on the write ups about women with the Civil Rights movement and the Vietnam protests. I'm not satisfied with those yet."

"Sounds good." Katherine recovered her faculties, yawned, and grabbed her cell phone. "Glad you still have energy. I'm done in."

MJ guided her to the doorway. "You get some rest."

Another yawn from Katherine. "I have time to grab a nap before William comes by. I'm anxious to see him. I hope those cops are leaving him alone. I'll go check on the café with the lunch rush."

"No worries, David's there. I'll help him if needed."

Katherine closed her laptop. "Great. Amber's late today after being on the search last night. I need to go check if she's finally here, and open the shop. I need her to prepare the shop's shelves and window for Valentine's."

Katherine dropped off her laptop in her office, rounded the corner, burst through the alcove, and bumped into the only guest browsing the shelves. The lady barely stood as high as Katherine's shoulders, dressed in a pretty, matching sweater and scarf set complementing her mauve leggings.

Flustered, Katherine reached out, "I'm so sorry, Charlene. Are you all right?"

Katherine helped her favorite Bayside hairdresser regain her balance and stilled the shoulder bag that swung from her elbow. Katherine recoiled in horror. Something squirmed inside Charlene's purse. What could have hidden itself inside? Two bright eyes and the wet nose of a toy poodle popped out and erupted with a shrill bark.

Katherine's arms sprung up against her chest, with hands tightfisted. Her head shook back and forth as she gazed at one of her most beloved designs, her 'Cinnamon Cherie' winter satchel inhabited by an animal.

Katherine's quickly calculated what it had taken in time, effort, and money to create. She turned her head to hide her pout of indignation. She'd accepted a Handbag Designer Award for that bag's acclaimed artistic and functional style. She recoiled over the months agonizing over the right shade of dark red to add to the vegan material to create that delicious, deep cinnamon color. The effort designing the shape with strategically placed exterior pockets. The dollars, beta trials, marketing, all for a portable dog bed? Katherine shuddered as Charlene lowered it to the floor.

The purse's occupant demanded all Charlene's attention. Her voice trembled, "Dolly? Dolly dear? Are you all right?"

The pet jumped out. Charlene addressed her dog in soothing and motherly tones. "Dolly almost took a nasty fall, but mommy saved her." Charlene reassured Katherine. "Dolly's all right."

Katherine muttered under her breath, "What a relief." She wanted to rescue the purse, not the pup. Amber chuckled. Purrada peeked her head around the counter and studied the guests.

Katherine reached for the bag. "Can I help you with your Cinnamon Cherie?"

Charlene paused squinting in thought. "Oh, you mean Dolly's bag." Charlene put the dog back in the purse, stood up, and lifted the strap back on her shoulder in one smooth movement. She giggled at Katherine. "I found it on my last visit, and it made my day. The perfect size for Dolly and so comfortable, especially in cold and wet weather. She goes everywhere in it. Today I wanted to browse on my lunch break to shop for a handbag for me."

Charlene took a dog biscuit from the outside pocket of the designer bag and dangled it before the dog. Dolly deftly grabbed it in her mouth. As she crunched, several crumbs tumbled into the purse's rich silk lining. Katherine had rejected multiple samples of silk material before making the painstaking decision on the final version. Charlene gestured toward the dog. "Would you like to pet her?"

Katherine felt her cheeks flush warm at the final indignity. She reached toward the satchel and petted an eager-faced pup, tongue hanging out, and soft eyes seeking her heart. Inside the Cherie Katherine heard the soft sweeping of the tail against the lining. She couldn't blame the dog for the crimes of the owner, and she could never stay upset with her friend Charlene. "She's a sweet dog."

Charlene nodded. "A little spoiled, but she's irresistible. Nice to see you, Katherine."

"You too. I need to get online and make an appointment. I'm convinced my hair grows faster in these cold winters."

"Science disagrees with you. Human hair grows

faster in the summer weather. The shop's been busy over the holidays. Call me if you have any trouble finding a time. I can always fit you in for a chat, snip, and style. Or check for a late afternoon time. Those are opening up suddenly."

Katherine frowned, curious. "Why?"

"Oh, poor Donna Ruiz, of course. I searched for a while yesterday. When I woke up today, I heard they'd found her dead, buried in the outskirts of town. No one knows how she died." Charlene scratched Dolly behind the ear. "How terribly sad. She became a regular customer of mine, you know. People are scared at the news. Many are canceling late afternoon appointments because they want to get home before dark. If you have trouble finding an open appointment time, book at the end of a day."

Katherine gave her friend a hug. "Thanks."

Amber leaned forward on the counter. "Katherine found Donna."

Charlene cuddled Dolly closer. "You did? Oh, how terrible for you. Thank goodness at least she can peacefully get laid to rest for her family. Where did you find her? How did she die? I heard that crazy Sophie Brody pulled a gun on her on New Year's Day. Did she shoot Donna?"

Reluctant to reveal too many details, Katherine decided to make it brief. "No, not a shooting as far as I know. We searched the fields out by the homes near route 104."

"A heart attack?"

"I'm sure the police will announce cause of death when they know."

"She seems young for a heart attack. That residential

area seems safe. Donna came into my shop for a trim and style so recently, on New Year's Eve. Such a beautiful and sweet lady."

"How did she seem when you saw her? Did she seem concerned or worried about anyone following her? Did she talk about any problems?"

"She didn't seem sick, didn't complain about heart pains. She talked about a new boyfriend dating her daughter. Donna felt uneasy about him. She didn't want them getting too serious too fast, but she didn't know how to stop it without upsetting her daughter. When teenagers get riled up, it can push them right into doing what you're counseling them against."

Amber grabbed a box from behind the counter and cleared her throat. "I'll take these extra totes to storage. I'll be right back."

Charlene blushed deep red as Amber strolled out. "I forgot Amber and Julia are friends. Anyway, the tension growing with Julia concerned Donna. She felt like the boyfriend resented her too. She made a resolution to spend more quality time with her daughter."

A shudder ran up Katherine's spine at the thought of time running out on Donna's loving resolution. "Anything else concerning her with her husband out of town?"

"Well, I'm sure you know about the trouble between them. She wanted to make light of it, but I could see through that. She wanted her hair done for a birthday celebration she'd planned to welcome him home. I fit her in New Year's Eve because the shop closed for New Year's Day. She wanted to have a special time with her husband."

"Marital problems?" Katherine wondered.

"She said it upset Tomás when she spent time with some other man. She tossed those accusations out of the way, like a stray curl over the shoulder, but he wouldn't let it go. I never figured out who the guy is. She spoke vaguely about working hard on a project and consulting. She said she wanted to celebrate Tomás coming home and put all accusations behind them."

"I'm sure she appreciated that you stayed late for her appointment."

"Oh yes, that holiday in particular brings lots of customers. Always a long day, but worth it for the extra tips. Even with the closed sign and the door locked, another woman knocked. I told her she'd have to wait. She changed her mind, pulled her hood up and left. She seemed desperate for a new style for the new year but guess she couldn't wait." Charlene laughed.

Katherine smiled. "Maybe she'll wander in here for a new purse for the new year too. Anyway, sounds like Donna remained optimistic for the new year, although she'd had rough times."

Charlene agreed. "She left in high spirits, and absolutely beautiful." Charlene patted Dolly's head. "Come on Dolly. We better get back to work or our next appointment will beat us in the door."

Amber returned to the counter and emptied the register. "Storage is all secured."

Katherine said, "Charlene, I'm so glad I bumped into you today." They both laughed. "Let's get together soon, and I'll make an appointment online too. I'm due."

Charlene said, "Oh yes, let's have lunch or something."

Amber handed a store bag to Charlene. "Here's the scarf and wallet you bought, both gift wrapped. Thanks for coming in today, Ms. Brown."

"Thanks Amber. Dolly and I will go out your side door, closer to the car. I heard there's a storm on the way tonight. You ladies stay safe. See you soon, Katherine. Bye."

Katherine walked across the room to the window, Charlene's remarks about Kevin ringing in her ears. How much tension had he brought on the family? She would follow up with him. What had happened with Donna's neighbor could have been life threatening. She didn't believe Donna could have an affair. There must be a misunderstanding. Why had Tomás secretly returned? Did he actually suspect Anthony held feelings beyond friendship for Donna?

Charlene stepped off the porch toward the curb, the Cherie bounced on her shoulder, a wagging dog tail popped out of it. Katherine crossed her arms. Couldn't Charlene find some knock off or linen tote instead? Everyone around town will see her Katherine Watson design abused this way. What if more pet owners copy her?

A smile slowly grew with the new opportunity—couture pet purses on parade. With the right marketing, there would be buyers. She could make a profitable line, while providing a product that appears to be in demand. She could call it, the Darling Dolly Doggie Line. Katherine made a quick note on her phone.

Amber stepped back over to the main counter. "Storage remains a little full. I'll rearrange the display by the alcove to fit in more." She stood with a far off stare.

Katherine put down her phone. "Can I talk with you a minute first?"

Amber's whole body stiffened. "I'm sorry I got here

late today. And I'm sorry, but I couldn't stay here and listen to her talk about Julia like that. I wanted to find a nice way to walk out."

"I understand. I want to talk about something else. Charlene said Donna's neighbor had a gun and threatened her? Did Julia mention anything to you? Or did Charlene embellish?"

"One hundred percent." Eyes wide, Amber emphasized each word. "She shot at me too. She's nuts. I walked up the driveway with the lattes. I barely got in the house alive. She says she's shooting at birds. That's bad enough, but she could have killed me. Donna said it happened before, and she called the police."

Katherine's jaw had dropped. "Terrifying. Thank God you got to safety."

"I never want to be on the wrong side of a gun again."

Katherine agreed. "No, never. The police stopped her?"

"They handcuffed her." Amber stepped back and gasped. "When I left, she yelled about getting revenge on Donna. Could she have shot Donna?"

The visual of Donna's body consumed Katherine. She couldn't burden Amber with the deadly details now, or her suspicions. Tomás needed to be the one to break that news to Julia, not her friend. Tomás would know about the plastic bag over her head from when he identified her body. Heart attack or gunshot could be eliminated as a cause of death.

Amber's question begged for an answer, but Katherine avoided it. "The police are working on it, but I don't think she got shot." Katherine mentally noted that besides checking more about Kevin, or talking to Tomás about returning early to Bayside, she needed to question this crazy neighbor. "In the meantime, I wanted to ask if you've heard anything from William and Nicky, about their interrogations. I haven't heard any details."

Amber turned to greet a couple of guests who browsed the merchandise. When she turned back, she gave her attention to a counter display, avoiding Katherine and briefly responding, "I didn't hear much about it."

Now she had Katherine's full attention. "I thought since you and Michael are together, you might have?"

Amber shook her head slowly and shifted to straightening a shoulder bag on the display. "I know they don't want to be questioned again."

Katherine stifled a yawn and her curiosity over Amber's stilted reaction. "I'm dead on my feet. I need a nap. William's coming over today. I'll hear about it from him."

A purposeful pause, in case Amber would say anything more. Instead, she went back to the cash register. Katherine moved into the hallway and there stood David.

"Hi, David. Do you need help with the lunch rush?"

"No worries. MJ and I are creating an oasis for wandering souls to bask in."

"That sounds good on a cold day like this. I'll be there later then. I need a nap after that long night."

"Sleep at peace. MJ said the cops are closing the case tomorrow."

"What?"

"MJ protest plans…already underway."

Chapter Twenty

Ringing up the ladies' purchases calmed Amber.
The customers took their new merchandise and walked
into the alcove toward the Clutch Cafe. Amber took
advantage of the quiet to relax.

She'd enjoyed her morning adventures with
William, sneaking into the professor's office and
searching for the missing phone, and other clues.
Although William had worked for the professor, he
couldn't be seen in the office now. Amber didn't want to
talk about William's troubles with Katherine. If William
chooses to, he'll fill her in.

The door opened behind her, and she happily
greeted her boyfriend. Then she wondered, "Michael,
why aren't you at work?"

"I had a delivery nearby. I wanted to see you." He
moved next to her and held her hand.

She sighed at the touch. "I'm glad to see you."

Michael moved his hand gently up and down her
arm. "Thanks for helping out today. You didn't have to,
but it'll help get those cops off our backs."

A group of ladies walked past the gift shop and into
the exhibits. Amber led Michael to a corner of the side
wall for more privacy. She lowered her voice, "Crazy.
Nothing like what I imagined. I thought we'd walk into
the professor's office and find evidence in five minutes.
William would find a connection to a drug deal, and all

would be solved."

Michael grunted. "You said you got nervous when I dropped you off in the parking lot. So, what happened?"

Amber interrupted, "I'm glad you parked at the other end of the lot, by the dorms. Not near the prof's office."

Michael laughed. "Worked great. You headed toward the dorm. I walked across the lawn, and the cop took the bait. I led him all over campus."

"You kept the stakeout focused on you, for sure."

"So, what happened after I left?"

Amber rubbed her hands together and showed a broad smile. "I let William out of the trunk. He leaped out, glad to be free."

"I bet. I had to sneak him in there early, while Stakeout Bozo followed Nicky to catch his van. Will got stuck in there a while."

Amber nodded. "Worth it, we got into the Prof's building unseen. We walked upstairs. The cops had finished searching the office, but the campus security guy hung out there. So, I went to work."

"How did that go?"

Amber giggled. "Terrific."

"That's because he wanted to believe it. Everyone wants to be a hero."

Amber continued, "I called out to him, and he showed lots of interest."

Michael frowned. "He better not show too much interest."

Amber rubbed her shoulder against him. "He wanted to know why I came there. I tried to cry as a distraction, then I gave him the rest of the fake story. I said my boyfriend dropped me off, and I saw a strange guy following him, and I'm so scared for my boyfriend. As a security guy he immediately tensed up with a big frown, I felt kind of bad tricking him. He wanted more information. I described the stake out cop. Then I pointed him in a completely different direction than where you went."

Michael laughed loudly, and Amber put her finger against his lips. He kissed her hand. "Perfect, and he never caught up to me. So, William sneaked in the Prof's office while you kept the guy busy? Did Will's key still work?"

"Big surprise, a wide open door. When the security guy left, I sneaked down the hall to the Prof's office, and when I got close I heard a voice. I couldn't tell what she said. I stopped outside the door. Then I heard William, so I went in."

"Who did you see him with?"

"The prof's wife had come in. The police told her she could pick up any belongings. What a sad lady. She said she didn't want to run into a lot of people. I felt bad. William suggested we could help her pack up what she wanted to take, and then she thanked him. That gave us a chance to see his stuff before she took it."

"So, you're packing. Did you see the phone? What happened?"

"So bizarre. She talked about her husband as such a different person. I mean, she seemed clueless about the harassment charges against him. Everything she packed she'd say he's smart, such a great teacher, a man doing valuable research work, a renowned science expert."

"When Will got the job, he said he'd be working for the best."

"We filled a couple of boxes of stuff. She wanted

pictures on the desk and hanging on the wall, and some mementos. I could see William tense up when she went through the desk drawers and pulled things out. I held my breath. If she found a phone, she might take it. William told me later, the more she talked the more he felt sorry for her, and he didn't want her to see what may exist on the phone."

Michael shrugged. "We need that phone if it proves he deals drugs without us. That's why Will needs to get it."

"She couldn't find his laptop either, so I guess he didn't have that at home. William thinks the cops have it. After she left, William shut the door and searched everywhere again."

"Found it then?"

"Nada. I figured we got on the wrong track, but William wouldn't give up. He even scooted under the desk and searched. When he came out, he had a new idea."

Michael checked his watch. "I bet the cops found it when they searched the car. They wanted to trick Will when they grilled him at the station."

"No, we searched the prof's research lab."

"Cool. What happened there, while I hiked all over campus in the freezing cold?"

Amber teased, "I bet you ended up at The Hub and ordered a venti hot latte."

Michael grinned. "Well, I did need to keep up my energy, right?" He hugged her and whispered in her ear, "You know me too well."

"While you drank," she paused with a laugh. "William and I went through the lab. We couldn't believe it when we turned up nothing."

"I'm telling you, it got left in his car."

"Then William walked over to a red bin attached to the wall labeled hazardous waste. Before I could shout stop, he opened it. He fiddled around under the lid. I told him to be careful that he didn't get contaminated. He said he thought he felt a button, like a spring. Next thing I know he's smiling at me and holding a phone."

Michael took in a deep breath and slowly exhaled. "So, our plan worked. You got the phone. What's on it?"

"William has it. We took off in different directions. You'll find out more from William tonight."

Michael gave her a hug. "You did great. I want to get those cops off that stakeout, and life back to normal. So, William knows the password on the phone, right?"

Amber frowned at Michael. "I don't know. I never asked."

Chapter Twenty-One

From the museum hallway, the quiet of the Clutch Cafe suggested an early closing for the day. David shut away the late afternoon dark by dropping the blinds. Katherine turned the lights up, and remembered Charlene's warning about a storm front moving in. People scurrying home before it hit, or rushing to get groceries in fear of an extended ice blast off the Puget Sound meant no time for a cheery latte stop. Yes, an early closing may be in order. She pulled out her phone to warn William to stay home and avoid the weather.

A familiar, gravelly voice blew in from the back patio, "Hi, Mom." William filled the doorway. Cheeks red, baseball cap dripping, ski vest hanging over jeans and damp from rain, or snow. He stomped on the mat, shaking mud off his trainers.

Katherine burst forward with a broad smile and a hug. "I'm glad to see you. I almost called you to stay home out of the weather, but I'm glad you're here."

A blind on the window behind them dropped to the sill with a thud. Katherine introduced David. "Splendor to meet a grandson of the Moon. How about a warmup, man? What can I make you to drink?"

"I'll grab my usual." William stepped behind the bar and held up two cups.

Katherine nodded with enthusiasm. "Thanks, I can use the caffeine jolt. I'm still catching up on sleep lost from last night's search."

As David watched with an amused grin, William banged and clanked a canister, pouring coffee beans. The grinder whirred, and steam hissed. Katherine waited in growing anticipation of the magical, hot concoction and eager to share time with her son. He mixed the liquids in tall, metal gray pitchers, and then poured into large mugs, which he brought to the table.

Katherine warmed her fingers around the mug. "Tell me what happened with the police."

William stiffened and leaned forward with elbows on the table. "Mom don't make a big deal out of this. We're handling the cops."

"I knew it was a misunderstanding." Katherine frowned. "Rob's column reported the professor died from a drug overdose." Katherine paused as her son took a long drink. "William, I'm so sorry about your Professor Randall. What a big shock for you to deal with."

He put the mug back on the table, fidgeted with it, then leaned back with a sigh. "Yeah. He could be annoying, but I liked working for a famous expert. I kind of glossed over some things to get to work with him and learn from him. I don't know how long I'd have kept working for him, but he didn't deserve to die."

Katherine frowned. "A smart man, tarnishing noble achievements, and it all ends in a life lost to drugs."

William stared at his drink. "There's something you don't know." Katherine felt her muscles tense again. "I saw him that night."

Katherine sat in silence, waiting to hear where this remark would lead. Her son took his cap off and hooked it on the back of his chair. "Randall called me. He had trouble with a file for an important meeting Tuesday. I met him at the office before I went to the beach party."

Katherine shifted in her chair.

"Mom, he was alive when I left."

"Of course." Katherine's stern response echoed in the quiet cafe.

"He didn't do drugs, and he didn't deal either."

"You didn't know everything about him. He might have kept it hidden. The priority remains getting you cleared, and the police to leave you alone. Nicky too. Thank goodness Christopher's not involved."

David meandered toward them and offered a small plate of muffins that they happily accepted.

As William helped himself, Katherine leaned forward. "I'm worried about you."

"Don't. I've got it all under control." He drained the remaining contents of the mug.

Katherine agreed. "Yes. You saw him at the office because of your job. You left before he left. Case closed."

"You're investigating?" William laughed. "Take me off the suspect list."

Katherine shook her head. "You never made the list."

David walked around the room with a towel and disinfectant spray, cleaning off tables. He walked past them, then continued working nearby.

"Mom, someone else saw him after me. Right before I left, he got a call."

"Do you know who?"

"I told the cops. When he hung up, he laughed and said we needed to finish. He said he suddenly had a date. He joked that work could wait because she couldn't." William blushed.

"Did you see her when you left?"

"No but when I walked out, I saw a guy at the end of the hall. No idea who. I don't know if he wanted to see Randall or what. I took off."

"You told the police all that too?"

"Oh yeah. They wanted to know where I went, with who, all that stuff."

"I mean you told them about the guy in the hall?"

"No."

"Well, according to Rob's online article the cops declared the case an overdose. Rob wrote in some loose ends, but it doesn't sound like there's much more to that story. I'm glad the police are done with you."

William shifted in the chair. "I told you not to worry. We're good."

MJ walked into the room and clapped her hands with a broad smile. A couple of tables away, David tossed the cloth up in the air and caught it. "Moonjava, did your creative energy reach its potency?"

"I'm enamored with my efforts on the display." She rushed forward. "Sweet William, you're here." He got up and hugged her. "Sit down and tell me everything you've been experiencing. I want to absorb it all."

"Next time. I'm meeting the guys. I had to stop by so Mom would feel better." He grinned. "Gotta go."

"Peace out then. I'll focus great vibes for next time."

William grinned. "In your old time talk, right on."

MJ held up her two fingers in the peace sign. "I feel your heart."

William gave his mom a thumbs up. "See you later. Don't worry."

As he walked out, MJ sat. "Why are you worried?"

Katherine wanted to share her concern, then David

sat down at the adjacent table and stared at his phone screen. Had he listened to their conversation all along?

Chapter Twenty-Two

An inventory of refrigerator contents revealed few choices for dinner. Katherine sighed at the empty shelves and bins. She had to cobble something together to encourage Julia to eat. Thank goodness Amber could stay and support her friend. A furry tickle against her leg interrupted Katherine's concentration.

"Purrada, I expected your sudden and affectionate appearance at the open refrigerator door, but dinner time comes later." Cautious as she stepped around the cat, she reached in for the leftover roast, gravy, corn cobs, rolls, and salad makings. The bowl on the counter still had some Washington apples, for dessert. Purrada meowed and wandered under the table.

As Katherine washed her hands at the sink, she glanced at her phone on the windowsill. Her fingers itched to call Anthony. The charming, calm, and endearing Anthony had disappeared in all they'd been through. Far from it. Why not invite him over after dinner? She could chat with him privately in her office. The anger he'd displayed through the past twenty-four hours felt so misplaced.

Katherine dried her hands and clicked Anthony's contact on her phone, wondering if he'd even pick up. When he did, the words slurred. "Hello. What do you want?"

"I'm thinking of you. Anthony, I know you've had

a terrible shock. You're not yourself."

A gruff laugh, followed by a gruffer tone, "Who am I?"

Katherine scowled. "Honestly, I don't know. What are you doing?"

"I'm on Main Street drinking my dinner."

"That only makes things worse. Put the drink down and order some food or come over here tonight. I'm putting together dinner now. After that we'll talk."

Silence on the other end. Then he said, "Donna should be alive. She should be here talking to me about the pharmaceutical research for my book. She should be laughing and talking and…alive. Killing her over nothing, that's what's so wrong."

Katherine frowned. "Anthony, you're right."

Silence in response, followed by resolve. "I finished my last drink. I'll eat something and drive over. Katherine, thanks."

"No, don't risk driving. I'll reserve you a ride share. I'll order it for an hour from now and have it drop you here. I'll give them your number to contact."

"I'll see you then."

Concerned and curious, Katherine put her phone away. What in the world did Anthony mean? Sincere concern stemming from Donna's research for the new book, or was there more to that story? Did he know more about her disappearance? Drunken ramblings? She'd never seen Anthony drunk. How had he reacted when he stopped by the Clutch Café, and heard Julia worried about her mother?

Amber stepped into the room, pulling Katherine back to the present, and dinner. "Fresh tea in the pot, Amber. Help yourself while I get dinner on the table."

"I'm good." She leaned on the counter. "Julia's coming down in a minute."

Katherine put the meat and veggies in the oven. "I hope she got some rest."

"She said she did. She can use a friend to talk to tonight."

"Well then, she's in the right place with the two of us. We're both good listeners."

Amber set three places at the table. "I wish we could have a do-over for this new year."

"Unfortunately, we have to play the cards we've been dealt."

Amber sat at the table. "Too bad MJ isn't around. I could use a meditation."

Katherine put a hand on her hip. "Play the cards you're dealt isn't groovy enough for you?" They both laughed. Katherine went on, "MJ and I worked on the 1960's purse exhibit today. We still have more work to do for the Valentine Power of Love grand opening party."

Amber leaned back in her chair. "February seems far away."

Katherine heard footsteps on the backstairs that came into the kitchen. She picked up the teapot. "Julia come on in. Would you like a hot cup of tea? Or there's some pop in the cupboard, or hot chocolate."

"Some tea. I could use the caffeine. Thanks."

Katherine poured. "Dinner's almost ready. I hope you're hungry."

Katherine tossed the salad as the two girls muttered and whispered at the table. Katherine left them to their secrets, even taking time to leave the kitchen for the pantry. She stared out the window of the back door at the dark winter night. As the wind rattled by, she checked the lock and briefly wondered if Anthony had stopped drinking. She could only hope. She'd find out when he got here. She fed Purrada an early dinner to stop her persistent meowing.

Through the archway, the girls sat in the kitchen. Katherine thought of Tomás, and how he must be missing Julia tonight. As she walked back to the stove she wondered again, why had he come back early but not gone home? She shook off her reservations about him and the trip. Time to serve the girls dinner.

Despite hunger pangs, Katherine forced herself to pull back and wait when she saw Julia put her elbow on the table and lean her chin in the palm of her hand. She stared at Amber, who stopped with her fork midway between the plate and her mouth. In sympathy, she lowered her fork. "I'm so sorry."

Julia wiped away a tear. "I'm sad. I can't stop thinking about…"

Katherine reached over to hold her hand. "We're all sad at the loss of your mom."

Amber pushed her plate away. "You might feel better if you talk about it. Go ahead. No one here will judge."

Katherine's curiosity perked up. "We're your friends. We want to make things easier."

After hesitation, Julia cleared her throat. "The last time I'll ever see my mom I got so mad at her. She felt mad at me too. Why did I act like that? I didn't know I'd never see her again. I can never even tell her I'm sorry." She burst into tears.

Katherine crouched down next to Julia and gave her a hug. "Your mother knew you loved her, and she loved you dearly. Your mother would never have doubted your love. Because of that, there's no need for a sorry."

More tears now as Julia continued, "She ruined my New Year's Eve. Then she stopped me from dating Kevin again. I'd never been so mad at her. Now I've never missed her so much."

Katherine embraced her again. "Everyone has disagreements. It doesn't mean you don't love each other anymore."

"Do you think she had time to forgive me and love me again, before…Do you think what I did that night, how mad I acted, caused her to…to…die?"

Katherine took both Julia's hands in hers and gazed into her eyes. "No. Absolutely not. Your temper had nothing to do with whatever happened. I know that. Amber knows it too. The police will prove it."

Julia's clenched hands loosened. "I hope so."

Katherine nodded for the girl who desperately desired some peace in her troubled mind. "Julia, I want you to put your hands over your heart." The girl did it. "Now close your eyes and see deep into your beating heart, because that's where your mom is. She's so close to you now. Can you feel her?"

Julia's lips turned up slightly, into a glimmer of a smile.

"Let your heart speak to her, of how much you love her. She will hear you." After a pause, as Julia's breathing became easier Katherine continued. "Julia, think of a time when you and your mom felt such happiness together. A peaceful time over her favorite daisies, she sure loved daisies. Or a joke you shared. Or a secret. Any favorite memory. Share it in your heart with your mom."

Julia's smile grew. She opened her watery eyes. Katherine smiled back. "You can do that anytime. Your mother will always be that close to you."

Julia said, "Thank you." She used her napkin to wipe tears away. "I'm a little relieved."

Amber reassured her friend, "That's good."

Purrada appeared from under the table and jumped onto Julia's lap. "Hi, Purr." Julia scratched behind the ear. The cat snuggled against the girl. "You want me to feel better too."

Katherine poured Julia some more tea. "Try some dinner. It seems a long time since you ate anything."

Julia grinned. "You're right."

Katherine picked up her fork and tried to pick up the mood too. "I'm hungry, does that make three of us?"

Purrada sat tail curled, eyes locked with longing on Julia's plate. Katherine shooed her off Julia's lap. "Guess that makes four of us." The cat indignantly left the room prompting a giggle at the table.

Conversation paused. Julia picked at her food. Katherine kept the conversation light. She talked with Amber about the gift shop. She talked fashion and the shocking trend of small wristlets, and young women carrying no purses, only their phone. Both girls shared a guilty look, then everyone burst into laughter.

Amber reached for the salt. "The shop's not as busy now as before the holidays. I've had time to reorganize and spruce up the displays.

"Business will pick up as Valentine's approaches. Thank goodness I'm almost done with my fall line."

Julia asked, "Fall? Isn't that too late?"

Amber shook her head. "She means next fall, for her designer line. She's always creating a couple of seasons ahead."

"Moving from Southern California has enhanced my understanding for how different the seasons are in a lot of places. The vibrant colors of fall, the desperate desires for warmth in the winter, the romance and mischief of spring, and bright summer delights."

Amber nodded. "I never knew much about fashion until I worked for you."

"My mom liked briefcases." Julia volunteered.

Katherine smiled. "She worked a valuable profession. I'm sure she commuted with things like her laptop and reports. She'd need a good bag for that. She did a lot of good in the world."

Julia teared up. "Yes. She bought that new, giant bag instead of a briefcase." She turned to Amber. "What did you call it?"

"Messenger bag."

Katherine put her silverware on her empty plate. "Your mom did a lot of good both at work and at home too. She raised a wonderful daughter."

Amber grabbed a tea mug for a toast. "Here's to your mom, and here's to Julia, a great friend."

Katherine clinked her mug against the girls' mugs.

"I love David's new drinks." Amber's comment came as a relief to Katherine. Barista changes are never easy, but who knows how long he'll stay. Amber spoke to Julia. "David's made awesome changes, the best new blends. I already have new latte favs. I'll get you a ginger latte tomorrow. You'll love it. David labels ginger one of the healthiest spices ever, and he adds some other spices too."

After dessert, Katherine cleared the table. "Amber, you might want to head home before the storm gets worse."

Amber stood at the sink. "I'll help you with the dishes first."

Katherine said, "I'll put them in the dishwasher. You go ahead."

Amber walked back to Julia, still sitting at the table. "Are you seeing Kevin tonight?"

"He's working."

Katherine dried her hands on the towel. "We'll have a relaxed evening here." The front doorbell rang, followed by several loud knocks. "Oh, I forgot, Anthony's stopping by tonight. That must be him."

Katherine went to answer the door, fingers crossed it would be a nice quiet evening.

Chapter Twenty-Three

As she walked through the hall to answer the front door, Katherine flipped on a couple of light switches to brighten the entry. Another series of knocks accelerated her pace, and she swung open the door, "Anthony…"

Three people huddled on the front porch. Tomás stood primed to bang on the door again, sporting a wrinkled, feverish expression. He wore a thick black jacket zipped to the top and jeans tucked into high ankle boots.

Next to him stood Cleo wrapped exquisitely in another designer coat, with a fur collar that she clutched at the top with one hand covered by a silky glove. Her hair swept up into a matching snow hat and her makeup elegantly applied. Cleo's tall husband stood next to her, partially turned away from the door and texting on a bright phone screen. The blue suit he wore had been exposed to the elements with the long, unbuttoned coat flapping in the wind.

Tomás blurted out, "I need to see my daughter. Please."

Katherine swung the door wide. "Of course. Please come in, everyone."

Tomás walked straight in, stood in the middle of the foyer, and crossed his arms. "Julia? Julia, please come see me."

Cleo followed, taking in every detail of the scene

with great interest. Stephen stood facing her, with his forefinger pointed in the air. Katherine wondered how long he expected her to stand with the door open and the heat escaping while he finished some text. The phone swooshed, as the text went. He pocketed the phone and stepped through the door. "Evening." She closed the door behind him.

Cleo walked around the area in a circle, taking it all in. She spied through the doorways to the exhibits, into the gift shop, down the hall to the office and kitchen, even glancing upstairs.

Katherine spoke to her first, "Another time I'd be happy to show you around, Cleo." She approached Tomás. "You want to see Julia."

Cleo put her hand on Tomás' arm. "We brought them dinner. How astonishing to hear he and Julia are separated at this difficult time. I suggested we bring him here immediately for a touching reconciliation."

Tomás stood silent during her proclamation. "I need to see my daughter now."

"I'm not keeping you from—" the doorbell interrupted Katherine. By the time she'd turned around, Stephen had answered it. Framed in the doorway stood Anthony and Kevin.

Anthony frowned. With a slight slur, he addressed the room, "Imagine my surprise when I went outside to get in my rideshare, and saw my driver." He stared hard at Tomás. "I believe you all know each other."

Katherine flinched. She didn't know whether to ask them to return later or encourage them inside so the door could be shut against the storm. Anthony resolved that dilemma as he gestured forward with one hand, "After you Kevin. You said you wanted to see Julia. Careful, you may have to move a mountain to do it."

The young man frowned, then cast aside trepidation and walked inside with determination. He stood silent, away from Tomás but squarely within the father's glare.

Anthony never took his eyes off Tomás as he spoke, "You invited me, Katherine." He stood across from Tomás.

Cleo held out her gloved hand to Anthony. "We haven't met. I'm Cleo. That's my husband Stephen who opened the door for you. He owns NRML Pharmaceuticals where Donna worked." Cleo nodded toward Kevin, "And your friend is?"

Kevin stammered, "A friend of Julia's."

Tomás raised his voice to Katherine, "I want to see Julia." He moved toward the stairs. "Julia? I'm here to see you."

Crossing the room and grabbing the door handle from Stephen, Katherine shut it abruptly. She turned back to Tomás. "I'm happy to take you to her."

Cleo said, "Best if she come here. Don't you agree, Tomás? We can all help her see reason."

Katherine stepped from the door. "For privacy, the cafe closed some time ago so the two of you could talk there. I'm sure Julia wants to see you as much as you want to see her."

"Yes, if you can show me where she is."

"Let me show you to the cafe, then I'll let her know you're here."

Cleo frowned, but before she could object Tomás said a terse thank you. Cleo sighed. "You're sure you want to chance an argument? I'm happy to play peacemaker."

A gust of wind blew leaves against the window,

followed by a terse exclamation, and then the doorbell. Katherine shrugged. "Tonight, I need a revolving door."

She ushered in the young woman she recognized from the search tent and struggled to remember her name. The woman had seemed more concerned with impressing Stephen than with searching for her boss or comforting Julia.

"Brittany." Stephen's warm tone and Cleo's deepening frown intrigued Katherine.

The young woman sported a hooded ski jacket, short skirt, tights, and a broad smile aimed at Stephen. Her knee high boots, almost stilettos clattered across the stone floor.

"Mr. Rider." Any suggestion of formality vanished in the tone of her greeting. Did Cleo hear the same? "Oh, Mr. Rider, I'm glad to catch up with you. These test samples need your wet signature for early tomorrow morning." Brittany tapped the case she carried.

"I appreciate your ingenuity finding me, Brittany. If you check your texts, I said I'd meet you at my house in an hour and sign them."

"Funny thing, as I drove by I recognized your car. I thought, why not stop in?"

Amber walked in from the kitchen with her coat on. Julia followed. "Oh." Amber stopped without warning. Julia peeked over her friend's shoulder.

"Julia, mi joya." Tomás held out empty arms.

Julia took two slow steps, then hurried over and filled her father's arms with a hug.

Katherine teared up. Across the room, Kevin stared at the floor. Anthony's face twisted with unmistakable outrage. Brittany's gaze locked on Stephen, who appeared eager to escape out the front door. Cleo stood

184

tapping a foot with impatience, examining Julia from head to foot.

"Papa, I need you."

"We are family. We need each other." They hugged again.

"Oh Papa, why didn't you come home New Year's? If you'd been home Mom would…"

"My dear, you know how medical emergencies go. I have to be where I'm needed."

"But you had come back."

"I didn't expect to get back early."

Anthony spoke up in a gruff voice, "You couldn't go home? Did your wife know you came back? She told me she expected you Tuesday."

Tomás held up a fist in Anthony's direction. "Why would my dear wife tell you anything." He held Julia by the shoulders, so they faced each other. "Julia, you've grown up a doctor's daughter, you know how it can be."

"But why did Kevin say he saw you with the professor who got killed the night before?"

He answered without letting her go. "We're family. We'll work all of it out. All of it. What's most important is we're together. I love you. Come home tonight. Come home now."

Julia's voice had a tremble in it, "I want to come home again…"

Tomás answered immediately, "Yes. We'll go. We'll give our thanks and…"

Julia pulled away. "Wait." She ran up the stairs.

Tomás moved to go after her, but Cleo stopped him. "Do what she says, Tomás. We'll all see what she has in mind."

Katherine thought fast, searching for an idea to clear

people out. "No need for everyone to stay while Tomás has time with Julia. Go home before the storm gets worse. I'll give Tomás and Julia a ride when they're ready. Anthony let's get together tomorrow. Kevin you can drive him home and see Julia tomorrow." Katherine felt like she did directing traffic New Year's Eve.

Brittany and Stephen both brightened at the suggestion. He gestured to Cleo, who stood stoic next to Tomás. Kevin took a few steps to leave, then hesitated.

Anthony shook his head slowly side to side to side. "No. Katherine, you invited me." Then he pointed at Tomás. "And you haven't answered my question."

Anthony should wait somewhere else, with some sobering coffee. Katherine considered how to motivate him to move, when Julia captured everyone's attention as she bounced back downstairs.

The girl carried a big, red messenger bag with a leather bow on the front. The attached daisy charm bounced back and forth on Donna's bag. "I can't keep Mom's bag now. I can't even hold it without crying." She raised her eyes over the bag and held it out to Katherine. "Will you put it in your museum? Please?"

Speechless by the girl's gush of emotion, Katherine's eyes brimmed with tears. "Oh, Julia, in time you'll treasure everything your mom has left behind. I'll keep it for you until you're ready to have it back. One day your memories of her won't bring pain. They'll be treasures. Your mom loved you so much, and I know your mom liked your new matching bags. I'll take good care of it for you." Despite her compassion for Julia, Katherine's mind wandered to the other unanswered question, where had Julia's twin bag ended up? Not on the trail where Donna must have been attacked. Not in the field where she found Donna. Not in her car.

"Thank you." Julia shoved it into Katherine's hands.

Cleo stepped forward. "Julia, are you sure? We can take it now and you'll have the bag stored away at your home, where it belongs."

Julia shook her head. "No."

"I'll put it in my office. It will be there whenever you want it." Katherine's fingers tingled as she took it. Did the police even realize which bag Donna owned? Had they searched the bag? She could check it for clues. Julia wiped away tears as Katherine shouldered the bag and hugged her. Investigation would wait.

Julia rushed to Kevin, and they embraced. She said, "I'm so glad to see you. I'm going home now, but can I see you tomorrow?"

He nodded. As Julia went to her father, the young man stared at her back.

Anthony waved a hand in the air. "I've had enough. I'm outta here." He took long strides into the exhibits room toward the cafe. Katherine frowned. He wants coffee now?

Cleo clapped. "All's well. Wonderful. We'll drop you both off, Tomás."

Julia said, "I need to go upstairs and get my things."

Cleo moved next to her husband again. "You're ready to leave, Stephen?"

Katherine left the messenger bag at the foot of the stairs while she whispered to Kevin, "Can you go get Anthony and drive him home? I'll update the app on my phone with the address and payment. I appreciate you helping me out."

"Sure."

Stephen asked, "Katherine can I use a table, so I can

sign off these tests and Brittany can go?"

She pointed down the hall. "You can use the desk in my office, second door on the right."

"Thanks."

Cleo stood poised at the bottom stair next to the bag. Katherine put it back on her shoulder. "Sorry to leave this in your way."

The woman's gaze drew past her, in the direction her husband had disappeared. "Do you mind if I help myself to a glass of water?" She pointed in the direction her husband had walked. "Through here to your kitchen?"

"Yes, let me get that for you."

Cleo said over her shoulder, "You've got your hands full. It won't take a minute."

Katherine shrugged and the bag shifted. "Glasses are in the cupboard to the right of the sink."

Tomás paced. Voices murmured from the exhibits room, and Anthony emerged unsteady and sarcastic. "Thanks for a great time, Katherine."

Kevin walked around him and out the door. The wind blew so hard it swept leaves onto the porch and into the house. Katherine shivered at the sudden drop in temperature. She patted Anthony's arm. "Sober up tonight. We'll talk tomorrow."

Anthony turned toward Tomás and pointed with a flourish. "I know what you did."

Tomás stood still with fists poised, ready for assault. Anthony stood unfazed. "An incredible lady, way too good for you. I know you sneaked back early, and you killed her." He walked out the door, hand in the air. "Hey kid, I'm coming."

Speechless, Katherine rushed over with the bag

swinging and almost falling off her shoulder. She closed the door behind Anthony and stood between it and a furious Tomás. For a moment she thought he may charge out despite her. "Tomás, he doesn't know what he's saying. He had too much to drink."

Tomás stared at the door. One fist tapped against his thigh. "Katherine, you need to watch out for that…for that…I don't trust him. All that time he spent with my wife? They didn't write some book." He clenched his fist tighter. "I'm figuring it all out too late."

"Please, Tomás don't torture yourself."

He launched himself toward the door and shouted, "He killed my wife."

"Please, stop." Katherine put a hand on his shoulder. "He's gone. You'll upset Julia if she hears you. Please. We don't know that Anthony had any involvement."

He stood still. "I know."

Katherine put the bag on the table and forced her shoulders to relax as she attempted to hide her growing doubts about Anthony. "I said we don't know, and we don't."

Tomás bowed his head, overwhelmed with emotion. "They had an affair. Or he wanted to have an affair, and my wife refused." His voice rose again, "So he killed her."

"Tomás, you're too close to this. Wait for the police to investigate, for Julia's sake."

He gazed at the top of the stairs. "The police are giving me news tomorrow. We'll have answers then, and if he did something…"

"The law will bring justice." Katherine changed the subject, "I'm glad Julia will be home with you."

Tomás waited for Julia to reappear. "Thank you for

taking her in, but she belongs at home."

"I'm glad I could be there for you both. I'm so sorry for your loss."

"I'll give Julia a hand packing her things." He slowly walked upstairs.

Stephen marched in carrying Brittany's case. "Everything all right? Did I hear shouting?"

"Everything's fine."

Brittany joined him. He gestured to her. "Thanks for your extra effort to finish the work tonight, Brittany. I appreciate it."

"Of course."

He held up her briefcase and as she took the handle, he lingered over her fingers. "I'll walk you to your car." He opened the door to the wild weather.

Amber emerged from the gift shop doorway with raised eyebrows. "I'll check on Julia."

Katherine pushed the door shut and stood by the window. Her hand rested on the messenger bag next to her. Stephen lingered at Brittany's car, despite the cold rain and wind.

When someone cleared their throat, Katherine pulled her sweater tighter. If only she'd raised the thermostat temperature. Cleo twirled around in the foyer. "Have you seen my husband? I seem to have misplaced him." She giggled.

"He finished signing and stepped outside to help Brittany back to her car."

"Oh." They stood uncomfortably together. Cleo scanned the bag on the table, the door again, the stairs.

Katherine checked her phone screen. "I'm sure you can head home soon. Thanks for bringing Tomás here. I like seeing Julia with her dad."

"We'll wait for Tomás. We'll drive them home." Cleo crossed her arms.

The front door opened, and the storm pushed a drenched Stephen inside. Cleo joined her husband. "Checking the storm?"

He shivered. "We need to get home."

Katherine offered to get him a towel. Then voices echoed from the kitchen. Julia and Tomás walked down the hall, followed by Amber. "You came down the back stairs."

Tomás said. "I checked your other door for Julia's boots."

Julia gave Katherine a hug. "Thank you for letting me stay."

"You're welcome here anytime. You know that."

The four remaining guests walked out without another word. Tomás hugged Julia to him. Katherine thought of the accusations he'd made. Anthony having an affair with Donna? Would he pursue a married woman? And if he did, and she refused? She'd never seen Anthony driven to violence.

What about Anthony accusing Tomás? He never said why he went to the college that night. Are the two sudden deaths connected by him? Why did he fly back early? Why didn't he go home? Katherine reconsidered whether Julia should have gone home now, with so many questions unanswered?

Amber joined her at the window. "What a night."

Katherine said, "Thanks for staying. I appreciate how you helped calm Julia at dinner."

"I feel bad for her."

"Amber, what do you think of Kevin? The anger he showed at the search concerns me, when he shouted at

Tomás despite the cops watching. Then the way he drove away with Julia, almost in triumph."

"Kevin's nice. They're a great couple, but he has a temper toward her parents. They've had some bad times. That last fight, Julia and her mom fought over him."

"Julia's serious about Kevin?"

"He's serious about her too. He has a romantic side."

"You like him then, for Julia?"

"They seem good together."

"You don't think he broke in and trashed their home in a rage?"

"He has a temper, but he told Julia he didn't do it. She believes him. She won't stop seeing him. They seem romantic."

"Could Kevin be mad enough, and violent enough, to attack Julia's mother?"

Amber stood still. "No, but she could have got run down by a car or something."

"When I found her…an accident is unlikely." Katherine stopped, worried she'd said too much, and realizing how certain she felt that someone had murdered Donna.

"Someone killed her?"

"Be careful Amber, until we know more." Amber took out her car keys. "Text me when you get home, and please be careful. Check for anything suspicious when you get out of your car at the dorm."

"I will."

She waved from the window as Amber drove away. The shrubbery surrounding the house waved and moved in all directions with the wild winds. Shadows from the outside lights jumped and weaved. Now that the crowd had left, the storm sounds roared through the walls and even rattled windows. A crazy storm could hide many threats. She locked the deadbolt and pulled the messenger bag back onto her shoulder. The weight of it dragged and tantalized. Perhaps an exploration of Donna's messenger bag would turn up a clue. First a hot chocolate in the kitchen to soothe the nerves after this evening. After that, she'd search for any helpful messages from Donna's fashionable accessory.

Chapter Twenty-Four

A police car parked in front of her house. Despite the weather, Jason and Hobbs sauntered up to the door. She smiled broadly as she let them in.

"Well, here's a surprise the storm blew my way. I didn't know you would stop by tonight, but how nice to see you. Both of you." Katherine grinned and gave Hobbs a gentle scratch behind the ear.

"I hadn't planned on it, but I'm glad to see you." Hobbs sat down and yawned, as Jason gave Katherine a lingering kiss, and then another. "I can kiss you better if you put down that gigantic purse. Do you need to carry a purse indoors?" He laughed.

"No, on my way to my office after a busy night." She put the bag on the side table and slid back in his arms. "Can you stay for a while? Hot chocolate for you, and a doggy biscuit for your partner?"

"We're on duty tonight, so I'll take a rain check. A real rain check." He hesitated and ran his fingers up her spine. "Although, I can't speak for Hobbs. He may want a biscuit, and another…" He grinned that irresistible, mischievous smile and leaned in for a soulful kiss.

She offered him her hand and led him to her office, as he signaled Hobbs. It always amused Katherine, when Hobbs entered her office with a quick and hopeful glance to the corner cabinet. She placed the messenger bag on the corner of her desk and opened the box of dog treats inside that cabinet. Hobbs gave a quick hop for joy as she gave him a small chew bone. He hopped again and then lay on the rug to enjoy. She put her arm around Jason's shoulders as she joined him at the bay window behind her desk. He entwined an arm around her and continued to gaze outside.

Katherine took a moment to relax and enjoy the festive neighborhood, filled with bright Christmas lights. She wanted a soothing break from the alarming accusations of the evening. Outside the window she ignored the chaos of the storm, enjoying the view past her own plentiful, cheery lights, to the houses across the street. With the new year underway, she'd miss the warmth of the sparkling colors when people took their decorations down. She stood on the brink of Bayside's final deep plunge into the dark depths of long winter nights. She'd take her lights down too. She vowed to check the forecast for the next dry day to get that done. She snuggled closer to Jason as a wind blast shook the window. He seemed focused on the patrol car.

"There's news. The department's planning a press conference tomorrow. They've concluded the case for Professor Randall." Jason's tone had turned professional.

"The professor? William told me the police stopped questioning him, thank goodness." She tensed and stepped aside. "You have something to tell me? That detective won't harass him again, will he? If William gets questioned again…"

"No one's questioning him. Tomorrow the chief will confirm cause of death as a drug overdose."

"I'm glad to hear it will be over and done with."

He seemed to ignore her comment. "That's only part

of the press conference. They'll be talking about the investigation around Donna Ruiz too."

Katherine gave a quick, eager gasp. "What's the preview?"

"I can't say much."

"I don't want you to get in trouble, but you came here to tell me something. Can I help?"

His lips tensed. "I'm here because you found Donna. You're one of the few people who saw her."

Katherine steeled herself for hearing tough news about an extended investigation, and a killer among us. She thought again of Tomás flying back but staying away from home. Then Anthony's accusation against Tomás came to mind, and that outburst from Anthony prompted the agonizing question of his suspicious behavior. Tomás seemed convinced of Anthony's guilt, or did he create a story because he needed to hide that he murdered Donna?

"Katherine, evidence can lead to several theories. Analyzing the evidence brings investigators to conclusions."

"Jason, what do you want to tell me? You didn't stop here while on duty to give me a lesson in solving mysteries. I know that crime solving takes analysis of clues. Wait, I know what you're here to say. The chief will announce there will be an extended investigation."

She attempted to display patience as he hesitated again. "No. The case is closed."

"They caught the murderer?" What a relief. So, it can't be either Anthony or Tomás. Instead, a temper driven, love crazed Kevin? Julia will need a lot of support and understanding.

"There's no murderer."

Katherine stood speechless, but only for a moment. "For heaven's sake, your chief thinks she killed herself? What? Jason, I found her. Suicide is not what I saw, and Donna would never do that."

He took her hands, and his sad eyes met her determined stare. "I wanted to forewarn you. I didn't want you to hear it later from people around town. Julia and her family will need you to be strong for them."

"Jason, you surely don't believe it."

"I'm not giving the press conference."

"Wait." Jason and Hobbs both watched Katherine hurry over to her design closet and pull out her large whiteboard.

Hobbs went back to work munching on the treat. Jason sighed. "Not the whiteboard. I have to get back to work."

"It won't take long."

"Right." He checked his dispatch phone, then sat in her desk chair.

She wrote Kevin's name on the board and pointed at it. "Do the detectives know he has a terrible temper, and he's mad that Donna doesn't want her daughter dating him? Can the police get access to the ride share records he keeps to see where he drove, and when?"

Jason remained silent. She stood still, debating whether to continue. "Amber said Donna's neighbor had a gun and grew furious when Donna reported her shooting. She almost shot Amber on New Year's Day. Could she have been crazy enough to take Donna hostage at gunpoint?"

Hobbs finished the treat, licked his lips, and rolled over for a nap.

Katherine paced, deep in thought. Jason leaned

forward, apparently ready to announce departure time. Katherine dared to jump in with both feet. "Did you know that Tomás stayed in town all that night? Here, and never went home. He never told anyone he had returned. The husband always gets labeled a suspect." She added Tomás to her whiteboard.

Jason checked the dispatch phone again. "Suspect everyone, but the husband may not always raise suspicions."

Katherine rubbed her eyes. What in the world did he mean by that?

Time to hold back now. No need to bring Anthony into the conversation tonight. She wanted to talk to a sober Anthony tomorrow.

The next name she wrote on the board had intrigued Katherine at the volunteer search center, and tonight. Donna's ambitious assistant may have thought she had much to gain with her boss out of her way. She added notes on Brittany's actions that could be clues.

"Brittany's got something for her boss. She's all over him, even in front of Cleo, his wife."

"You wrote down she wanted a promotion."

"A promotion, or an affair, or both."

Jason rubbed a palm against his chin. She wrote CEO on the board.

"Since you added the CEO, you should add the CEO's wife too. Suspect everyone. The CEO's wife could have blamed Donna for not controlling her assistant." Jason grinned.

Katherine slapped his knee, and he pulled her into his lap for a long kiss. Then he hugged her close and whispered, "Too bad I have to go back on duty."

They stood up, and Katherine added the CEO's wife

to the board. "Possible she aimed for Brittany, and Donna got in the way."

Hobbs watched from a comfortable recline, as Jason stood next to her. They both faced the board and Jason put an arm around her. "I have a couple of comments for you."

Katherine's hopes flickered to life. Jason tapped on the column she'd titled "neighbor". "I'm aware of the incident on new year's day. That neighbor spent twenty-four hours in a cell at the station waiting on bail. In terms you'll appreciate—she has an alibi."

"Good to know. That's helpful."

He lingered over the other names and comments. "My recommendation—skip the press conference." He pushed the whiteboard back into the walk-in closet. "Come and walk me to the door. I need to get back on duty." He took her hand and signaled Hobbs.

At the front door, the couple shared a tender kiss. He brushed stray hair locks over her shoulder. "You've had a couple of tough days. Can you get to bed early tonight?"

She shook her head. "I'll be burning the holiday lights into the early hours of the morning. I'm behind on the final details for the Rodeo Drive show, and the L. A. staff can't wait much longer." She glanced out the window. "Be careful in this terrible storm."

He caressed her cheek and grinned. "I'll be in the neighborhood."

"Good to know. I'll keep the decorations on for you."

After Jason and his partner left, Katherine went straight back to her office closet. She added a column for Anthony, drew a line through "the neighbor" and scribbled a few more notes. She stood back in contemplation, then decided she better get to work on her runway show. She didn't want to be late sending her updates to staff, and she didn't want to be late to the press conference tomorrow.

Chapter Twenty-Five

Katherine sipped from her third mug of hot chocolate and paused to absorb the coziness of her home office. Rare when Katherine couldn't concentrate on creating fashion but tonight proved the exception. The allure of Donna's bag on the corner of her desk enticed her, but dire fashion deadlines required restraint. She'd vowed to get her work done first. She studied an email from L.A. about remaining tasks and deadlines for fashion week in New York, followed by Dubai the next month.

Yet another bright lightning strike broke across the porch and through the glass French doors. She mentally counted seconds to the thunder crash. Boom. So close.

She comforted Purrada. The cat seemed in two minds, enjoying the attention versus hiding under the desk away from the storm. Purrada nestled in her lap. She'd worked for hours, but her weariness came from the tension of the never-ending wild storm. The rain pounded heavily on the porch overhang, and sideways against the windows.

Her screen had gone dark, and now it gave no response. Katherine hadn't plugged it in, and the battery died. She grabbed the cord out of the bottom drawer. Her cell phone dead too. She'd meant to charge it when she got home but never got around to it. The wind slammed the rain against the window again, a low rumble of thunder, and the room went pitch black.

Katherine groaned and whined out loud, "Not a power outage. Come on." With a swivel of her chair, she turned to stare out the window. All her pretty holiday lights had turned off. When she leaned forward to see down the street, indignant Purrada hightailed it off her lap.

Lights blazed across the street. All over the neighborhood decorations glowed, streetlights beamed, porch lights shone, and two spotlights shone on signs for businesses down the hill. Only her property stood in the dark.

A creaking in the house and Katherine's whole body stiffened. With the power off, her alarm system and camera would not be working. She sat alone with no way to reach anyone.

The road appeared dead quiet after midnight. She could drive for help or check the fuse box herself. The storm calmed as suddenly as it had flared up. More creaking, closer. A chill ran slowly up Katherine's spine. She felt a presence. What a ridiculous MJ kind of thought, but she could not dismiss it. Behind her, did someone enter the room?

Katherine sank behind her tall chair back, motionless, holding her breath. A flashlight beam hit the wall mirror and lit Katherine's reflection. The intruder remained in the dark. She plunged to the floor behind the desk as a shot blasted. The desk shook.

She crawled around the desk corner. The light beam rested on the messenger bag. The thief picked it up by one strap and swung it over a shoulder, then moved toward the hall. Nothing recognizable stood out with the intruder dressed in black from head to toe including hat, gloves, turtleneck, pants, even the shoes.

Anger and adrenaline charged Katherine forward. She reached out blindly, grabbed both sides of the messenger, and pulled with all her strength. She couldn't see the red bag well, but she felt the stiff leather firmly between her fingers. The bag jerked as the thief spun around and pulled back hard.

The thief had covered their face. Two small holes for penetrating brown eyes to glare through. Katherine's deafening scream echoed in the dark. "No!"

She lost her grip. The smooth leather slipped through her fingers. Desperate not to lose Donna's bag, Katherine ran forward. She caught the curve of its flap and pulled. The strap gave way with a pop. Katherine fell on the floor. Hugging the prize close, she lay ready to fight for it. She heard a distinct click from the hammer of a gun.

"Freeze. Stop. Hands in the air." Jason's voice commanded. Fast, heavy footsteps, and the thief ran past Katherine, who clutched the messenger tight. The French doors swung wide. Jason turned on a powerful light beam then tripped and fell. The light rolled under the desk, shining out on Jason's entanglement with Katherine on the floor.

"Katherine? You're okay?"

"I think so."

"I didn't see you on the floor. When I heard that shot…I thought…" His voice had an unusual husky tone. "Give me your hand."

Suddenly she felt overwhelmed with exhaustion, drained of energy. He took her trembling hand. Her other hand lay on top of the bag as she leaned against him, and they sat on the floor. He hugged her to him. "God, I'm glad you're all right."

She nestled against him, feeling comfort and warmth. "How did you get here?"

"You said you'd keep your lights on for me. When they suddenly went out, I pulled in the alley wondering if I should check on you. Then I heard that shot." He squeezed her even tighter.

Cold air rushed into the room. He leaned her against the desk and retrieved the flashlight.

Jason pushed the familiar vest button and opened Hobbs' car door. Almost immediately came the click of animal claws on the kitchen floor. Jason called Hobbs, and the dog appeared. He wrapped an arm around Katherine again and pulled her close. "I've got to check your fuse box. Wait here with Hobbs. Hold my phone. The light doesn't shine bright, but better than nothing."

He hurried past the dog after giving him a command. Hobbs watched his partner, then focused on her. A professional dog now, not wasting a single glance on the treat cabinet. Apparently Purrada had made a clean getaway. She managed to drag herself to her feet. She picked up the messenger bag and gingerly placed it back on the corner of the desk. The broken strap drooped and dangled in her hand. She took some deep breaths to calm herself.

Who would break into her house to steal Donna's bag? All those who had come to get Julia tonight knew she had it here. Anyone else? She squinted momentarily as the power came back on and the dark turned bright. She leaned against the desk and focused again on the bag, considering each visitor who saw Julia giving it to her. Why did someone want Donna's bag? Why would someone want it so bad to shoot her for it?

Sirens blared. Jason returned. "I called for backup. I told them to dust the back door for prints. Why didn't you keep it locked?" He stood and gently rubbed her arms. "I need to track with Hobbs. The perp has a big lead on me. Did he touch anything? Your bag?"

Katherine let go of the broken strap. "Yes." Jason never knew about Donna's bag, and she didn't want to tell him tonight.

"Please, step back." He snapped his fingers. The dog jumped up and sniffed Donna's bag. "A home break in and shooting…" Hobbs barked twice and without a word they raced across the room. "Don't touch these doors. They may have fingerprints." And with that they ran across the porch and vanished into the night. Keep the back door locked? Jason had that wrong. She had locked the back door, when she made dinner for the girls.

Outside the bay window two patrol cars parked. Her thumb bumped against a rough, warm, jagged edge on the bag. Her jaw dropped. A hole in the corner of the bag. That thief had almost become a killer. Her hands shook as she examined the hole through the bag. She weaved a bit unsteadily, realizing she could be dead right now. The bag had deflected the bullet and saved her life. Where did the bullet end up? Her head ached.

The officers got out of their car and scoped out the scene in all directions. Despite the lights shining brightly again, they used the car's searchlight to light up the yard, and then flashlights playing on the ground and shrubbery as they continued searching on their slow walk to her front door. Katherine lowered the bag below the desk in case they could see her through the window. If she showed it to them now, they might take it away as evidence. She needed time with it first. When she slipped it inside the closet, Purrada meowed from its depths. A whiskered face tentatively peeked out from a group of next winter's model totes.

"Purr, thank goodness you have nine lives." The cat stared. Katherine crouched. "Come on kitty. Come on." Purrada sat up, gave her front paw a few licks, and strolled forward. Katherine picked her up with soothing rubs, then glanced at the whiteboard of suspects. The cops didn't need to see that, or the messenger bag either. Katherine shut and locked the closet door.

Chapter Twenty-Six

Bayside Police Station overflowed with unaccustomed activity from press, concerned citizens, even a surplus of officers. Katherine yawned and took a sip of her second latte. Today she'd avoided a David Sure creation. She needed her own highly caffeinated design. The energizing effects still had a way to go. A long crime review with the officers last night, calming her nerves after being shot at, a restless sleep, and an early press conference took a toll. She gripped her latte tighter, shifted her bag higher on her shoulder, and maneuvered her way past the information desk to the meeting room.

The door to the chief's office stood ajar. He checked himself in a mirror on the wall. She gently edged her way through a gap in the crowd and entered the sterile conference room.

They'd roped off the front row and a sign indicated "Press only". Reporters perched on the edges of their seats, checking notes and equipment. Some stood and posed in suit jackets and jeans with the podium behind them as they spoke into microphones.

Spectators filled the rows of chairs behind the press. Standing room only at the back of the room. Loud voices blended into a dull roar of separate conversations.

She gave an inaudible squeal of delight, when she spotted a vacant chair in the third row. Then an officer sat and relaxed in it with a coffee and donut. A lone hand waved from across the room. Judith Sanders. She sat by the windows, with an empty seat next to her. Katherine sprinted over. She sat and leaned back, balancing her purse on her lap.

"Hi, Katherine."

"Judith, hello. Thank you for the chair."

"Of course. I heard you're the one who found poor Donna. How upsetting." Judith's ulterior motive for gathering news immediately floated to the surface. Katherine's guard rose.

Although Judith had been absolved of previous accusations of wrongdoing in the investigation of the city council and the building heights limit, Katherine remained uneasy about confiding in her. "I'm glad the family can have some closure."

Undeterred with the lack of details, Judith leaned closer. "Have you heard from Tomás or Julia? I hope today the police announce they know how she died. What a precarious time."

"I haven't seen the family today."

Judith tilted her chin up as she squinted back. "I heard they uncovered a surprise during the investigation, and they've taken Detective Grace off the case."

Katherine frowned. Jason hadn't mentioned anything about that. He didn't know? Or Judith could be confused?

"The police consult the city council on cases now?"

Judith shifted in her chair. "Of course not. However, concern about the safety of its citizens takes priority as an issue, especially if a killer roams free. Rumors spread like mayonnaise and blanket the community in fear."

Katherine pointed to the podium. "Are they getting

ready?" Judith's attention shifted. An officer tested the microphone. Katherine grabbed her cell phone from her purse zip pocket. She wanted notes in case of new information.

Katherine mentally designed how the press conference should proceed. The assigned Detective should give a complete update on the investigation. Then poor Tomás should plead for help from the public to catch his dear wife's killer. The chief can then issue instructions for Bayside's citizens on what to do for their own protection, while assuring them the police are doing everything possible to catch the killer, so remain calm. End by answering questions. Katherine already had a few. And, what about news on the professor?

Her cell phone swooshed with an incoming text. A fleeting reminder from Rodeo Drive about the New York Fashion meeting that afternoon.

A glance out the window revealed a frosty scenario. Moonjava steered Tomás and Julia from the station personnel door to the sidewalk. Their pace toward the street crept slower than Purrada rising from a nap. A deep conversation consumed them. Julia dropped her arms hard against her legs in an exasperated motion. Tomás pulled her closer to him.

A weight on Katherine's arm for a fleeting moment as Judith pressed to follow Katherine's glance out the window. "Why are they leaving?"

Katherine remembered Tomás' bitter accusations against Anthony. Had he been right? Anthony in custody? Last night Jason warned the chief would announce that he'd closed the case. Had Jason got the murder part wrong?

The small group stood at the curb. Katherine sighed

and whispered with halfhearted enthusiasm, "They seem too overcome with grief to stay." Had the detectives asked Tomás questions he didn't want to answer?

Judith agreed, "Of course they're in the midst of a terrible time. I'll reach out later today to comfort them. I'll invite him to the next city council meeting, where he can thank the community for their search and ask for any other help needed. We're all here for them in their time of desperation."

A familiar compact car pulled up. Amber ran around from the driver's side. Before Julia got in the car, she hugged Moonjava. She seemed to cling as if to draw strength. They all got in the car, except MJ, and drove down the road.

Judith pulled a tissue out of her satchel bag and dabbed her eyes. "That poor girl. Will Moonjava speak on behalf of the family?"

MJ faced the station, her clenched fist raised to the sky. Her shout muffled, unclear. Katherine reached over and opened the window panel. The sputtering engine of a passing truck and then a passionate, measured chant, "There is no debate. You need to investigate!"

Katherine's face burned. The crowd's attention veered from donuts and coffee, from press cameras, from an officer checking the microphone. Everyone stared at her mother. Katherine fumbled with the window handle and managed to pull it shut.

Judith continued her running commentary, "Freedom of speech thrives in Bayside, but I don't get what she's protesting. Do you?"

"No idea." Katherine avoided the crowd's attention by searching through the contents of her calico leather shoulder bag. Of course they're investigating. This briefing will confirm what they've found and what they'll do next. Wouldn't be the first time MJ misunderstood and made a fuss. Conversations resumed. A friend greeted Judith and monopolized her attention.

Katherine finished her latte. Grabbing a tea offered a good excuse to get away from Judith while waiting for the briefing. "I'm getting some tea. Do you want anything?"

"No thanks."

Strategically settled in the first row, Rob fixed a camera onto a stand and aimed it. Then he walked around and spoke into a microphone while facing a camera. Rob stopped and checked out the crowd. When their eyes met, he flashed a grin at Katherine and turned the camera toward her. How annoying. She frowned and walked back to stand by her chair before he took another shot.

Jason walked through the door at the back of the room, with a couple of fellow officers. They grabbed coffee and donuts from the table. His stare rested on Katherine at mid-bite. He greeted a few people as he weaved through the crowd.

Katherine smiled as Jason greeted her. "Doubly nice to see you, after last night."

Judith's eyes widened. Katherine ignored her and focused on the fervor in Jason's voice. He put an arm on her shoulder and whispered, "Thank God you're safe, but do you need to be here? Does MJ?"

She sat down and put her purse on the windowsill. "I'll find out the news one way or another, better to hear firsthand. I can't speak for MJ. No one can."

As he leaned against the windowsill, he bumped her bag onto the floor. They both grabbed to retrieve it, and their heads tapped together. Neither could stifle a laugh.

Judith, ever vigilant for information, leaped in. "Jason, do you have a preview on what we're about to hear? Anything about a killer? Have they determined the cause of death?"

"I'm not the detective on the case, so I don't know the up-to-date facts."

"No, but you've heard things, right?"

Jason grinned. "Nothing direct from the chief."

Judith persisted, "Any unexpected developments?"

Curiosity waved over Katherine. Had he heard more since last night? "What?"

Tapping on the microphone quieted the crowd. Jason pointed to the front of the room. "The chief's ready. The Information Officer will introduce him."

The chief entered. Next came Stephen in a black business suit with no tie, holding Cleo's hand. She wore a somber gray turtleneck dress with a long string of pearls and dabbed an eye with a handkerchief. Brittany followed carrying a light briefcase bearing the company logo In her other hand, an electronic notepad. Her cobalt blue skirt and matching jacket fitted at the waist gave off a professional air, with a hint of spirit as the skirt's hemline bounced. Her teal streaked hair bounced too. Her shirt's neckline plunged. Stephen motioned for his wife to sit in the chair by the podium. He sat between Cleo and Brittany. Anthony entered the room along with two officers. Anthony in custody?

Jason whispered in her ear, "Brace yourself." Katherine's eyes widened and she took a breath to calm herself. The usual sparkle had disappeared from Jason's dark brown eyes. He nodded at the podium and whispered again, "The family went home in shock. The report...what they're about to announce...the family could not bear it in public."

The officer at the front of the room announced introductions and media instructions.

Chapter Twenty-Seven

The chief placed one hand on the front corner of the podium and straightened his posture. Positioning shoulders back, he stood slightly sideways and waited for the room's full attention. He didn't have to wait long.

Anthony moved to the back of the room as the chief cleared his throat. So, the officers did not hold Anthony in custody. Katherine moved to catch his eye, and he gave her a sheepish expression. He made a beeline for the coffee. She resolved to catch up with him later.

The chief nodded at the press, then expanded the scope of attention to the full audience. "Welcome everyone. Thank you for your interest in the Donna Ruiz and the Professor Nathan Randall cases, and for your help in searching for Donna. I want to begin by extending my sincere condolences to the families of both victims." He briefly bowed his head.

The press sat poised, recording with phones and tablets in hand and questions at the ready. Taking full advantage, the chief droned on about the skills and tenacity of the department, and the professional conduct of the investigations under his leadership. Tomás and Julia may have left to avoid the current publicity spectacle.

Activity outside the window caught her peripheral vision. David arrived in MJ's car. They unloaded wood from the trunk and sat on the lawn hammering together signs with painted messages. A sinking feeling of dread weighed down Katherine's belly.

The chief positioned himself straight at Rob's camera. "My important message today—Do not fear a killer remains on the loose. You can feel safe in Bayside."

Audible sighs scattered through the room, including Judith who visibly relaxed in her chair.

Rob's hand shot up in the air, phone extended. "Are you saying you have someone in custody for both deaths?"

The chief shifted weight from one foot to the other and back again. "Please save your questions for now. Our investigation has concluded. Both deaths— determined as self-inflicted. I won't comment further here, for the sake of the privacy of the families."

Murmurs of confusion and heightened curiosity swirled. The only calm presence flowed from the trio seated next to the chief. Brittany leaned into her boss and whispered to him. She handed him a piece of paper she'd pulled from her briefcase. Cleo subtly put her hand on her husband's thigh and tapped on it until he turned to give her his full attention.

Judith turned to Jason. "No wonder Tomás left, and poor Julia."

Katherine blurted out to Jason, "Double suicide. No."

Jason stared straight ahead when he quietly responded to both ladies, "Unexpected."

After her official statement, after what she'd seen and described? Outraged beyond a whisper, Katherine folded her arms in disgust. "Unexpected? I'd say wrong."

A commotion at the back of the room. Anthony apologized for spilling coffee on someone.

The chief ignored the waving hands of the press and once again stared straight into the camera. "I ask that you all respect the privacy of the families during the time of this sad development. I assure you of Bayside's safety. Come join us for our January winter events and enjoy our shops on Main Street. We've closed these cases."

The chief turned to the seated guests. Stephen gave him a nod. The chief gestured for quiet, as he resumed. "Your attention again, please. I'd like to introduce Mr. Stephen Rider, owner of NRML Pharmaceuticals, Donna Ruiz's former boss."

Within a couple of quick strides, the CEO possessed the podium, which prompted an immediate hush across the room. Brittany and Cleo both watched him in rapt attention. The chief reluctantly stepped back.

Outside a few people gathered around MJ. Some took signs and MJ led a march up and down the sidewalk. Katherine opened the window again and their repeated chant drifted in, "There is no debate. Someone must investigate."

As Stephen addressed the crowd, Brittany silently mouthed what he said. "Ladies and gentlemen, at this solemn time I want to pay tribute to a dedicated, skilled, kind, and caring woman, Donna Ruiz. A treasured person and employee, gone too soon."

Some of Donna's friends stood and clapped. Others quickly joined in, some brushing away tears. Most of the room joined their applause. Stephen waited, and as people sat down again, Cleo dabbed at her eyes with a handkerchief.

His voice remained strong and professional, "The

work she completed at NRML Pharmaceuticals, clearly a service to humankind. I cannot begin to review all her accomplishments here. I do want to highlight her most recent, groundbreaking endeavor. She'd recently completed testing on a revolutionary drug treatment for depression. There's no telling how many millions of lives will be renewed and saved as part of her legacy."

Stephen gestured to Brittany. "My thanks to Brittany Felton, Donna's talented assistant, who availed herself of the final test results, documented her additional findings, and presented to the board on schedule. Her work allows Donna's project to continue forward toward sale to the public without delay." The acclaimed assistant rose to her feet, beaming at the praise. She remained standing until the reporters had time to get their pictures.

Stephen continued, as Brittany slowly sat. "With gratitude, and in honor of Donna Ruiz, today I'm announcing the move forward of the new drug to be commonly referred to as The DR named after Donna Ruiz. Thank you." Cleo jumped to her feet applauding. Her expression glowed, transfixed on her husband. She hugged him.

The chief stepped forward, eager to regain the microphone. Before he could say a word, Rob leaped up. Immediately followed by Katherine. The chief ignored her, then pointed to Rob. "Yes, I can make time for a question from the press."

Katherine sat down again with a thud of exasperation. Rob kept the camera filming as he asked, "Chief Harrison, your department's finding of a double suicide raises additional questions. Are these two suicides connected? Did they each leave a note?"

"No notes found, but other evidence points to the final conclusion. I'm not indicating any link between the two cases."

As other reporters waved their hands for attention, Rob remained standing. "A follow up. When will the autopsy results be available to the public?"

The chief paused and stared at a couple of officers before addressing Rob again. "In our state, an autopsy gets performed only if the Medical Examiner determines the necessity for it, in order to determine the exact cause and manner of death. The Medical Examiner's report can be viewed online on our media release page."

Katherine searched for the media page on her phone while she muttered, "How can they possibly determine Donna committed suicide? I found her. I know what I saw, not suicide."

The chief turned further away from her. "No other questions from the press?"

Jason moved a hand onto her knee. Katherine appreciated the gesture of support, until the slow shake of his head and frowning lips. He meant to communicate caution. She moved her knee to the side and resumed her phone search.

"Stacy here, with The Baysiders Press. Did the two deceased know each other?"

"They worked together on projects for NRML and developed a relationship from that work."

Anthony moved up the aisle in the middle of the room. Now he echoed the implication, "Exactly."

The chief gave an impatient glance at the front row. "Thank you for the final question."

Katherine stood at full attention, and her shocked stare shifted from Anthony to the podium. "Are you implying more than a work relationship? You can't substantiate that." He needed to retract that outrageous claim.

Jason leaned forward with elbows resting on his legs, face down.

The room of spectators turned to her, and Katherine gave an emphatic nod. As she insisted, the chief abruptly turned and pointed to a man in the press row. "Did you have a last question."

"Gordon Dale with the Free Press. What's next for these cases?"

"Archive. I'm officially closing both cases. Thank you everyone."

With a brief wave, he left the podium. Katherine would not be ignored. "You have no proof. Donna did not kill herself. Donna truly believed in life. She fought despair for those who did not have the strength to fight alone."

A murmur grew in the crowd.

The chief addressed the room. "On behalf of our department, with remorse I announced today's solemn news. Our hearts and prayers reach out to each victim's family and friends. We don't want to make things any harder on them."

As he left the room, Katherine replied in rhythm with the protestors, "There is no debate. Someone must investigate."

Chapter Twenty-Eight

Katherine remained standing. Defiance screeched from her crossed arms and determined frown. Stephen motioned to Cleo, and they strolled over to the local television station's reporter. The camera lights went back on, for an interview. Brittany stood close, as if she expected to be included at some point. The rest of the press packed up. Others in the audience left to face their normal day's routine.

Jason handed Katherine her purse she'd knocked to the floor in her exuberance, then he stood up. "I'm headed home. I've had a long shift. Turns out I can't see you tonight. Another time?"

Determined not to let her disappointment show, Katherine pretended to search her purse for her keys. "Another time, of course. Did you get stuck with another night shift?"

Jason said, "I'll text you later. Keep your doors locked after closing."

That pointed remark reminded her, how did the thief unlock her back door?

Jason moved for a hasty exit. "Nice to see you, Judith."

"Excuse me, Katherine." Judith hurried after him. "Oh Jason…" A couple of bystanders stepped in Jason's path, and Judith caught up to him. Katherine smiled, amused by the foiled escape attempt. She focused in on her own target. Anthony sat alone, busy on the phone. She walked over and stood behind him.

Jason had made it out of the room, and Judith sought her next victim. Anthony hung up and put the phone in a pocket. As he stood, she firmly pushed down on his shoulder. "Katherine, I applaud you for giving the chief a hard time. He deserved it." She sat down next to him. He winked. "You and I, we're on the same page."

"No, we're not. You owe me a conversation about last night." Judith walked past them and remained within earshot.

"I suppose I do." He sighed. "Not here. I have to do something else."

"That's right, you have to talk with me."

He glared at her and raised his voice, "Not now."

"When?"

He stood up. "I'll call you."

She stood next to him. "Make sure you're sober." He stormed out of the room.

Judith gasped, scanned Katherine from head to toe and pursued Anthony.

Rob's laughter grated on Katherine's nerves, and his clapping. "For that performance, I applaud you. So where will you investigate?" He pocketed the press credentials he carried. "You can talk to me off the record."

"No time now, Rob. Later."

"Oh, you'll call me later, sober?" Then they both laughed and sat down together. "You obviously disagree with the cops. Why are you so certain they're wrong? They're implying an affair that went wrong and a double suicide."

Katherine shook her head. Although few people

remained, she lowered her voice. "Donna would not have an affair, and she certainly did not kill herself."

"How do you have no doubts? What did you see when you found her?"

Katherine frowned as others from the Press strolled past them. "Not here."

Rob grabbed the camera. "Come on. I parked in the back." They quickly walked outside and sat in the car with the windows rolled up against the cold and against anyone wandering by. Rob turned the key and turned up the heater. "So, there's something about how you found Donna."

"Off the record, you promise." Katherine crossed her heart with her right hand.

Rob patted over his heart. "All right. We're collaborating. Free exchange of information. We're on the same side. We both want justice for Donna and the professor."

Katherine hesitated, then freed all her pent-up frustration. "Could the professor have overdosed intentionally? I don't know, but someone murdered Donna. The evidence can't be clearer. The chief has hidden something up his sleeve." Katherine went on about the plastic bag, and the missing purse. She didn't mention the attempt to steal one of the two purses last night. "I heard Donna had a concussion too. Someone hit her with something hard."

"My story will blow the police department wide open and require an investigation of the chief and... oh, wait a minute, she could have got a concussion from losing consciousness from the plastic bag and falling hard on the ground."

"No. Someone hit her. And no, you can't blow the

case wide open now. You agreed you'd make our talk off the record. Keep it off the record until I prove a few things, like the concussion. Otherwise, you'll hurt Julia and Tomás even more."

Rob said in a low tone, "Brutal way to die whether suicide or murder. Tape the bag to your neck, so you can't change your mind and pull it off as you lose consciousness. The more out of it you get, the less chance you're conscious enough to break the bag open."

Katherine responded, "Especially if the killer prevents you from fighting back."

Rob said, "A source told me the examination documents her ankle as broken. She could have stumbled as she committed suicide and couldn't get up."

Katherine gave him a sideways glance. "Broken ankle? I didn't see that. Did she break it running from her attacker? And I still don't understand why she would park her car and walk about 5 miles away to commit suicide. She didn't."

Rob muttered, "I have a Pulitzer worthy story."

Katherine sighed. "The police won't help…"

"Not even Jason? Come on, you must have convinced him. Did he see what you saw?"

Katherine grabbed her keys out of her purse. "Like I said, the police won't help, so I want to follow up with people close to her."

Rob nodded, "Like the last man to see Donna alive, your friend Anthony."

"What?"

He shifted further sideways to face her. "I have it on reliable authority. Anthony met her for coffee that morning, at a place she used to go on her way to work. She didn't use the drive-through that day. She went inside and sat down with Anthony, at the Coffee Hut."

Katherine frowned. "Hmm. In a public place close to the transit center."

Rob turned the heater up. "Yes, and my source says they left together."

Katherine paused for a breath. The last person to see her? She thought about Donna's bag in her office. "I've got some clues to pursue before I talk with Anthony." She got out of the car.

Rob grabbed the camera and ran around to her. "I've got some investigating to do myself, but let's stay in touch."

Katherine stared directly at him. "I don't want to see any of what I've told you in the news. You said off the record."

Rob slowly nodded. "For now. In the meantime, I'll get some footage of your mom's protest."

They walked away in opposite directions. When Katherine glanced at the Police Department building, the chief stood in the window staring at her.

Chapter Twenty-Nine

After the shocking events that started January with a bang, the week after the press conference kept Katherine huddled at home over a drawing board. Her new crossbody line had deadlines to meet. Besides that, she felt newly inspired to design a beautiful and functional designer baby bag for new mothers. And of course, she also had high hopes to create a Dolly Doggie Line. As her designs continued to gain widespread praise and devoted customers, commitments required her attention. Deadlines fast approached for decisions on final spring show details.

Both the Clutch Cafe and the Museum ran short staffed these days. Compelled to fit in protests at City Hall, and other high visibility sites in Bayside, MJ and David had less time for creating treats and supporting exhibits. After running ragged, Katherine decided to end the week with pleasant errands on Main Street. She insisted MJ join her, tearing her away from the handful of protesters at the police station.

MJ leaned her protest sign against the nearest tree and turned to the small handful of fellow citizens marching in a line up and down the sidewalk. "I won't take more than a quick break. Keep up your passion, my friends. We'll convince them." She raised her fist in the air. "Someone must investigate." The others cheered and continued the chant.

Katherine tugged on the sleeve of MJ's heavy jacket. "I thought a walk would be nice, but with the cold I wish we had the car. I don't know how you all can stay out here for hours in drizzly weather."

"Dedication to what's right warms the heart, and the spirit." MJ pounded her chest.

"But not the body. I wish your protest had reopened the case by now. I thought you'd get more traction with your interview in Rob's news feature."

"When the fuzz pretends they can't hear, then we need to shout louder."

Katherine pulled her coat closer against the weather. At least no snow fell. "Fortunately, Sandy's bakery always hugs customers with extra warmth. It'll be a relief to finalize the menu for the February party." Katherine quickened her pace.

MJ held a thumbs up. "The '60s love-in. I dig all the plans and the cool exhibit."

Katherine shook her head. "One people won't forget."

"Go with the flow, Katherine. It may not be your favorite period in history, but you can't deny all it inspired and changed."

"Of course. And so many women contributed purses from their families to help show the story of those times."

"And their own purses too."

"Yes, including your luscious, suede, peace sign shoulder bag."

In a tone of deep reverie, MJ said, "That bag has seen a lot."

Katherine's voice quivered. "I can only imagine."

"And you call it shoulder bag, but you could call it

crossbody. We needed to be hands free for marches and many things."

Katherine agreed. "Well, definitely fringe, and now you rely on a fanny pack when you're on the march. Thank goodness we're here. Okay, Sandy, here we come. I'm ready for a break from the rain."

Katherine opened the door with her mittened hand, and they stepped aside for parents with two young children leaving, clutching bags of baked goods. A cheery greeting from Sandy, and the irresistible scent of freshly baked muffins and cookies drew the women in.

After exchanging hellos, Katherine leaned against the glass counter. "Oh Sandy, everything always tastes delicious here, and we're both ready for a treat."

"What can I get you?"

MJ spoke up. "A slice of that whole grain banana bread for me, please."

With a smile, Sandy served it up as Katherine repressed her desire for a frosted lemon cake slice. Instead, she hoped a cranberry oatmeal cookie would satisfy with fewer calories.

Sandy gave her a cookie, and Katherine paid. "How have you been, Sandy? Have you recovered from working hard over your busy holiday party season?"

"I'm grateful for lots of business."

MJ added, "How satisfying to know you've helped fill homes with love."

"It doesn't feel like work, if you know what I mean."

"Yes, I get that." Katherine said.

"How are you, Katherine? It must have been a terrible shock finding Donna. I still can't believe she's gone."

"An incredibly sad time, devastating for Julia and

Tomás."

"Donna never sounded suicidal, only the opposite. She worked to ease depression in people. She ordered a birthday cake two days before she disappeared. I never thought it would be the last time I'd see her."

Katherine put her cookie down. "How did she act then?"

"She wanted a special cake for her husband. He'd been out of town over the holiday, and she wanted a nice family celebration when he returned. I could see her excitement to have him home again."

"They always remained a close family," Katherine said.

"I made a beautiful cake for Tuesday pick up. Closing time and still no Donna. I never heard from her, so I called. No answer. I tried leaving a message, but it wouldn't take one. I never heard from her. The next day I found out she'd gone missing."

Katherine shook her head. "I have my doubts about suicide."

Since no other customers came in, Sandy walked around the counter and gestured to sit at one of the tables. "I've been on edge, like all the rest of Bayside. Rumor says she might have been murdered. What do you think?"

MJ slapped her hand on the table. "Of course, the cops do nothing. I'm outraged by the lack of protection for innocent citizens. You should join our march against City Hall."

Sandy's face turned red. "They're doing nothing?"

Katherine wanted to reassure her somehow. After the break-in at her home, she wanted to reassure herself too. "They closed the case. I'll set aside time to investigate myself. What you tell us about Donna's cake order adds to other concerning evidence."

Sandy took a deep breath. "I'll get my catering suggestions for your big event. We'll finalize plans, then you can get our mystery solved without delay."

After a productive review of the food plans, Katherine and MJ thanked Sandy and prepared to leave. Katherine picked up her purse. "Sandy, you'll spoil our guests with your wonderful creations, as always."

"I'm happy to be part of your event. Keep me posted on your investigation, Katherine. I worry about coming to work early in the morning through empty streets, and especially in winter darkness. It makes things worse if a killer hides out there."

MJ hugged Sandy. "Keep your phone handy. Carry mace. I'm wishing you positive energy."

Katherine patted Sandy's shoulder. "Take care. I'll let you know what I find."

Two women entered the store deep in conversation. Sandy greeted them and returned behind the counter. Katherine turned to MJ. "I'm headed for the tea shop next. Gran's rooibos blend disappears fast."

MJ smiled. "I haven't seen Joyce or Darla for a while. I'd be interested in a new blend for these long nights, something with a darker taste. I want a taste more harmonious to the seasonal oscillations. I'm sure Darla will create the perfect combination for me."

Katherine pulled the door open. "No matter what new challenge you dream up, she manages to make it happen. Darla's a true artist with her teas."

Before she followed MJ out the door, Katherine glanced at Sandy slicing a devilishly chocolate cake for the two women and sharing more than dessert. "Not an accident, someone told me she got murdered. When I saw Donna that week…"

Katherine braced herself against the cold again. As news of a killer spread, would pressure build to force the police to defend their suicide claim?

People walked by on the sidewalk, taking advantage of the January rain instead of snow. Not many umbrellas. Unlike Katherine, true Pacific Northwesterners instead kept jacket hoods up, hands in pockets, and walked at a brisk pace.

Cynthia brightened with a smile of recognition as she walked toward them. The tote hanging from her shoulder displayed the distinct line—Booked at the Bayside Library. A bag from the batch Katherine had designed and produced for fundraising. She juggled a grocery sack in the other hand and a bag from the local toy store.

Katherine gave her a quick hug, accidentally hooking her umbrella handle to the strap of Cynthia's bag and pulling it off her shoulder. She caught it and put it back for her friend. "Oops! You know, holiday season ended already. You don't have to buy for another year for your adorable kids."

"Post-holiday sales are great for my son with a January birthday. What are you doing?"

"We came from Sandy's, finalizing the menu for our February Museum event."

Cynthia gave a coy smile. "What are you planning now?"

MJ waved her hand in an arc to illustrate. "A love-in, celebrating the new '60's decade exhibit."

Katherine shifted her umbrella against the rain as the breeze shifted. "Lots of music and food…"

MJ added, "psychedelic sounds of the '60s, and people expressing themselves while communing with the universe."

Katherine shuddered. "It'll be music, poetry readings by a few locals, and an open museum featuring a unique new exhibit. You may be surprised by the extraordinary and dramatic events of that decade."

Cynthia nodded. "How good to see you both. Last time we met up at the search. I can't get over what happened with Donna. I had no idea she felt depressed. I wish I'd helped."

Katherine shook her head. "All terribly hard on the family."

Cynthia stepped closer and lowered her voice, "I heard lots of talk at the library about the press conference. The chief failed to answer some tough, awkward questions."

Katherine said, "That was me."

Cynthia shifted her bags into her left hand and pulled the hood on her jacket further forward. "I thought so, even before they mentioned your name." She shifted her attention to MJ. "And you've been protesting at the station?"

"Yes, I am. Donna treasured every life and would never end her own."

Cynthia turned to leave, then hesitated. "Donna taught a hands-on science class at the library. She stirred up excitement in the teens and preteens. She'll be greatly missed for that too. Always such a positive person, but last week she seemed stressed. She admitted problems at work and said test results aggravated her. She loved her job, but it may have defeated her."

MJ shook her head. "I can't see her giving up."

Cynthia shifted the weight of her bundles. "I better go, but great to run into you both."

Katherine stepped aside. "Happy birthday party." The trio parted.

The tea shop smelled spicy and warm. The lighting brightened the cloudy day, revealing novelty tea sets, sweet snacks, and packaged mixes, along with Bayside postcards and souvenirs. Mounted along one wall, spanning the full height and length of the room large jars of different tea leaves and spices lined up to be chosen, or mixed into magical blends.

In the doorway, MJ clapped her hands together. "Hello, Darla. Would you take me on a quest to discover a new blend, a dark taste begging for steamed milk, like a stormy night allowing streaks of moonlight through."

The striking brunette behind the counter replaced the top on one of the large tins used to store tea leaves. "Moonjava, welcome in. Katherine, good to see you." Slim Darla in the mauve leggings and gray pullover sweater beamed, as she stepped briskly to the long side wall. "I'd be delighted to guide you in a new selection."

From the other side of the room came a cheerful hello from Joyce. "First time we've seen you two in the new year."

MJ laughed. "Didn't see you, Joyce. The inventory has you hidden away on your knees."

Katherine greeted them both. It hit her again what a perfect yin and yang these partners made. Creative Darla, a connoisseur of the blends, paired with sharp businesswoman Joyce who ran the tea shop. Her fitted beige pantsuit included a puffy cream colored blouse padded at the shoulders, retro period chic.

MJ and Darla studied the tins and Katherine

remembered, "Could you please bag Pam's favorite rooibos too?"

Darla raised her hand in acknowledgement, "Of course." Then she pointed out a trio of leaves to MJ. They conferred longer, then agreed on a combination. Darla carried the tins to the counter to blend. "You'll love this creation, Moonjava. I recommended it to a college professor last fall, and now others on the faculty order it."

MJ breathed in the scent of one of the tins again. "Such peaceful vibes."

Darla weighed the bag. "Tragic what happened on campus. I heard Professor Randall died from a drug overdose." She paused, pensive.

MJ nodded. "My grandson William worked for him."

Darla sympathized. "How traumatic for him."

Katherine sighed. "Yes."

Joyce carried over a box of bagged merchandise. She answered Katherine's questioning stare, "Now we have a to-go delivery for online orders. I recently struck a deal with a ride share to deliver."

Darla added, "Another brilliant Joyce idea."

Her partner blushed. "Some of our customers love the convenience. I'm betting the results reflect good business sense, but too early to be sure."

Darla handed her purchase to MJ. "I do miss seeing the people though. Before New Year's we had a run of online orders from my campus friends, but I didn't get to see anybody. Instead, we called ride share Kevin, that's what I call him." Darla laughed at herself.

Joyce grinned and sealed one more package. "I didn't hear any complaints from you New Year's Eve when we gave the orders to Kevin, closed the shop, and got home early."

Darla tapped a finger on the counter. "You'll never hear me complain about leaving work early." After a sigh Darla continued, "You know, that's the last tea order I'll ever blend for Nathan Randall. He loved experimenting with teas. Poor man."

Katherine broke her silence. "Did he have a favorite?"

Darla answered, becoming animated as her excitement grew. "Oh, he had several, but often he'd ask me to surprise him with something new. That night I sent him my Countdown Chai." Katherine stared at her blankly. "You know, count down to the new year." She laughed. "An Indian blend, containing exotic spices and sweets. There's a kick from the caffeine for dancing past midnight."

Darla swayed to music only she could hear. Joyce giggled and moved her hips and arms as if she danced on a disco floor. MJ gave a couple of twirls and began her own groove. Katherine raised her arms and conducted an imaginary band. They all laughed. Katherine got out her wallet. "What do we owe you?"

Darla flipped the register display to show the total. As her credit card processed, Katherine pondered the information the ladies inadvertently handed her about Kevin on New Year's Eve. He had a connection with both Donna and the professor. When did Kevin arrive with the tea? Who or what did he see? Did he deliver drugs too? Katherine put her credit card away and walked out the door with more than she'd bargained for.

Chapter Thirty

"All right, Katherine. Where do you want to meet?" Defeat echoed in the tone he used.

"Meet me at the Coffee Hut, right before the south freeway entrance. I'll be there as fast as I can."

"Near the transit center?" Anthony sounded anxious to get off the phone.

"Yes, that's the one." Katherine toughened her tone. "I'll be there. Don't stand me up." She grabbed her keys. The Coffee Hut, where he'd met Donna on the day she disappeared, according to Rob. The final touches on the illustration of her newest design would have to wait. Turns out obtaining answers from Anthony tops today's priorities.

Light traffic allowed for record time across town. The place stood empty except for the server behind the counter. Katherine recognized Christopher's friend. "Darren, nice to see you. Happy New Year. Did you enjoy your holidays?"

"I had a good time and picked up more shifts to make some extra money."

She asked, "Lots of customers?"

"It gets busiest right around Christmas, and we had a night shift during the volunteer search. You heard about the missing lady?"

"Yes, I went to the search."

"Real sad when I heard she died. I normally work

mornings, before classes. She drove through here a lot. Nice lady. I used to kid her because she always ordered the same thing."

Interesting. Katherine set her purse on the counter. "You knew her."

"A little."

"She always drove through? She never had time to come inside before work?"

"She'd come in if the drive-through got backed up. She came in the last time I saw her. She had the day off work, because she sat down at a table and talked with some guy."

"Black wavy hair? Broad shoulders?"

"Black hair. He dressed up in slacks and a jacket. He ordered the same as Donna, and a breakfast croissant. They talked for a while."

"They left together?"

Darren replied with a sharp, "No."

Katherine frowned. Rob got it wrong? Did Anthony leave and then lie in wait for her? Could charming, romantic Anthony have a hidden, violent nature? Darren fiddled with the stack of cups and checked the drive-through camera. Katherine took the obvious hint and ordered a drink for herself, and something for Anthony similar to what he liked at the Clutch Cafe. She thanked Darren and included a generous tip.

Darren prepared the drinks and handed them across the counter. "So, if you want to see that guy, he walked in now from the parking lot."

Katherine shuddered knowing it must be Anthony. She checked the door and gulped hard at the sight of Tomás. She asked Darren, "That guy?"

"After the first guy left, another guy joined her. I

remember him because he didn't order anything. He walked in kind of mad, but they left together."

"They drove off together?"

"We got busy. They sat there. Later when the morning rush ended, they'd left." Darren shifted weight onto the other leg.

As she picked up both drinks, Katherine felt a surge of enthusiasm for an opportunity to quiz Tomás about such a quiet return to Bayside. Hopefully Anthony's late. Tomás shuffled to a table and slumped in a chair. Dejection lined his face.

He gave no recognition of her, only a vacant stare as Katherine sat across from Tomás. She slid a drink toward him. "Tomás, I'm sorry about the police findings." With no response, Katherine prodded him. "I find their conclusion hard to believe."

"Yes." The gruff tone of that single word answer communicated a dark mood. The fingers on his cup jerked back and forth in quick, short movements over the smooth tabletop.

Katherine took a long sip. He leaned forward and whispered. "I told you who killed her."

Katherine stiffened, knowing Anthony could arrive any time. "Tomás, why did you fly back early but never go home?"

He squinted at her. The eerie silence lasted too long. Katherine opened her arms before her, palms up. "Let me help you."

He leaned back now, eyes watering. "I don't want to go on without Donna. I need to be strong for Julia, but I don't know how." He rubbed his forehead. "I needed time to myself. Next thing I know I'm here, the last place I saw my dear Donna."

Katherine sat stunned at the sudden confession. "You came here that morning? You saw her before she went to work on Tuesday?"

He continued, almost in a dream state. "I thought someone had come between us. We sat together, very tense. I hardly recognized her personality at first. She blamed it on work."

Katherine held back the onslaught of questions on her mind and remained quiet. Tomás needed someone to listen. A couple of giggling young ladies entered and headed for the counter. Darren turned from the drive-through window with a cheery greeting.

"I wondered for a while about all her night meetings and texts. It had to be that professor. I'm out of town, and thoughts of them drove me wild." Surprise jolted through Katherine at Tomás' accusation.

He leaned forward, face down in trembling hands. "I sank so low as to go see that professor." Tomás suddenly stared straight at Katherine. "That's why I came back early, to confront them both. I stood at the end of the hall, hidden around the corner, summoning the courage to face what I might see."

"You had second thoughts?"

He shook his head. "A young man came out, a student. He left in the other direction."

Katherine frowned. William said he'd seen a man. Tomás? Or someone else? "What happened then?"

"Silence. Complete silence wrapped around me, as I thought of breaking down that door and beating him unconscious. I could hardly breathe. The building temperature felt comfortable, but I sweated."

Katherine gripped the arms of her chair. Her stomach tightened.

Tomás pounded a fist hard on the table. "I'll never know if I could have. A door slammed."

"Oh no." Katherine groaned at the pained expression he wore.

"I peeked around the corner. Some woman covered in a long black hooded coat and stilettos slipped into his office. A champagne bottle and glasses clinked in her hand. Her graceful stature, her familiar curves, the scent of her favorite perfume, all missing. Obviously not mi carina. My Donna."

"Wouldn't that make you happy? You could go home."

"I missed my wife."

"Oh Tomás." Katherine's body relaxed into a puddle of empathy.

"I wished for home, but I'd solved nothing. Still convinced she'd betrayed me, but with who? My anger simmered. I wandered the campus, then the neighborhoods, then the bar."

Katherine resisted the lonely image he portrayed, although deception did not seem his intent. "When you left the college, what direction did you walk? Into which neighborhood?"

"Nowhere in particular. Don't you get it? I wanted the love of my life, but she didn't want me. I drank too much. I spent a long, rough night in the motel across the street. How could my Donna cheat on our love? And with whom?"

"Couldn't you go home the next day?"

"I passed out for most of the day. When I pulled myself together to walk back to my car, students stared at the building. They said the professor died. I panicked. I rushed back to the motel."

"You never saw your family New Year's day."

"Very early morning I summoned the courage to face Donna. Not at home. Not with Julia. I figured Donna would stop here."

"You talked to her?"

"I came in after I saw him leave."

"Him?" Katherine steeled herself for the answer she expected.

"There he stood in broad daylight. I had accused the wrong man. When I saw that scum Anthony with my Donna, it made sense. He got away too fast for me, but I confronted her."

"You gave her a chance to explain?"

"She denied it and said I'm ridiculous. She insisted she must leave for an important work meeting. I refused to let her put our future on hold."

Katherine's brow wrinkled as her body tensed. "So, you grabbed her hands? Did you pull her out the door and force her into your car…"

"What? I embraced her. I kissed her with all my heart. We sat, and I gazed into her eyes, and I believed her. I'm sure that scum Anthony chased her, but my floreciente, my blooming flower, she loves only me."

Katherine wiped a tear from her eye. "You reconciled. Then why did she leave?"

"Some questions raised on her drug test results concerned her. She insisted she must present the correct data to the CEO at her office meeting that morning."

Katherine took a deep breath. "So like Donna to put duty first."

Tomás leaned against the palm of a hand, staring at the tabletop. "Her passion for helping people remains unmatched. I couldn't stand in the way of something so critical to her. We agreed to go away together soon and reconcile as a family."

Katherine leaned back in her chair with the weight of a heavy thought. Donna missed the meeting, and her assistant had stepped forward in her place. Brittany didn't stop the drug from moving to market. According to Stephen, Brittany endorsed the drug test. Sounds like a career advancing move. Could ambition be her driving force, perhaps moving her to murder? Or instead of murder, Brittany's involvement may reflect ignorance about the reliability of the test results?

Tomás had formed one hand into a fist. "He attacked her and killed our future."

Katherine held her breath, then let it out asking, "Who?"

"Aren't you listening? That murderer, Anthony."

"Why do you think…?"

"Donna didn't speak of him. She wanted to spare me, but I know about dirtbags like him. When my beautiful Donna refused him, he became enraged with a jealous fury. I know he killed her that day."

With his voice raised, Katherine could imagine the level of fury Tomás might have achieved that morning. He says he reconciled with Donna, but Katherine only had his word for that. Her concern grew as she noted Tomás' reddening face and tense expression. Attempting to calm him, and not convinced he'd told the truth, she lowered her voice, "Where did you go when Donna left for work? Did you follow her?"

Tomás pounded the table. "Not him." One hand shook as Tomás pointed. "He killed mi carena."

Tomás bumped the table. Katherine steadied it. "Goodbye, Katherine. I will not tolerate him." Tomás pointed again and moved toward the door.

There stood a sheepish Anthony. As Tomás approached, he reached out with both fists and shoved Anthony back against the wall. Darren sprang to life from behind the counter shouting, "Hey. None of that here. I'll call the cops."

The barista hurried toward them, but Katherine beat him to their side. "Stop it." She grabbed Tomás' arm. Anthony stood frozen against the wall, hands up as if in surrender.

Tomás shook Katherine off and stared deep in Anthony's eyes. "You won't get away with it."

Anthony said, "You're wrong, Tomás. Donna and I shared a dear friendship, nothing more." Those words fell on deaf ears, as Tomás stormed out the door.

Darren cautioned, "No trouble here, mister."

Anthony offered the familiar, charming smile. "We're not here for trouble. We're here for lattes."

Darren gestured to the counter. "That I can help you with."

Chapter Thirty-One

Anthony turned to Katherine. "I owe you a latte, and an explanation. I haven't been myself. I'm sorry."

"Apology appreciated. I already have a latte, but I'm thirsty for your explanation." Katherine motioned to the table. Anthony bought a drink and joined her.

One hand loosely looped around the bottom of the venti cup, and a forefinger rubbed up and down in an absent-minded way. He stared down at the table. "Rough times."

"That's when people should stick together, not strike out at each other." Katherine intended to hold him to a full account for all recent behavior.

He returned her stare. "Have some sympathy, I've lost a dear friend."

She responded without hesitation, "Tomás lost his wife, and Julia her mother. Any empathy for them?"

He chugged a long drink. "I saw Donna here that morning because I worried about her. She tried reassuring me. When I saw through that act, she admitted concern over a morning meeting. She knew the CEO wouldn't like what she had to say."

Katherine smiled. "Sounds like the Donna I knew, always doing the right thing."

Anthony shook his head. "Reading between the lines I sensed it might mean her career."

Katherine frowned. "A strong woman like Donna?

A disagreement with her boss wouldn't stop her."

"Professional stress can be tough, and when all sides of your life are stressed…Her disagreements with Julia over her boyfriend escalated. She described a New Year's nightmare. She would have done anything to give her soul some relief."

That dire pronouncement came as a surprise to Katherine. "You think she killed herself? And the professor too? Don't tell me you now believe the love tryst line?"

"Don't be ridiculous."

"So, we agree there's a killer who needs to be stopped."

Anthony paused and gulped his drink. Katherine decided to open Pandora's purse wide open. "Anthony, did you two have an affair?"

He seemed to take the question in stride. "No. An affair with me, or anyone else, grew from a figment of Tomás' imagination. She wanted to patch things up with hubby. She didn't know how to convince him to drop all suspicions."

Katherine dug further to test how deep Anthony buried the truth. According to Darren and Tomás, Anthony left the cafe alone, but did he wait for Donna? Did he follow her? Did he…"Where did you and Donna go from here?"

In a fast moment Anthony gave Katherine a most intense and angry glare. "My God, Katherine. You suspect me? After your talk of not striking out at people."

"I want to find missing pieces of Donna's puzzling day."

"You're outrageous. I'm not a missing piece."

"Where did you go with her?"

"I left without her. She said with all the complaints from Tomás, it would be better if we didn't meet for a while. She gave me the name of another doctor willing to consult on my mystery." He groaned. "As if I cared more about my book than her. We hugged. I never saw her again."

"You're one of the last people to see Donna alive."

Anthony raised his voice, "But not the last."

They stared across the table at each other. Anthony took out a phone and flipped through the screens. "All right, Nancy Drew, I talked on my phone with my agent that morning. We had an appointment on a book appearance in Seattle, which I kept." He flipped through another screen and displayed a personal calendar. "My agent would tell you I arrived early." The screen flipped to another calendar page. "At the signing, I happened to meet an enticing young woman. I reserved lunch for two at the restaurant next door. Enjoyable, and then we…"

"I don't need to hear more."

"I didn't need to tell you any of it. Drop your accusations. We need to solve the mystery of a suicide that's murder."

Katherine raised her latte and spoke as Anthony clicked his drink against hers, "Not one, two murders. We're up against a serial killer that needs to be stopped before there's another."

Chapter Thirty-Two

After vows to collaborate soon on potential clues and murderous theories, Anthony drove out of the lot. Katherine moved in eager anticipation of free time to finally examine the contents of Donna's messenger bag.

As she unlocked her Mustang, a ride share car parked on the other side of the road caught her attention, because of the familiar crowd surrounding it. Her son William stood talking with Amber who held Michael's hand. Julia spoke to the driver who stood beside the car. Now she recognized her boyfriend Kevin. He signaled for them all to get in. William took the lead, and the others went for the back seat. Katherine wondered if she should make time for a visit to their All Man's Land tonight. Jason had broken their date again. She could bring some food and catch up on their news. Katherine waved. Too late for any of them to see her. The car drove off.

Amber shifted in the seat to give Michael a little more room. No decision had been made yet on where to go. First they needed to be sure no one followed. She glanced at Michael, knowing how hard everything felt to him after last year.

Julia leaned forward from the back seat and put her arms around the driver's neck. "You're a doll for picking us up."

"I didn't know you had company." Kevin blushed.

Amber clicked on her seat belt. "We cheered her up. William, did you see your mom across the street?"

He glanced in that direction. "Where?"

"I saw her outside the barista, as we drove away."

"Hmmm, missed her."

"So, where can I drop you?" Kevin slowed the car.

William twisted to face the back seat. "We need to break into the prof's phone."

"You could all come to my house," Julia sat forward and rested her hand on Kevin's shoulder, "but my dad's there."

"A back table at the library?" William suggested.

"I have an idea" Amber said as they approached a stop sign. "How about the Purse Museum, and go upstairs, out of sight."

Michael shook his head. "No way. The cops must be watching William's mom."

Amber added, "I haven't seen them there. They might think Jason will report if he sees anything, but Jason hasn't been around."

William pointed at her. "I went there yesterday. I didn't sneak in, and no cops. If we can go without being seen, we could bust into the prof's phone there."

Amber offered a plan. "I'm working today anyway, so it'll appear normal for me to go in. I'll scope it out and let you know if it's all clear." Amber relaxed.

William said, "I'll walk in with you. If the cops are there, I'll ditch the plan and talk to my family."

Michael frowned. "I'll wait for the all clear."

Amber directed Kevin to the top of the side alley. "No one will notice your car here. We'll cut through the yard and scope it out." They got out, and Julia moved into the front seat.

Amber went to the gift shop's side door, as usual, but today she heard a surprise greeting. "Far out. The universe positioned me to receive a couple of my favorite people." MJ spread her arms wide. "Hugs all around."

The long, beaded necklaces around MJ's neck clicked against each other as she straightened her brightly colored floral tunic hanging over her bell bottom pants. "I baked my coveted cupcakes, before resuming my protest at the cop station. Are you hungry? We can commune as we indulge."

William smiled. "Love those cupcakes. I have something on the agenda if it works out. Do you have a lot of guests today? Any in uniforms?"

"Uniforms? No. I'm in sync with your anti-establishment vibe. What's up?"

William gave a quick glance at the front entry. "Mom's not here, right? So, no Jason."

MJ flashed a conspiratorial grin. "No fuzz, not even Jason. What are you hiding?"

Amber texted Michael. William patted the backpack and whispered, "Professor's phone."

"Why?"

"Your friends," William gestured air quotes, "the fuzz…"

MJ grinned. "Friends?"

"They're harassing us, saying we're dealing drugs with the Prof. They're constantly in an unmarked car on our street and follow us when they want to. We've had enough."

"You took the professor's phone?" MJ crossed her arms.

"I'm not turning it over to them until I see what it shows. Randall never dealt drugs, or if he did it'll show

248

nothing about us."

"Then you think these cops will have to back off. How do you break into a phone?"

Michael came into the shop. William said, "We'll work on it upstairs. Don't let anyone know we're there."

MJ gave a thumbs up. "I go with the flow. I'll keep an eye out down here and let you know if any cops show up." MJ held up her hand for them to wait, and she walked through the front hall and into the first exhibit room.

Amber took off her coat and put it on the counter. "I'll be down here until store closing, but text me if there's good news. I hope you can break that password."

William said, "Nicky's coming by after work in case we need more techie skills. We'll get in one way or another."

MJ returned, glancing furtively around. "Front stairs are all clear."

As the two men walked by, MJ raised her hand in a peace sign. "Show 'em you're not gonna take it anymore. Right on." William gave her peace sign a fist bump.

Chapter Thirty-Three

MJ stood in the back hall, uncharacteristically head down over her phone. Interrupted when the door closed, she greeted her daughter. "Wishing you peace on a troubling day."

Katherine put her keys back in her purse and paused her eagerness to examine Donna's messenger bag. "Same to you. Your protest over early? Or taking a break?" Katherine shifted her weight from one foot to the other, then tapped her foot as she stared at her mother. "Am I interrupting something between you and your phone?"

"I saw you on it, as you parked and walked in. You drove up the alley a little fast. Take your time and enjoy life."

Katherine silently counted to five before answering. "What's so exciting on your phone? Hello? Can we enjoy our conversation, or should I move along to my office?"

MJ held her phone up, showing her screen. "Amber set me up on a neat app with the outside cameras. I'm warned about all who come and go."

Katherine sighed. "For what good it may do you."

MJ turned her phone back and kept it handy. "A Shakespeare philosophy?"

Katherine ignored her comment over her movie reference. "You want to predict rushes on Clutch Cafe orders, or something?"

MJ glanced at her phone. "I'm on a specific mission, monitoring the establishment."

Katherine frowned. "Are you protesting later?"

MJ leaned against the wall, staring again at her screen. "I might."

"Who are you watching for?" MJ's annoying silence reminded Katherine of childhood, and she snuffed out her wish to stomp a foot for her mother's attention. Her own protests had never worked anyway. "I'm on a mission, so if you and David don't need me I'll be in my office for a while."

MJ mumbled, "Good idea."

Katherine walked in the opposite direction from the cafe, and asked over her shoulder, "You said Amber set up your app? She's at the shop then?"

"She's here."

Katherine closed the office door behind her. She picked Donna's bag up from the shelf in her closet. She immediately felt the weight of it in her hands and in her heart. Donna had no idea she'd packed up her bag for the last time, and in her rush to work she'd grabbed the wrong one. Now Julia left her mother's bag here for safe keeping. Katherine knew Donna as a caring person. She solemnly put the bag on her desk. She sat down and stared at the front. What message from Donna would she find?

A deep breath and Katherine inspected the bag. She recognized the designer's vegan style. She shared an ecological commitment. The vegan leather had a brand new stiff feel. With use and age, more flexibility would develop. Until then the huge messenger mimicked a formidable opponent, daring her to break in. She refused to be intimidated.

What's inside, and the purse itself says things about a woman's personality. Katherine stared at the gigantic, blood red bag. A key ring dangled around the handle of a giant red leather bow drooped across the front. Other than the bow, a utilitarian bag. Donna personified the importance of her work in no-nonsense science. Devoted to helping those suffering physical and mental illness, she held a strict belief in the do no harm promise. Yet, she had a soft side seen through her love of family. Katherine played with the cute daisy charm on the key ring and thought of how her beautiful flowers delighted Donna. She'd added a matching charm to Julia's bag too. Where did Julia's bag end up?

The handle on top allowed carrying the bag like a briefcase. An adjustable strap added the more traditional option over the shoulder, the way the bike messengers had made them famous.

The clasps to open the bag hid underneath the front flap at an awkward angle. She'd design one of these differently, possibly for next year's line and in her own styling. First, she'd add an easy access zip pocket on the back.

She pressed the two clasps and flipped the panel over the top, expecting it to stay out of the way. It didn't. She pulled the heavy purse on her lap and tucked the flap against the desk to keep it open. Katherine paused to admire the beauty of the gorgeous vegan leather again. She'd design a way to lighten the frame. Katherine sat straight up in her chair, unzipped the top, and peeked inside.

The bag divided into three sections. The middle included padding and inside nestled a laptop with plug-in cord for charging. A prominent sticker on the laptop showed the NRML Company logo and two bar codes, one labeled as asset class and the other as serial number. No doubt it would be password secured. She placed it on the desk.

The front section contained several items. Katherine pulled them out one at a time and set each on her desk. First, a bound notebook with about a hundred single spaced pages. The title, *Independent Review* held little meaning, but she immediately recognized the name of the author printed underneath—Professor Nathan Randall. In a folder, a few pages stapled together showed an agenda for a NRML meeting dated January second. Also attached, some introductory remarks that appeared to roll straight into a presentation but cut off abruptly. Katherine searched in the bag for loose pages, but found none.

One inside slip pocket held pens and a small notepad. The other held a lipstick. Katherine's hand shook to hold such a personal item. She imagined Donna using it, not knowing she'd never use it again. Katherine moved to the last interior pocket. She barely felt something at the bottom. She pulled out a key attached to a ring with a daisy charm.

All that remained included two slip pockets on the front panel of the bag. An electronic tablet slid out of one, along with a charger, and glasses, and a romantic birthday card for Tomás. The tablet seemed like Donna's personal, and also Donna's reading glasses. The last pocket contained a wallet. Katherine unsnapped it and stared at Donna's picture on her driving license displayed in a clear plastic covered slot. Other slots held credit cards and a couple of membership identification cards. Almost one hundred dollars in bills remained inside. A receipt from Sandy's Bakery noted pickup for a custom cake on Tuesday.

Katherine hugged the empty bag, leaned back in her chair and stared at the contents on her desk. The full impact of a missing item stunned Katherine. Not everyone may agree on its significance, but it increased Katherine's conviction of murder. No suicide note, birthday plans for her husband, and preparation for an important business meeting. Donna did not walk three miles away from her car to attach a plastic bag to her head with red tape and commit suicide.

Katherine fingered the tear made by the bullet in the messenger bag. A confident smile grew as Katherine remembered how hard she'd fought. Then she frowned. That bullet had been meant for her. Luck and Donna's purse diverted the bullet, and then Jason ran in. Donna's belongings lay on her desk, next to the booklet authored by Professor Nathan Randall, also dead.

Chapter Thirty-Four

Amber ran upstairs to check on progress. William and Michael sat across from each other at the desk in the spare bedroom and stared at the professor's phone lying between them. William obviously deep in thought. Michael slumped deep into his chair, tapping his fingers in a bored rhythm.

"What's happening?" Amber aimed to sound cheerful and encouraging despite the mood permeating the room. "Any breakthrough?"

Michael perked up at the sound of her voice. "The good news…it fits my charger." He tilted the phone to see the screen. "Almost a hundred percent."

William shrugged. "Still can't get in. Man, I've lost count of all the things I've tried. I'm out of ideas."

Michael checked his own phone. "Half an hour ago Nicky texted he left to meet us, confirming no cops in sight. No word from him since."

William paced. "We need some tech skills. I can't figure out the password, and I don't know how to bypass. Without Nicky's skills we may be stuck."

Michael put an arm around Amber. "How about the office desktop password?"

William stared out the window. "No good."

Michael persisted. "You tried the code for the pad to get in the building? Or the phone number? His birthday, or address?"

"None of those worked." He leaned against the window.

Amber felt Michael's body suddenly tense. "You don't see the cops, do you?"

William looked both ways. "No cop in sight." Then he laughed. "Gotta give it to Nicky. He always finds a way."

Michael moved away from Amber toward the window. "You see him?"

"Yeah, on a scooter with full out ski mask, junky coat, old boots."

Michael commented, "A disguise. Smart."

William nodded. "I recognize the scooter. He painted those purple wheels for Deeanna."

Michael leaned on the sill. "I thought he broke up with Deeanna."

William said, "He's turning the corner."

Amber said, "He might come in the back way."

William muttered at Michael. "Deeanna…hot Deeanna…oh yeah." William grabbed the phone. He clicked on the screen then stared at it with a grin. "We're in."

Michael laughed. "How did that happen?"

"The Prof's obsession with women, he'd yack about bodies." William glanced at Amber with a blush. "He used to mutter 36-24-36 like a meditation. We've got the password."

Michael said, "Let's check out the texts. Let's get rid of those cops."

Amber said, "I'll find Nicky and bring him upstairs."

William and Michael huddled over the desk, as she walked out.

Amber found Nicky unmasked in the kitchen and getting a glass of water from the sink.

"Any trouble getting here?"

He laughed. "None. I skipped the van and bused it from work instead, then I got off at a different stop. Anyone watching the transit center totally missed me. What did you figure out?"

"They're in. They're checking out the phone now. They're upstairs, second bedroom on the left at the top. I have to get back to the shop until closing."

Nicky gave her a thumbs up. "I left a scooter inside the back door."

"I'll lock it in the inventory closet and catch up with you guys later."

Chapter Thirty-Five

Now that she'd seen everything in Donna's bag, Katherine knew she needed to turn it over to the police. She leaned back in the desk chair. These items might convince them to reopen the investigation.

Little chance the chief would listen. Katherine frowned. Detective Grace may give a sympathetic ear, but the best chance felt like a soulful, convincing talk with Jason. If he'd given her the time to lay out all her facts, he'd have agreed with her. She'd take the time to prepare and finish reading the professor's report. Good thing Jason called back asking about a late date tonight, after the late work shift. Perfect. She'd be ready to convince Jason.

In the meantime, her growling stomach suggested a snack. She locked Donna's things in her cabinet. Reluctant to carry the gigantic bag around with her, she grimaced as she compromised her style sense and heaved it over her shoulder and crossbody. She silently scolded herself for leaving it unguarded all morning. Someone wants it. She must protect it and treat it as evidence, and a sentimental legacy for Julia. She fingered the lifesaving bullet tear again. She'd ask her team on Rodeo Drive to mend the bag good as new, for Julia. She took a firm hold of the bag leaning against her hip.

The line of mid-afternoon latte drinkers at the Clutch Cafe kept David occupied and MJ finally off her phone. Chatter filled the room. A round of ladies' laughter erupted from the center table.

Peggy clapped her hands together. "Those were the days, ladies."

Winifred noted, "We're talking last summer, not long ago."

Peggy said, "Exactly. Welcome to a new year Winny. Keep up."

Another round of laughter and Pam waved. "Katherine, where have you been? Join us."

Katherine warmed to her grandmother's invitation. "I'd love to."

The ladies murmured delight to see her, and Katherine pulled out a chair to sit. Judy pointed at the bag. "A new favorite? You're carrying that courier bag like a Cold War spy."

Peggy giggled. "A fancy bag for a spy. What a big bow."

"To throw off suspicions." Judy laughed.

Katherine slipped the bag off and sat down with it on display in her lap. "I'm toying with the idea of adding a messenger bag to my line."

Judy stroked the side of the bag. "I always call them by the old courier bag name."

Peggy asked, "This blueprint model appears ready to wear."

Katherine said, "Not a model, Julia Ruiz asked me to keep it for her."

Judy set down her drink. "I cherished my friendship with her mother. It breaks my heart Donna's gone."

The ladies echoed her sadness, "Far too young." and "Her poor family."

Judy said, "Donna had a brilliant thirst for life and

for learning. How dedicated she remained to her life saving medical research work. I remember her sense of fun too. We enjoyed some dear adventures together."

Eager to hear more, Katherine rested the bag sideways beside her in the chair. "Tell us about your friendship."

"We met at a Library Friends meeting and hit it off right away. The speaker presented information about historical fiction. Our families both came from Germany and left during the Cold War. Donna and I got together sometimes after that. Last year when Liz and I visited Russia we returned through Berlin. Donna joined us there. We visited some of our families' beginnings."

Liz leaned back with a smile. "What a bustling city."

Peggy said, "I remember seeing your pictures, and hearing your stories about the intrigue of the Berlin Wall."

Margaret jumped in. "I like spy novels about Berlin during the Cold War." She turned to Katherine. "We should suggest that to Anthony for the new book."

Katherine's mind ricocheted back to Donna's mystery and her conversation with Anthony earlier. "The current work in progress seems to have a thriller twist."

Margaret straightened in her seat. "Oh?"

Judy shifted her gaze to Katherine. "Messenger bags without bows are used by military, diplomats, and other officials too."

Margaret noted, "I've read about spies carrying secret information hidden in the bags."

Judy said, "I have a messenger bag from back then."

Katherine said, "I'd love to see it."

Margaret grabbed Donna's bag and held it out to Judy. "Where are the hiding places? Show us on Julia's."

Katherine kept a wary eye out for any sudden moves from others in the room. Judy leaned forward eager to demonstrate. "Do you mind, Katherine? I'll be careful with it."

"No problem, Judy. I'm interested too."

"Well, the seams along the sides of the shoulder strap leave a space across the middle. The inside of that strip spans large enough for a small, folded note or in the Cold War days a ream of developed film. Or it could hide a vial of poison or other drug."

Peggy noted, "These days I bet you could slip a USB drive in there, if you want to smuggle some data."

Judy stared at the bag. "A giant bow can detract a bystander's interest, but an opposing spy or official would not be fooled. Oh, a pretty little charm." Judy fingered the hanging ceramic daisy. "Donna loved her flowers." With her eyes downcast, she gave a sad sigh. Her hands slid along the sides of the bag. She cleared her throat. "You can see how thick these leather sides are."

Katherine nodded. "Yes, the gussets."

Judy continued her tour of the bag. "Within these could be hidden pages, letters, even a small weapon. We'd have to destroy the bag by taking it apart to get it, so in that case the bag could not be used again." Judy flipped open the flap and unzipped the top. "In World War II tamper evident locks or seals on these courier bags, gave an alert. Nothing like that on any contemporary model. Some of the old bags sport wide zippers, and thick for hiding something."

Margaret slapped the table with her hand, broadcasting her enthusiasm. "So many opportunities for intrigue."

Judy tilted the bag, so everyone glimpsed inside.

She tugged on the lining. "Of course, there's lots of room behind here to sew in something you want to smuggle. These partitions for the separate sections can also be torn apart to reveal a hidden surprise."

Margaret spoke up, "They could put in a false bottom."

Judy agreed. She closed the bag and handed it to Katherine, who vowed to examine the bag again in greater detail.

Amber approached the table. "Ladies, your ride has arrived. I sent it around to the back so you can walk out the door here."

Pam said, "Lovely to see you all today."

Katherine agreed. "Yes, and thanks for the handbag tour."

As the Ladies of the Round Table said their goodbyes and headed out the door, MJ sat at the table and asked Amber, "Closing up shop soon?"

Amber said, "Yes, been slow today. No reason to stay open late."

Katherine fingered the hole in the handbag. "Business will pick up again. Clutch Café stays busy." Katherine meant to reassure Amber. Just then, Amber specifically stared at MJ, swept her glance up to the ceiling, gave a discreet thumbs up, and walked out.

MJ ignored Katherine. "The ladies all had a good time. How about you, Pam?"

"Very nice. And I enjoyed David's drink concoction too."

MJ sat forward. "Good. He had a busy afternoon behind the bar. If you both don't mind, I'll wrap things up and go work on the new exhibit for a while." She quickly moved to the door and disappeared.

Pam raised her voice, "I'll see you later?"

Katherine put her hand over her grandmother's. "Can I get you anything?"

"No dear. I'll finish my cup and head home for dinner."

Katherine winked. "I'll head after MJ and see what mischief she's up to with that exhibit."

"You two have fun."

"I'll check on you later." With the messenger bag on her shoulder, she hurried after MJ.

The new exhibit room stood empty. Katherine found her mother in the kitchen making sandwiches and putting them on a tray. Katherine sauntered into the room and eyed the heaping plates of food. "You're planning on eating all that? You did work up an appetite."

"Don't sneak up on me like that. Usually, I sense you near me."

Katherine crossed arms over her chest. "What are you up to? Don't say nothing."

MJ continued putting sandwiches together. "Your friend Jason expected here soon, or any of your friends in blue?"

"No. I'm seeing him late tonight. He's pulling extra shifts or something. Why?"

MJ glanced furtively out the window then stepped back peering down the hall toward the front door. "No special reason."

"Don't give me that. And I saw some signal Amber gave you…wait. Who could be upstairs?"

MJ picked up the tray. "The anti-establishment gathered, and they've had a breakthrough. Come on."

Chapter Thirty-Six

A round of hushed cheers greeted the tray of sandwiches and drinks Moonjava carried through the upstairs bedroom door. As the others dove for the food, William held back, when his mother walked in. "Anyone else coming up?"

Katherine put her hand on his shoulder. "No. What are you all working on?"

Amber explained, "They needed some privacy. I thought here would be a good place."

William defended Amber, "I wanted to work here. I didn't think you'd mind."

Katherine rubbed William's shoulder. "You're at home here, and I'm always here if you need me."

As the others munched on the sandwiches, William emphasized, "We don't want any police involvement."

Katherine cocked her head to the side. "You mean Jason? He's not here. The police stopped bothering you, didn't they?"

William glanced around the room at his housemates. Michael swallowed a mouthful of sandwich. "Tell her. She helped me when they locked me up. She might have a good idea."

Katherine sat down on the edge of the bed, and MJ sat next to her. William faced them. "We're not being questioned, but we're under suspicion."

Katherine protested that outrage, "How could any of

you possibly be involved? They declared it a drug overdose."

William hurried to continue, "They're not saying we killed him, at least they haven't said that yet. They think the prof dealt drugs. They want to prove we did deals with him."

Michael added, "They have a stakeout at the house all the time and follow us too."

Nicky said, "We had to sneak around to get here today."

Katherine bit her lip and forced herself to stay calm, although fury grew that Jason had allowed the surveillance without saying a word to her.

Michael put an arm around Amber's waist. "We had to come up with a sneaky way to break into the Prof's office too, so we could check it out and the cops wouldn't know."

Moonjava's arm bolted upright with her fist high in the air. "Right on."

Katherine pulled MJ's arm back down. "You broke into the office at the college?"

William stood up. "We didn't break in. We didn't want the cops to know we checked it out or stop us. We have to prove we had nothing to do with all this. The professor did not deal drugs, and neither do we. His wife came to the office. We helped her pack his things, and we searched for clues."

Katherine's curiosity pushed aside her concerns. "What did you find?"

William sat again. "He had a personal phone stowed away in a hiding place." He gestured to the desktop. "This afternoon we figured out the password, and we've been checking it out. Pretty interesting."

Katherine leaned forward. "That's either personal property his wife should have or evidence the police should be given." Katherine fingered the strap of Donna's purse, kept from the police in order to search it. Like mother, like son.

William said. "After we clear ourselves, then we'll give it to the cops."

Michael groaned. "We'll copy whatever clears us, then they can have the phone. We need to make sure we're in the clear, and no more stake outs."

Katherine frowned at William. "Why didn't you tell me about the trouble they're giving you? I'd call it harassment. I'll complain. I'll get it stopped."

MJ turned to her. "We'll have a sit-in at City Hall. I'll text out a call to action."

William waved them off. "Hang on, both of you. That suggestion will get the cops mad." William spoke directly to his mother. "Your good intentions can't solve all my problems."

Katherine nodded. "Let me help."

William paused before responding. "It makes sense to keep quiet a little longer, until we prove they're on the wrong track. Then they'll leave us alone. We may be close."

The intrigue hooked Katherine. "What have you found?"

Michael said, "Nothing on that phone shows drugs."

Amber's voice tinged with anger, "Pictures of girl students, including Candace."

Nicky added, "With all this crap on his phone, the work file stands out."

"Why clutter up a porn cell with work?" Michael laughed, then suggested, "He could have saved it there by accident. Or on purpose to hide it?"

Katherine asked, "What kind of work?"

Nicky said, "I recognize the information from my company. I don't know why he'd have NRML test data."

William scrolled on the phone screen and held it up to Katherine. "Remember the appointment we found? The prof texted Julia's mom about attending her company presentation."

Katherine rushed over. "Texts with Donna? Donna Ruiz?"

William handed her the phone. "They're strange texts. Clandestine. She didn't sound happy about him attending the meeting. She said she had it handled."

Nicky said, "I don't get that. At NRML everything's on the cloud, so what would be different from what Brittany presented? The professor talks about compromised tests and no time to waste."

William said, "Donna texts back—fake."

Nicky added, "and a placebo effect…"

William continued, "In one text she sends a blunt plea about patients dying and accusing him of a problem, or she could be convincing him? I can't tell. They're texting in some secret language only they know."

Nicky said, "It could be some kind of code because they don't want anyone else to figure out what they're saying. Fierce competition between pharmaceutical companies exists, for real. There's lots of money involved. They'd want to keep secrets from other companies' spies."

Katherine said, "Amber, you said Donna rushed away upset on New Year's when you told her the professor overdosed."

"Yes. A total, radical reaction."

Katherine stared at the text on the screen. "I haven't mentioned to you, but I've been investigating something else."

William grinned. "Let's see if we can help you."

Katherine leaned over his shoulder with a hug. "We can help each other. I've been investigating Donna's murder."

That created a collective stir in the room. "Murder?"

MJ answered, "Yes, murder. Not suicide."

Katherine added, "This accidental overdose attracts a scent of intent." She motioned for everyone to gather closer. "Let me tell you what I know about Donna."

Chapter Thirty-Seven

It didn't take long for Katherine to give her update on what she'd discovered about Donna. No one had moved or said a word as they took it all in.

Amber cringed. "Hard enough for Julia, thinking her mom killed herself, but now the idea someone else may have killed her."

Katherine responded, "There's no rush to tell her, or her father, anything until we know more. They have their hands full with grief either way."

MJ added, "The value of life is the love freely given, not the means to the end. Julia knowing and feeling her mother's love brings resilience."

William tapped on the messenger bag. "You found something interesting inside?"

"The contents are locked in my office." Katherine led the parade down the back stairs. They surrounded her desk, as she unlocked the cabinet and put Donna's things on the desk.

Amber wrapped her arms around herself, as her bottom lip trembled. "I didn't know it would be so hard to see Donna's things, with her gone." She wiped away a tear.

William asked, "Can I hold the bag?" He fingered the bullet hole. "Are you sure you're safe here? What if that thief comes back?"

"I'm keeping the place locked, the alarm on, and my

phone charged. I'm planning to give the bag to Jason tonight."

MJ said, "We must hold those cops accountable and protect the innocent. I'll text for a sit-in at City Hall. I need my phone." She marched out of the office.

William shook his head. "Mom, you should stay somewhere safer, not here alone." He jiggled the daisy charm. "Have you uploaded the file yet? What did you find?"

Katherine sat in her chair and laughed. "Find in a decoration?"

He pulled the bottom stem on the daisy and revealed a USB drive. Nicky stared. "Man, no one uses those anymore." William handed it to him, and he held it as if holding a rare antique. "Better not upload it now. It could be malware."

Katherine asked, confused, "What do you mean?"

"You know, a virus or something that can totally mess up your laptop. I'll check it at work where I can view it in the tech lab." Nicky stuck it in his jacket pocket.

Katherine sighed. "Thanks. I didn't think of that."

Nicky grabbed the key off the desk. "This key shape matches keys to old lockers at NRML It might go to one in Donna's test lab. I'll see."

Katherine held out the laptop to him. "Why don't you take this too? You might access company information that reveals something about Donna's last days."

Nicky dropped the key in a pocket and zipped it shut. He put the laptop in his backpack. "I'll let you know what I find out. Amber, where did you say you put my scooter?"

"Follow me." Amber led the way for Nicky and Michael.

William hesitated at the door. "Are you sure you're safe here tonight? I can stay over."

"Don't worry. MJ's here." Katherine remembered with a laugh that MJ had walked out. "She's here somewhere. Don't worry. I've got work to catch up on, before I go out for a little dinner. If I get nervous, I'll call you. I promise. Love you."

William said, "I'll check on you later. Love you." He closed the door behind him.

Chapter Thirty-Eight

Thunder rumbled again. Katherine hovered over her laptop. Nicky had sent a video file. She understood about every tenth word of the NRML information Nicky had emailed to her. As head of the department, Donna waded through a lot of paperwork and research results. Her meetings with her technicians and pharmacists sounded like a foreign language. Deciphering her notes and comments on reports strained the mind. Katherine stretched and wiggled her toes in her slippers. Under the desk sat a trembling Purrada. She picked up her pet.

"Not bedtime reading, unless I can't sleep and need help." Katherine yawned. "Don't be nervous, poor kitty. The thunderstorm lurks outside, and you're inside in the warm."

She wanted to finish reading through a couple more department meeting notes before getting ready to see Jason.

The screen lit up. Joanne Taylor—presentation of testing results update, the next agenda item on the weekly meeting notes for Donna's section at NRML. Katherine steeled herself for more medical jargon as she clicked on the link. Another presentation, another PowerPoint.

The screen split between a presentation, and a video camera view of the presenter. In the corner of the screen another camera view showed the conference room filled with about half a dozen people wearing lab coats. Katherine flinched at the frozen image of Donna sitting at the middle of the conference table. She happened to be staring directly at the camera. Her confident smile and attentive posture showed her happily in charge. Katherine pulled her glance away from Donna and clicked on the arrow to watch the video.

Joanne spoke, as another bolt of lightning brightened Katherine's office, and the next crack of thunder hit hot on its heels. Katherine stroked Purrada and focused on the video. Blah, blah, blah. Some kind of results of drug testing. Clinical trials. For heaven's sake, Katherine couldn't even figure out what the drug could cure. Something about testing results in clinical trial participants. The graphs and data in the referenced PowerPoint screens didn't help. Donna asked a question about criteria which drew Katherine's attention back to the people in the conference room.

All business Donna, serious and even commanding insisted on getting answers. Next to her, Katherine recognized Brittany.

Donna shook her head. She addressed the room in a low and heavy voice. "These are not the expected results. We need to take this one back to the drawing board."

Brittany abruptly stopped typing. "After three years of research and development work, it can't be the drug. Preliminary test results showed perfect."

Donna continued. "We can review the test procedures again. I'll assign an objective subcommittee to do that review and report back."

Brittany replied, "I'm happy to work on the committee."

A couple of others at the table raised their hands. One woman adjusted her glasses and then touched her blonde hair wrapped in a tight bun. "Donna, I didn't participate in the testing at all. I worked as a consultant on the original research. I could give an objective review of the testing set up and execution."

The young woman next to her volunteered as well. "I have some recent class experience from my graduate studies at the University."

Donna gave the group a brief smile. "Brittany, Vickie, Anna, I appreciate having volunteers. I will give careful consideration and notify everyone who I name to the committee. In the meantime, I've put the project on hold."

A quiet but audible groan sounded from the group, and all eyes fell on Donna. Even Joanne Taylor stared wide eyed.

A man sitting on the far end of the table, the only person wearing a business suit spoke up, "An indefinite hold puts us at a disadvantage in our market negotiations. You know the vicious competition. With the huge sunk cost, we can't afford a negative ROI."

A bolt of lightning through her bay window punctuated the man's comment. While riveted to the meeting, Katherine subconsciously waited for the thunder to follow. Return on investment she understood.

Donna addressed him directly. "I understand your financial concerns, Jim. You have to see the danger approving these clinical trials without further investigation."

Jim leaned forward. "With the appropriate project management, we can minimize the loss and still beat competitors to market. I'll make a proposal with the financials to back it up."

Donna closed the lid on her laptop. "That won't be necessary. The medical deviations override the financial forecasts."

Jim frowned and responded, "You can present your medical decision, and I'll present my recommendation. We'll see what Stephen's final decision is."

Donna stood up. "Thanks, Joanne. Thanks everyone. That's all for now."

Everyone left the room in a hurry, except Brittany who continued to type on her keyboard until the video ended.

Deep in thought, Katherine swiveled her chair around and stared at the storm while scratching Purrada behind the ear. They both tensed when a click of the door handle swept the door open. Purrada jumped from her lap with a snarl and ran for the closet. The hall door closed with a whoosh, followed by a thump. Katherine realized who'd arrived and her stiffened shoulders relaxed. "Hi, MJ. Where did you disappear to?"

"Maybe we're more alike than you think my dear Ms. Katherine, How did you sense me? Your connection to the universe grows and broadens."

"The resounding clunk of your protest sign has no equal. You missed the kids leaving. You've been goneawhile."

"You missed your grandmother. She's fixing roast beef and Yorkshire pudding for Julia and Tomás. Here, I brought you a soothing latte from David."

"That's nice of him." Katherine turned to face her. MJ's hand shook, as she put the drink down. Katherine "I'm no expert, MJ, but your aura appears stressed."

"I'm outraged. I'll need extra yoga time to center

myself. Cops waste time hunting innocent kids and ignore a two time killer in hiding."

Katherine wrapped her hands around her steaming cup. "I've been analyzing clues."

MJ leaned forward and shook her head. "I protested in the lobby at the cop station, but they won't re-open the case."

Katherine surprised herself by commenting, "I admire your determination."

MJ snorted. "When my protest began, a small group of people joined me. It became too easy for the establishment to ignore us. The others gave up. They want to believe a murder didn't happen. Real danger happens when people seek reassurance by altering the truth they believe."

"Sounds like your meditation of the day?"

MJ asked, "Why don't you come protest with me tomorrow?"

"I have investigative plans for tomorrow." Katherine hesitated, then decided to plunge forward. "We need to do something that will get results. Let's whiteboard our clues."

MJ's face lit up. "Yes! I'm with you."

"I have my own clue board. I could use your ideas."

MJ methodically inhaled a couple of deep breaths. "Bring on the board."

Katherine wheeled it out of the closet and sat on the edge of her desk while MJ got comfortable in the rocking chair. "So, what have you heard from Jason on all this? Does the company yes man blindly agree with department policy?"

"I haven't talked to him about it much, mostly because I haven't seen him. They have him pulling extra shifts."

MJ sat against the back of her chair. "At work? For what, when they're not investigating what's right in front of them? I have an inspiring meditation that fits. Don't let someone dim your light simply because it shines in their eyes."

"Okay, let's keep our own light bright." Katherine sipped again from the latte. "I like that extra something David added."

"You might mean the cinnamon."

"Nice." Katherine sighed as her tummy rumbled. "Hungry? I didn't get any of those sandwiches you made the kids. I'll get us a snack to munch on while we're detecting. Check out the board, and I'll be right back."

"Some pistachios sound good to me."

"I'll warm up some of that leftover quiche too."

With MJ's quick thumbs up, Katherine headed for the door. She heard a low hum, confirming MJ's mood had improved.

While the quiche warmed in the oven, Katherine wandered the quiet exhibit rooms of her museum home. She smiled as she passed the new 1960's room. The Valentine's month of love celebration couldn't come soon enough. With everything almost ready, Katherine made a mental note to reconfirm the menu with Sandy.

Final details for spring shows along with summer marketing and fall planning all at once sometimes overwhelmed. Yet, she loved the fashion business. Different worries propelled her now, though. Those kids needed to be out from under the cops' suspicions. This should be a carefree time of their lives, not their every move under a microscope. What if they're framed as guilty? Katherine shuddered, but not from the cold outside the window.

What about those texts, and that encrypted report? Had Donna and the professor discovered the problem with the drug? Did that information threaten a killer who's still on the loose? How many people using that treatment would be seriously injured? Or could their lives be at risk? The tragedy could reach much further than the professor's family. Further than Julia and her father. Then Katherine shook her head and gave a sigh of relief. No, Brittany had presented the findings at that company meeting. They would have caught any testing problems and refused to move forward. Right?

The timer on the oven buzzed. Katherine went back to the kitchen. She pulled the pan out, set it on the counter, and cut two generous slices of quiche. A sudden thought pushed her to double check the pantry back door. Happy to see it remained locked, she grabbed the plate and a bag of pistachios and returned to her office.

MJ stared unflinching at the whiteboard as she rhythmically rocked. Katherine leaned against her desk, and her glance rested on the opposite wall's display of her favorite purses. She smiled about the lovely story behind a couple of them.

That priceless, colorful wallet and checkbook holder set that her sons had decorated one summer. Such a sweet surprise. Words tumbled out as the excited young boys spoke over each other, telling about finding them at a garage sale and painting them. The wallet showed a fire breathing dragon, and the check holder framed a knight ready for the fight.

MJ stopped rocking. "Okay, how about Kevin? What are you thinking?"

Katherine crossed her arms as she gathered her

thoughts. "After I found Donna, he came there with Julia and created a terrible, public spectacle. He has a temper, and he doesn't care who sees it. His feelings for Julia are strong and her parents wanted to keep him away from her. His ride share business gives him easy mobility around town."

MJ stopped shelling pistachios. "You're focused on Donna. There's also the professor, and we know Kevin drove to the college office that evening with the tea. Did he have drugs too? Could they have been dealing drugs like the police seem to think? A disagreement?"

"Kevin spiked the professor's tea over a deal gone bad, and then killed Donna for spite? I don't know. He has a hair-trigger temper, but would he hurt Julia by killing her mother? At his public spectacle near Donna's body, Kevin accused Tomás of being near the college office that night."

MJ sat back. "Would Tomás know the professor through Donna?"

"I talked with Tomás, and Kevin told the truth. Tomás went to see the professor that night." Katherine paused to eat a bite of her quiche.

MJ went to the whiteboard to update the Kevin and Tomás columns. "What did Tomás tell you?"

Katherine brought her up to speed with Tomás' confession of jealousy, the revelation, and his own accusation. MJ's notes slanted a bit crooked as she absorbed the information. "What? Tomás believes Anthony and Donna…ridiculous. Anthony's a Virgo."

Katherine gave her mother a blank stare. MJ laughed. "She's a Gemini. In a romantic relationship, those two signs will only get on each other's nerves. They wouldn't have an affair." She put the cap back on the pen and sighed. "Don't you see? Consulting on a book would never turn romantic between them. The stars don't show it. Besides, what would he have against the professor? I don't believe Anthony did either murder."

Katherine paused. "Our friend Peggy would agree with you, but Tomás accuses him. Anthony may have met Donna at the wrong place and at the wrong time that morning, all in innocence. I checked, and he did have an appointment with his agent and a book signing, and a restaurant date."

"A man with an alibi. Can we put a line through him on the board, like the neighbor?"

Katherine wanted to, yet she hesitated. "Anthony told me he wants to work with me to solve the case, as Donna's friend. Or, because he wants to frame someone else for his crime?"

"Katherine, you surprise me."

Remembering Jason's comment, Katherine opened her eyes wide. "Everyone's a suspect."

"Don't say that to me." MJ laughed.

Katherine finished her snack. "No one can convince Tomás, but Anthony vehemently denies any affair. For me, I see Donna devoted to her family, not clandestine." Katherine leaned back. "Anthony and Tomás, the last two to see her that morning."

MJ sat down and stared at the whiteboard. She played with the pen in her hand. "Or so it seems."

Katherine leaned back. "Tomás accused Kevin of breaking into their home. Julia doesn't agree. A random, untimely robbery? Or did someone break in for a specific reason?"

MJ said, "Julia's in love."

Katherine continued, "She and Kevin hang out

together whenever possible since her mom died. Poor girl, she believes Donna committed suicide and carries tremendous guilt."

MJ shook her head. "The shock of it all affects her judgement. Kevin stays on the board. You mentioned Tomás came back early from a trip."

"Right. Strange returning to town without telling his family."

MJ waved her forefinger in Katherine's direction. "Do you believe what he told you? If Tomás convinced himself of the affair, could he murder in a rage? Then could he murder the woman he loves? With a broken heart, vengeance creates a powerful drive against a wife and her lover. He may have changed his story about that night with the professor to avoid confessing."

"According to Tomás, when he confronted Donna that morning they vowed to work out the tensions between them. Then she said she couldn't miss work that morning, but they would be together after."

MJ straightened her back and sat cross legged in the rocker. "He saw her right before she disappeared?"

"No, Anthony did."

"Unless Tomás waited where she always parked. Last person to see the victim…"

Katherine tapped the back end of a marker against the board. "That brings us to Donna's work. After today, her job takes on greater importance."

MJ went back to shelling pistachios. "Quite the revelations."

Katherine added some notes to the board as she spoke. "Her boss draws interest. Donna designed Tuesday's important meeting specifically for him."

MJ said, "That meeting connects Donna and the

professor because he texted Donna he wanted to be there."

Katherine said, "Her boss has shown concern for Donna and her family. He and his wife went to Tomás' house and offered help and sympathy. The company donated a coffee truck at the search. He said nice things about her at the press conference. His wife seemed concerned about reuniting Tomás and Julia, and driving Tomás over here to reconcile."

MJ interrupted Katherine's train of thought. "What if the CEO colluded with Bayside's blue badges to sweep bodies under the rug? He could have gone to the transit center that morning."

Katherine raised her eyebrows. "There seems to be something between Stephen CEO and Brittany Administrative Assistant."

"Brittany who?"

"Donna's assistant. She goes out of her way to catch up with her CEO, chasing him for something. She couldn't stop talking with him at the search. She found him here when they brought Tomás over that night, almost stalking him. She sat next to him behind the podium at the news conference."

MJ rocked in her chair again. "Her boss isn't even cold, and Brittany's wanting a promotion?"

Katherine paced. "He seems happy to be around her too. When they're together his wife Cleo gets clingy." Katherine made another note. "Did the CEO and Brittany know about the professor working with Donna?"

"Brittany sounds like a prime suspect."

"We still have questions. Hopefully Nicky can get me into the building."

A knock on the door before it swung open from the

hallway. David stepped in and gently placed his hands over the rocker onto MJ's shoulders. "I closed the cafe and cleaned. Bayside shimmers with peace from the delights we served them."

Katherine gestured to him and MJ. "Thank you both. Word spread fast about your incredible lattes. I see our crowds growing." David purposefully read the board. She moved to block his view.

David said, "The community buzzes with life while they're at the Clutch."

MJ stood next to David and pointed to her sign leaning against the wall. "Tomorrow, we need to protest again. Someone must investigate."

Katherine's heart warmed over their time together. "Thanks for your ideas, MJ."

MJ gave her daughter a hug. "Why don't we stay here tonight, in case you need us."

Katherine shook her head. "Don't worry about me. I'm fine. In fact, I need to get ready to go out." Katherine picked up the messenger bag and decided to keep it awhile longer. It would be safely locked away with the board for the short time she'd be gone tonight. "I'm seeing Jason after he gets off work. He thinks we're on a date. After what I heard from William, and Nicky, and everyone, I have something else in mind."

Chapter Thirty-Nine

Katherine walked right past the clingy turtleneck short hem dress and black nylons she'd laid out for her late date with Jason. Instead, she smoothed her Purse Museum sweatshirt over the waistband of her skinny jeans. She reached past the sparkling strapped high heels and grabbed the ankle boots.

He'll meet his match tonight. He needed to stop that stakeout. Then he needed to get on board with her and get Donna's case reopened. He needed to listen to her, admit regret about how fellow officers conducted their questioning and the stake out, and confess to the mess they'd made of Donna's case. Once Jason sees the light, they'll solve the case together. Then she'll wear the enchanting heels and celebrate.

While waiting to hear from Jason, she worked at her office desk. She'd successfully completed final details for the imminent spring fashion shows and sent instructions to her staff. She leaned back and imagined her newly designed vegan baby bag as the most talked about surprise for the shows. She held high hopes for her new crossbody as best design. Once she'd conceded to carry a crossbody in her line, sheer determination inspired the unique features she'd included. She paused in thought about turning a utilitarian wristlet into a creative statement.

The doorbell from the back door rang out. Jason,

finally here. She took a moment to recapture her resolve. With a deep breath, she flexed her hands in and out of fists and thought of her sons. The bell rang again. He's in a hurry to be schooled. She grabbed her small, gray clutch.

Katherine turned into the pantry, as Jason jiggled the knob and raised a hand to knock on the glass in the door. She leveled her eyes at him. "No need to pound."

He stepped inside. "Too much action on the scene, couldn't break away until now. Sorry, I'm later than expected." He pointed to the door. "Glad to see you're keeping the door locked."

"No problem. I'm so happy to see you."

Jason smiled. "Me too."

Katherine grabbed her coat off the hook on the wall. "I thought we'd take a drive."

His smile faded. "Sure." He paused. "I just want to say how great those jeans are on you."

He helped her with the coat. "Thanks. You're out of uniform. You went home and changed?"

As she stepped across the threshold, he asked. "Where do you want to go?"

"Let's head to the marina." She jangled her keys. "I'm driving. It would be great if your patrol car stayed in the driveway, in case someone wants to break in while I'm gone." Katherine specifically thought of the hidden messenger bag.

She closed the door as Jason backed up. "Good idea. Are you hungry? How about that new restaurant on Main Street? I'm starved."

"We can hit a drive-through on the way."

While Katherine parked her Mustang on Sunset Drive next to the Bay, she admired the beauty of the moonlit night. Jason unclenched his jaw and released his grip on the passenger seat. Always such a critic of her driving, Katherine used those actions to fuel her mood.

Jason opened the fast food bag and pulled out burgers and onion rings. He handed Katherine her salad. She snuggled into her driver's seat and stared through the windshield. Small waves moved along the lit pier and bounced the sailboats anchored off the beach. The hum of a private airplane buzzed overhead.

A momentary vision captivated Katherine. The Museum's February Love-In filled with Baysiders having fun, including Jason and herself holding hands. MJ playing her guitar and singing some groovy songs. She'd lean into Jason's arms. Surrounded by music and joy, they wouldn't have a care in the world. Her sons enjoying the party with their friends. Her sons…yes, time to talk.

Jason wolfed down the food. He'd finished a burger and half the rings already. She added dressing to her salad. Katherine turned on the defroster in the idling car so the windshield wouldn't fog up.

He wiped his mouth with a napkin and stared back at her. "Haven't eaten since lunch." He leaned back.

"What do they have you working on? Tell me they're reopening Donna's case."

Jason held a hand up to stop her. "I'm searching for the words about something hard to say." He stared at the remaining onion ring, then sighed. Katherine waited, hoping for good news.

Jason slowly broke the silence, "I'm torn. I have to make a choice, and either way I choose could bring huge regret." He stared straight ahead through the windshield. "I don't even know how to tell you, Katherine."

She sat forward. "I thought we could say anything to each other."

His enchanting, dimpled, mischievous smirk broke through for a moment, then clouded over. "I'm trying." He took her hand in his. "I've achieved so much I've wanted in life, even more than I hope. Here I am riding my motorcycle on the road to happiness. Up ahead, there's someone on the overpass threatening to drop a giant rock on me. Do I swerve away safely and let it destroy the next innocent person? Or do I race up there and stop them?

Katherine's impatience took hold. "You're philosophical tonight. Of course you'll save the day. That's who you are."

"Answers come so easy to you. Can I stop the inevitable? What if I'm determined but the car behind pushes me out of it?" He stared beyond her, out the window. "There are things out there I want to do. I'm being held back, pushed out."

The sincere yearning reverberated within Katherine's soul. She responded, although he didn't seem to be listening. "What are your dreams?"

He never changed his gaze. "Helping people in great need, making a difference, adventures, danger, challenges." He hesitated. "Love."

Katherine waited, but he stopped abruptly. She filled the void, "I know about wanting more, but Jason, be proud of all you've done. Your work in the army, overseas, all that you do for Bayside. You're too young for a mid-life crisis like this."

He laughed and brushed her cheek with the back of his hand. "You don't schedule these feelings for the middle of your life. I'm not like organizing a fashion show or launch. And who said crisis? I started something, I don't know if I can finish."

A famous Coco Chanel quote skipped through Katherine's mind, "fashion changes but style endures." Katherine straightened up in her seat. "All your talk sounds like a declaration you need to find yourself. That isn't the Jason I know. That's MJ. She's been searching for herself her whole life. God knows where 'herself' is. Even Google doesn't know, I've tried."

"Katherine, listen to me." He dropped her hand and gestured as he spoke, "I'm on my bike. My engine's revving. I don't know which way to drive." He shook his head in slow motion. "With the mileage on these tires, I don't know if I can get there. I know where I want to go, but then I may lose it all."

Katherine sat unable to move. "I don't know what in the world you're talking about."

He leaned back and rubbed his left palm slowly over his jeans. "I know. I don't know how to say it to you." She followed his gaze into the crisp, winter sky, lit by a half-moon. She basked in the scene and the thought of her recently finished half-moon bag design. Her first venture into a crossbody line, ready in time for Spring Fashion Week. Yes, she'd got the moon shape right, a bright orb with gray pockets.

An ever-vigilant cop, but did he even notice his surroundings? She should steer him toward restored purpose and success. A surge of inspiration hit. She could push him to stop the police harassment of her sons and solve the real murder case. Then he'd be celebrated, happiness would return, and romance.

"Jason, I know what's getting you down."

His shoulders gave a shudder at the sound of her

voice. He squinted, leaned on an elbow, and rubbed the side of his forehead. "A minute ago you said you don't know what I'm talking about."

"Listen, I'm on the verge of solving Donna's murder, and with your help we'll do it. Then you'll feel happy and invigorated, and so will Bayside. You can make something happen at the station. Tell them to stop the stakeout against William, Christopher, and their housemates."

"You're concerned about that? I'm not involved in that assignment in any way. If they're not doing anything illegal, then the stakeout will be called off in due course."

"If? What do you mean if? Of course they're not doing anything illegal. That's why you should tell your department to spend its time and resources in productive ways."

"You said there's nothing illegal, so it will get stopped at the appropriate time."

Heat rose in Katherine's face. "You won't intervene?"

"They're following orders. I don't give the orders."

"I'll have to file a citizen's complaint then."

Jason turned down the defroster and unwrapped another hamburger. Katherine groaned and vigorously stirred her salad, spilling some lettuce down the side of her driver's seat. She groaned again, and stabbed a hearty leaf with her plastic fork, breaking off half the tines. They ate in silence.

Katherine swallowed and turned to lean on her shoulder and face him. "You're asking me for help, and I can help. You're unhappy about how they handled Donna's case, and you know I am. We need to protest. Come sleuth for Donna."

Jason turned to her. "Donna's closed case is tragic."

"Go on." Katherine waited, but he said nothing more. "Tragic? Jason, I'm telling you it should not be closed and neither should the professor case. Let me tell you what I've discovered. I know you'll agree."

"Katherine, tonight I want understanding, not an exchange of murder theories."

"And I want help protecting my sons from an intrusion that could erupt into a terrible misunderstanding, or worse."

Jason shook his head. "I don't tell you how to sell purses."

"And what about Bayside? There's a killer on the loose."

"A killer on your whiteboard?"

"Sarcasm? Yes, as a matter of fact. The best way for change comes from within the system, but if no one within will stand up, then change has to come from outside."

"Now you sound like MJ."

Katherine slammed the lid on her salad and punched it onto the floor behind his seat. She put the car in gear and screeched out of the parallel parking spot.

Pushed against the backrest, Jason urgently checked at his side mirror. "Katherine, careful. Slow down." He gripped the arm rest. "Pull over, calm down, and put your seat belt on."

She slowed but continued to her destination. She needed to get rid of him. A couple more blocks, then she pulled up to the curb outside the police station. She released the automatic lock on Jason's door. "Please go in and tell them to stop the stakeout."

He sat still. "Come on, a few more blocks. Take me

to my car, and I'll drive away."

Katherine shifted into park gear. "Someone has to do something. I can go in with you."

Jason stared at her as if to say something, but he didn't utter a word. He calmly unbuckled the seat belt. "No." He picked up the fast food trash and got out. Turning back, he leaned against the roof and said in a surprisingly soft tone, "Belt up, calm down, and drive slowly home. Good night." He pushed the door shut and stood on the sidewalk. Would he go inside? Apparently, she wouldn't get that answer tonight. Katherine put the car in gear and headed home.

In her bedroom and almost ready for bed, she heard an engine outside her window. She peeked through a slit in the curtain, as the police car backed out onto the side street.

Chapter Forty

The funeral brought together Donna's friends, associates, grateful recipients of products she'd helped to market, students she'd advised at Bayside Library, community leaders, and press. Unlike the professor's private ceremony last week, here the chapel's pews overflowed and left standing room only. Tomás and Julia sat in front. Katherine felt honored to sit directly behind them, along with Amber and some of their other friends.

Pam and The Ladies of the Round Table sat toward the back, with MJ and David. They wanted to pay their respects for such a fine woman as Donna, support Judy who had been a close friend, and also show their support for Julia and her father. Behind Katherine and breathing down her neck sat prominent staff from NRML, along with their top man Stephen and Cleo. No surprise that newly promoted Brittany sat with them.

Next to the pulpit, a wonderful, enlarged picture of Donna smiled out to everyone. Her closed casket rested in front of the altar. On top of the casket, a cascade of daisies. A most amazing display of daisies decorated the church everywhere. Donna's favorite flowers embodied her spirit and stood as a great tribute to a great lady. The ceremony brought reverence, beauty, inspiration, tears, and love with heartfelt speakers, music, and the clergy's soothing words.

Then Stephen Rider got up to speak. Mostly a

canned replay of the accolades he'd delivered at the press conference, about Donna's accomplishments. He used a tone and expression attempting to personalize the loss he felt. Yet, he left Katherine as if she'd heard a marketing blurb from NRML public relations, instead of a last farewell from a friend and associate in an important healthcare endeavor.

At the close of the ceremony, the clergy invited Tomás and Julia to join him. They knelt before Donna's casket and received a final farewell and blessing. "As we come to the close of service, let us remember the love and the memories we shared with Donna Ruiz, dear wife and beloved mother. Though we say goodbye today, Donna's spirit remains with us always." Julia cried and her father hugged her to him. When they stood again, the clergy presented Julia with a pretty daisy bouquet that she clutched to her heart.

Stephen and Cleo had planned the wake at their home. Before they left the church, they encouraged people to join them there. Cleo reminded Tomás and Julia of their invitation and her wish they would come. Only the family would go now to the burial. Katherine had offered to wait for Tomás and Julia, but he told her to go ahead.

The Ladies of the Round Table became visibly moved by the service. They decided to skip the wake. MJ and David decided to take them back to the Clutch Café for a light lunch. Katherine drove with Amber to the Stephen and Cleo Rider mansion. Katherine had no idea of the opulence the pharmaceutical CEO lived in. It even exceeded the luxury of Cleo's wardrobe and accessories. The lengthy driveway ended in a circular covered entry to a gorgeous estate at the top of a hill with a tremendous view of Bayside, Puget Sound, and the Olympic Peninsula beyond.

Katherine parked her car next to others on the lot. Staff greeted them at the front door and took their coats. Most of Bayside appeared to have arrived, enjoying the surroundings and the never-ending buffet. As they walked farther in, Katherine recognized Nicky talking in a group. From the conversation she overheard, they appeared to be workmates from NRML. Anthony came over and pulled Katherine aside. She excused herself, and Amber went over to talk with Nicky.

"I'm sorry, Anthony. A final goodbye for a dear friend sticks in the throat, and heart. What a beautiful service. She had so many friends."

Anthony cleared his throat. "Seeing all the people Donna touched, and there's so many more than this, it makes me all the more determined that her killer will be caught. I want to do everything I can to help with that. I'm digging into a few things about her work. Can you believe the boss' home? I guess legal drugs can be very profitable. I'm learning more about her family tensions too. Speaking of which, I need to get out of here in case Tomás arrives. I don't want any more confrontations."

Katherine scanned the room. "I agree with you there. I've got some clues about the professor too."

Anthony nodded. "Let's get together soon and compare notes."

"Yes, I'll call you."

He turned toward the door, then froze in place. "There's Brittany. I want to talk with her. That boss always hovers over her, but not now."

Katherine interrupted, "They hover over each other." Anthony left her to talk with Brittany.

Katherine browsed the buffet to ease her hunger pangs. Some of the finger foods tempted her, but she decided instead for a cup of tea out of the silver set. She strolled across the wide dining room and through the sunken living room to stand in the corner by the floor-to-ceiling windows in the corner. She sipped the warm, soothing brew.

A movement caught her eye. Their host walked in her direction. Keeping pace at his side strode Rob, talking a mile a minute.

"Rob, I'm hosting a wake here. Your inappropriate questioning has no place in civilized company. We'll finish this encounter in my library, and then you'll leave the premises."

Stephen walked past Katherine and through the doorway behind her. Rob gave her a broad smile, and an arched eyebrow as he entered the library. The door remained open. Katherine put down her teacup and saucer on the side table and followed Rob, closing the door gently behind her. She unobtrusively sank into a large armchair inside the room.

"I deliver an incredibly touching eulogy for my friend and colleague, and you want to focus on some kind of made up past history to tear me down? What's wrong with you press people today? You want to stir up trouble, not report real news."

Rob pulled an electronic pad out of his backpack. "My sources report you've been involved in trouble with drug patent legal problems before. My reliable sources…"

Katherine couldn't stop herself from sneezing, and Stephen turned to see her. "You too? You both come into my home, I offer an opportunity for family, friends, colleagues to come together for support, to share memories, to celebrate her life, and you want to slam me with false accusations."

"As a member of the free press, I'm requesting your documentation concerning your drug patent infringement. My understanding suggests exclusive rights to sell, use, manufacture and distribute new drugs stays in place for up to twenty years. You did not abide by that law, did you? So, you lost your prior position. Then you had to relocate, hiding your identity and history and establishing your new NRML Company here."

Stephen's face turned red, as his eyes squinted with rage at Rob. "That's slander. If you print that your career ends, and you'll find yourself in court."

Katherine asked, "Rob, how would that relate to murder?"

Stephen turned with shock to her. "Murder? What are you talking about?"

Rob explained, "Patents are a legal way to incentivize research and development because it guarantees almost a monopoly on market sales for a period of time to recoup investment and make a profit."

Stephen gasped. "I told you I've had no legal troubles like you're describing. I've had enough, and in my own home."

Rob quickly replied, "The new drug you're rushing to market, You had some patent deal on it? Did Donna disagree with it somehow? Did she get in your way?"

Katherine leaped out of the chair. "What? Stephen, let us see your morning schedule on the day Donna disappeared. Did you drive near the transit center?"

Stephen walked toward Rob, who grabbed his

backpack and back pedaled. "How dare you. Get out, both of you." He unceremoniously pushed them out the back door, onto the cold patio. "And don't come back."

After the door shut, Katherine said to Rob, "Interesting information."

"Solid too. I'm after a Pulitzer."

Katherine paused. Did Stephen gain something with Donna's death? Did he need to silence the professor for some reason? She texted Amber.

—*Time to go. Meet me at the car. Can you get my coat?*—

Chapter Forty-One

Always happy to get a call from one of her sons, Katherine sighed with relief. William had made her day. The final touches on her design could wait as she savored the good news. The police surveillance of the housemates stopped three days ago. Other than the watchful eye of Gladys across the street, they lived free from observation once again,

Closing the case had not been enough to make this happen. Jason. He'd listened to her after all. He'd advised the chief to stop.

The day after she'd made him get out of the car at the station, outside the back door she'd found a small pot of deep purple pansies with a note. "I miss us. The pansy, from the French word *penser;* think, reflect, consider."

Jason must have thought about it and acted. What could she do for him as a peace offering, and thank you? She'd bring him the messenger bag and its contents, and explain it belonged to Donna. Then they could get the case reopened. Katherine checked her make up in the mirror and pulled on knee high leather boots. She buttoned her heavy coat over her turtleneck and wool skirt.

Hearing an incoming text swoosh, she read an update from Nicky. Donna's drive contained class outlines for the STEM classes she'd volunteered for at the library. Nothing else. Katherine sighed. More investigation needed. First, reunion with Jason. She stashed her clutch under her arm, picked up the messenger bag from the closet, and headed for her car. She stopped for a box of donuts on the way.

Katherine breezed past the group huddled around the front desk in the station lobby. The officer at the metal detector eyed the bakery box. He gestured for her to stop. "Please put your keys and other metal objects on the tray. Then you can step forward."

She complied, placed the box on the table, and stepped through the machine. Surprised to hear the buzzer alert she suggested, "It must be something in my bag."

The officer put on latex gloves. "Please place them both on the table."

He scanned her clutch with a wand first. Silence. "Your other bag please."

Distinct beeps resulted as he scanned the messenger. He opened the flap and pushed it toward her. "Please empty the contents."

Katherine gingerly took out each of Donna's evidence items. He scanned each item. No beeps until he waved the wand over the messenger bag. Katherine picked it up, turned it over, then brought it right side up again. "Oh, the logo on the front, I bet. It must have metal in it." She pointed to the branding on the bottom right corner of the bag.

The officer felt the inside, along the lining. "Go ahead."

Katherine carefully put away the contents. She stood patiently in front of the officer, then pointed at the bakery box on the table. He slowly reached for it. "Here you go."

Katherine opened the lid. "Help yourself to one.

There's plenty here."

His face lit up as he took a napkin and chose one. "You brightened my day. Thanks."

Down the hallway, Katherine stepped inside the Patrol Room. A couple of people sat inside, but not Jason. She didn't recognize the officer deeply engaged on the phone, but Jason's friend Brian greeted her, "Hey, how are you? Haven't seen you in a while."

Katherine tugged the strap of the heavy messenger higher on her shoulder. "Good thanks. How about you?"

"All good, except the drudgery of writing reports. Stopped by for Jason? He headed home."

"With all the extra shifts he's been working, I thought he lived here."

"He's working overtime?"

"I'll catch him at home. Care for a fresh donut?"

"You bet. Thanks." He made a choice in an instant.

"Good luck with your paperwork." Katherine waved. She decided she'd better get out of here before word spread there's a donut box at the station. She walked back to her car and drove north toward the outskirts of Bayside.

When Katherine turned the Mustang onto the quiet road to Eagles Bluff, the vast Puget Sound water view delighted her. Several trails meandered over the steep incline down onto the beach. Glimpses of the dull winter sun cut through holes in the shrubbery and tall pines. Scattered mailboxes gave the clue to houses along the way. Jason loved Bayside, but he'd been overjoyed to discover a scenic rural area close by. Katherine smiled. Same reaction as customers buying one of her Bayside totes, then finding a free matching wallet inside.

No one could ever take the city out of Katherine

Watson, but she appreciated visits to the beautiful countryside. The peace, serenity, and especially the solitude had pulled Jason to this location. Katherine tapped her finger on the steering wheel. He never talked to her about his war service in Afghanistan, not even after she'd located his military service dog Robby. She'd never seen Jason so happy as the day he brought Robby home from the Air Force Base. The devoted dog had more than earned a happy retirement. The dog hardly left Jason's side at home and got along well with Hobbs.

She turned onto the long gravel road where the sign declared a "Private Drive." She steered away from mud puddles. Hobbs bounded across the field with tail waving, barking an excited greeting. Robby followed, trotting with his body close to the ground, a smooth and fluid movement forward like a wolf on the hunt, with tail straight out behind him. She stopped the car. The dogs sat outside her door, quietly pacing and waiting.

The trailer home stood at the end of the driveway, with a shed next to it for the coveted motorcycle. The back of the truck stuck out from behind the shed.

The trailer door opened. Both dogs turned and trotted off to their man. Relaxed and comfortable in jeans and a sweatshirt, Jason held a large mug and gulped from it as he waited. He said something to the dogs and gave each a pat as they sat down. He stood up straight again and looked through the windshield into her soul, without a smile.

Katherine missed her car heater the moment she stepped out. The full force of the wind blasted her back a step as it swept up and over the sheer bluff. Why he wanted his trailer right on top of a bluff, unprotected by trees or any barrier matched the Jason trademark. She thought of his forthright nature. Of course he lived on a precipice. He always wanted to see in the distance anything coming at him and face it head on. He didn't like surprises.

Katherine reached in for the purses on the passenger seat. She turned the volume down on her cell phone. She didn't want any interruptions. She put the clutch inside the larger bag. With that on her shoulder, she grabbed the box from Sandy's bakery. She leaned into the wind and her long hair flew. Against the Pacific Northwest's winter attack, styling didn't stand a chance.

She gave Jason a hug. He held her briefly. "What an unexpected surprise seeing you today."

Katherine dangled the box before him. "I brought a peace offering. Can we talk?"

He gave her another hug and whispered in her ear, "A peace offering? I didn't know we're at war. Come on inside."

They left the dogs to roam the property. Katherine appreciated the stoic charm and functional comfort of Jason's sturdy trailer home. The bay view over the bluff always took her breath away. She left her winter boots by the door and wiggled her toes in her warm socks.

He poured her a cup of coffee and gestured at the kitchen table. "Have a seat. What's up?"

Katherine cringed at the blunt tone. "Thank you for the sweet pansy plant and card you left."

Jason sat at the table. "Did it get you reconsidering?"

She pulled out one of the wooden chairs with the matching cushion set. What did he say? Change her thinking? Hadn't the card meant he'd reconsidered and spoken out about the stakeout? Tentative, she hung

Donna's bag on the back of the chair and put the box on the table. "Donuts from Sandy's."

Jason offered napkins and plates as she sat. "From Sandy's? That's worth the extra workout afterward to stay in shape. Thanks."

He helped himself. Katherine cut one down the middle and put half on her napkin. "We haven't talked all week. Did you see my texts?"

Katherine shifted in her chair meeting that blue eyed stare and steeled herself for a response. "I saw your texts. You didn't want to talk. You wanted to tell."

Katherine sighed. "I didn't mean it that way. I don't want any disagreement to come between us." She shifted uncomfortably in silence. "Thank you for stopping the surveillance on my sons."

Jason leaned forward and put a hand on her knee. "I had nothing to do with that."

"Nothing? I thought you'd…"

"No, and I don't want to talk about Donna's closed case either."

Katherine put her hand on his. "Can't you consider for a moment a mistake happened in the investigation? I mean, why don't you trust my judgment on the case? Listen to what I've uncovered and what I've analyzed. Then you'll agree to a further investigation."

Jason sighed and leaned back. "Trust has nothing to do with it."

Her hand trembled as she put the rest of her doughnut on a napkin. "Yes, it does."

Jason crossed his arms. "You don't know what you're up against. You, and your friends, and MJ. You should stop her protesting. Leave investigation to the professionals."

"You mean the professionals who closed Donna's case? You mean the pros that are blind to the true connection between Donna and the professor?" Her anger erupted as she stood up. "They're not investigating. They're eating donuts."

"Katherine, you're taking it the wrong way. Because of my job, I can't discuss any case with you. You should step back from it. Your place had an attempted robbery. You've been shot at. Your own case remains open and active. We need to arrest that robber, and you need to keep a low profile until we do. That bullet in your desk came way too close. Don't take any more risks."

Katherine fingered the strap on the messenger bag. She'd brought it to give as evidence to Jason, to open Donna's case together. She wanted to explain to him why her house had been broken into, why the intruder fought her. How ironic, they're both talking about arresting the same person, but he has no idea the so called robber moonlights as a serial killer. Her hand formed a fist around the strap of the bag. The messenger held the key.

Obviously, he had no intention of listening. She put the bag on her shoulder and fingered the hole from the bullet. She could do more with this evidence than he would. She'd keep it longer. She'd keep it until she solved the case and caught the killer.

The dogs barked loudly. Jason got up to check on them, and Katherine moved to the door and slipped on her boots. She could feel his eyes on her as she hesitated at the threshold. She took out her keys. Silence permeated the void between them. Suddenly his home suffocated her. Could their relationship ever recover?

She felt the weight of the bag on her shoulder. "MJ once told me the biggest risk is not taking a risk." She walked out the door alone.

Chapter Forty-Two

In her rear view mirror, she saw the dogs watching her drive away. She turned onto the main road, and the messenger bag toppled over for the second time with the label's side up. Too pained to reflect on what Jason had put her through, Katherine thought fondly of the Ladies of the Round Table and Judy's exploration of the messenger bag.

Someone wanted the messenger bag enough to kill for it. Why? Katherine pulled the car into a deserted rest area above the cold Puget Sound waves. Her eyes threatened to overflow tears. She blinked hard and wiped away her sadness. Reaching for the messenger bag, she dumped the contents onto the car seat. She firmly positioned the bag on her lap, determined to give it a thorough review. "Tell me your secret message. I want to hear it. I will find the killer."

She reached for the emergency case of car tools on the floor of the backseat, then searched Donna's bag from every angle and depth. She knew her crew could put the bag back to mint condition for Julia, so she tore the lining, broke apart straps, pulled apart pockets, ripped the zipper, and tore into the bottom. No false layer. Her efforts produced nothing.

She stared at the designer label, regretting her impulsive actions. She polished the metallic emblem with her sleeve. Loose after the intense search, it wobbled. A snap closure? Yes. Pulling on the top, it unsnapped and pulled forward revealing a pocket. Inside hid a USB drive. Katherine gasped with hope. She patted the top of the messenger, inserted the drive back into the secret pocket and snapped it shut.

She grabbed her phone. Monday and he would be busy at work. What if the drive reveals important information about NRML and his boss? She called Nicky.

"Hello?"

"Nicky? Katherine."

"Hi. I texted you about the laptop. So far nothing suspicious there." He sounded hesitant.

She dove in, almost breathless. "I've found another hidden drive. The one Donna texted about, I bet. Can I bring it to you at work."

The pause on the line teased Katherine's impatience. She kept her lips shut. A moment later Nicky's voice returned at a lower volume. "When can you bring it?"

"I'm about twenty minutes away."

"Text me when you're parked. I'll meet you at the reception desk."

"On my way. Thanks."

She clicked off and put Donna's things back into her bag. She patched things back well enough to be able to carry it. She needed to keep the bag safe in her grasp.

Her phone rang. "Hi, Anthony."

"You want to hear what I found out."

Katherine sat straighter. "You found something?"

"Donna's so-called great boss got fired from two other pharmaceutical companies before he created NRML Company. Those other companies secured the details, so I can't see what he did to get fired. I'm digging to find out more about him and his employees."

Sounds like Anthony's been talking with Rob. Katherine switched her phone to her other hand and put her key in the ignition. "I'm onto something myself. Can you come over tonight and compare notes? We may be ready to catch a killer."

"You bet."

Her car's engine roared as she pushed the speed limit. She had to park a bit of a walk from the door. She texted Nicky. She debated taking her umbrella. The sky threatened to open up with a deluge any time. She grabbed it. Katherine hauled her messenger bag with her into the NRML Company lobby.

Nicky leaned against the receptionist desk, talking with the security guard. "Hi, Katherine. If you show ID, Sam can give you a visitor's pass and we'll head upstairs."

"Thanks, Nicky." She showed the guard her driver license and pinned on the badge with the prominent word "Visitor".

Nicky gestured to the hall to her left. "Let's go to the elevators. Thanks, Sam."

The guard gave a brief wave and answered a beep on a screen display. At the elevator bank, Nicky pressed the up button.

"Thanks for meeting me, Nicky. I hope what I found answers some questions."

When one of the elevators arrived, Nicky pressed the button and held his NRML badge over the scanner. "The company officers are all on the top floor. I work on the third floor, same as Donna's office."

The doors opened to a large sign declaring the company name, and its CEO, Stephen Rider. They walked down the hallway, past the panel listing door numbers including the main test lab, sales office, and a conference center. Nicky led the way to a generic office door and opened it as Katherine waved the USB in the air about to hand it to him. Then they saw a surprise.

Katherine recognized Brittany right away. The heat rose in Katherine's cheeks as she visualized Brittany's name on her suspect whiteboard.

Nicky stopped abruptly as he took the USB. "Brittany. I didn't know you're here."

With a flip of her shoulder length teal hair, her stare intent on the messenger bag, she leaned forward in her chair. "Yes, I wanted to ask you about…" She paused. "Katherine, Nice to see you again. Funny to see you here at NRML. What's on the USB drive?"

Katherine gripped the messenger bag strap a little tighter. "I don't want to waste your time. I don't know the content. I thought Nicky could preview it and see if it has anything to do with NRML. I don't think it does."

Brittany walked around the desk and pointed at the computer keyboard. "Let's find out."

Nicky sat at the desk. "We don't have to do this now. Let me answer your question first, Brittany. Then you don't have to wait."

Brittany didn't move.

Katherine sighed as she placed the bag on the edge of the desk and leaned in for a better view. Names of several saved files popped up. "Well ladies, any preference where to start?" Brittany immediately pointed to one. Katherine took a deep breath as her stomach churned. She studied the text with an intensity reflecting the bright lights in the room. Nicky scrolled. No one said a word. They gave each file brought to the screen the same level of concentration. Katherine's level of understanding dropped when reading the technical data, test results, and industry language. There could be no misunderstanding about the file titled Drug Withdrawal Required. Its contents included a visual presentation and notes for a meeting dated the morning Donna went missing. Her intent could not be mistaken.

The visual remained on the screen as Katherine reached for the drive and quickly pulled it out. She replaced it in the label pocket.

Brittany put her hands on her hips. "NRML owns that information."

Katherine put the bag strap across her body. "No. Donna's family owns her personal property. This drive didn't come from her office."

Brittany pulled her hair back and focused on Katherine. "You're asking for a legal fight. I recommend you give it back now."

Nicky stood up. "I'll take you back to the reception desk."

Brittany stood in the way. "Stephen needs to see the data."

Katherine's every muscle tensed.

Nicky asked, "Should we go to his office?"

Brittany sighed. "With all that's gone on he's worked long hours. He left for a break, but he'll be back tonight."

"Katherine, can you let me make a copy?"

Her attention darted from Nicky to Brittany and back again. "No." She ran to the door, desperately hoping she would not be followed. She continued up the hallway and turned the corner for the elevators. She caught sight of both of them following her. She pushed the down button, and a door slid open answering her prayer. She rushed inside and pressed the close door button several times. Nicky slid inside, and the door closed on Brittany's angry expression.

Katherine pushed the lobby button. "We must treat Donna's personal file as evidence."

"You suspect Brittany?"

"We'll see."

He stared at the elevator doors. "She's loyal to the company. She won't let it go."

"I'll take my chances." As they reached the lobby, another elevator arrived behind them. Katherine rushed forward, pulling her visitor badge off. She wished she didn't have to leave in such a hurry. If only she could search more of the company.

Katherine and Nicky stepped up to the guard's desk. Nicky greeted him. The guard reluctantly interrupted a phone call. He spoke to Katherine and pointed to a slot built into the desk, "Return your badge in that slot."

The guard resumed the phone call. Katherine made a move with her badge toward the drop slot. She secretly pulled the hidden drive out and hid it with the visitor badge inside her closed umbrella.

Katherine felt reverberations of Brittany's words. "Stop her. She's stealing NRML property."

The guard abruptly ended his call. "Excuse me?"

Brittany continued, "Search her bag. I saw her put it in there."

Katherine shook her head. The guard turned to her. "I need to check your bag."

Katherine handed it over. Brittany smiled and pointed. "There. Pull that forward, and you'll find a drive that belongs to our company."

The guard followed her instructions, and in full view the pocket revealed nothing. Brittany gasped. "What?"

"There must be some mistake." The guard handed the bag back.

Katherine grabbed it with both hands and hurried toward the door. The guard raised his voice, "Excuse me, your badge please."

Katherine answered, "You told me to slide it in that slot."

He waved her on. "Thank you."

As he returned to the phone, Nicky unsuccessfully struggled to hide a smile. Brittany moved to follow Katherine. "Nick, stop her. Search her."

"That's above my pay grade."

Katherine wasted no time rushing to her car and driving home. She parked next to the other car in her driveway. Anthony had beaten her home. She saw him in the Clutch Café window. She took out the bag and carefully carried the umbrella.

She joined him. "Have you been here long?"

"No, but I'm impatient to hear your news."

"Let's go to my office." Katherine gave David a happy greeting.

Anthony grinned. "Thanks again for the snack."

David paused in wiping the counter. "May your evening bring you peace."

Anthony gave a thumbs up. "That would be great."

In her office, Katherine put the messenger bag on her desk and carefully removed the contents from inside her umbrella. "Thank goodness it rains so much here."

"What's that?"

Katherine held the drive between her thumb and forefinger and waved it back and forth. "My friend, let me show you some evidence. I have a story to tell you."

"I'm all ears."

"Let me give you a preview. That meeting Donna told you she had to go to would have been a revelation of flawed testing. She planned to demand a pre-market recall of the new drug about to splash on the market nationwide. The same drug the CEO announced at the press conference would be named after Donna, shows dangers in testing. The flawed drug Stephen Rider rushes to release now on the unsuspecting public, with Brittany's assistance, Donna wanted to prevent from release. It all smells of cover up."

"Corruption from the top then."

Katherine pulled out the suspect whiteboard. She crossed off Anthony's name first, then Kevin, then Tomás.

Anthony stepped closer. "About time you crossed off my name." He checked the board. "Three names left, Brittany, Stephen, and Cleo. They all connect to that company. So, work killed Donna."

"Her dedication to doing the right thing, and those who fought her, killed her."

Anthony frowned. "If only we could get inside that company on our own to investigate."

Katherine walked back to her desk and held up the visitor badge. "You busy tonight?"

Chapter Forty-Three

Anthony parked his car a block away from NRML Company. He and Katherine hurried to the doors of the high rise. Her hand shook as she pulled the coveted visitor pass out of the messenger bag's outside pocket. Katherine wanted to carry out whatever evidence they found tonight in Donna's bag, if the quick patch up job would hold together. Hugging the bag closer, she swiped the badge, and the door swung open. No guard at reception after hours. Perfect.

He followed her inside the ominous silence of the large lobby with the raised ceiling. As they rounded the corner, Anthony slid one hand along the top of the guard desk. "You know, a place like this late at night would make a great setting for the opening scene in my next book, quiet and shadowy at night."

"Not now Anthony. You can plot later." She proceeded to the elevators and pushed the button. "Let's split up. You search Donna's office. Check for anything helpful from Donna but especially check for anything suspicious from Brittany's office."

Anthony shrugged. "With her boss dead, Brittany may have moved into Donna's office."

Katherine's eyebrow instinctively rose. "As soon as you're done, come meet me in Stephen's office. I'll be going through everything there too. Divide and conquer and we'll cut down on our time in the building."

Anthony gave a thumbs up. "I've been to her office before, on the third floor."

Katherine thought logistics for a moment. "We'll use the badge in the elevator to hit the buttons to both floors. Then, you take the badge and use it to join me on the top floor." The doors opened and once inside Katherine held the badge up with one hand and crossed her fingers with the other. "Hope the elevator reads both floors." She gave a little victory cheer when it did and handed the badge to Anthony. "Good luck."

"You too. Be careful. I'll join you soon." His serious expression surprised her.

When he stepped out, she braced herself for the rest of the ride. "Donna if you sense me at all, know I investigate for you."

The sign on the wall pointed to Mr. Stephen Rider's office. She moved fast, with determined steps. She passed two executive offices with doors open. Roomy interiors and lavish, with banks of windows boasting a view spanning suburban lights, and a westward facing Puget Sound. Stephen's office loomed in the corner. She launched herself straight through the wide open doorway, stopped short, and gasped.

The desk loomed between them in a grand office. The wall behind him featured a painting of the company's prolific logo. It stood out as familiar to Katherine as her own signature. After all Donna and her family had endured, that framed icon of hope-filled hands offering a tray of pharmaceutical miracles disgusted her. No true regard for their customers. Donna and Randall murdered. What next for profit? Katherine couldn't hide her disgust for him.

A litany of framed credentials on the wall

showcased the impressive Mr. Stephen Rider, corporate professional. Not a single picture of family, no memento of non-work times, nothing human. In an attempt at bravado, Katherine placed the messenger bag deliberately on it. She squared her shoulders, planted her feet firmly in place, and stared him down. Interesting how he ignored the evidence right in front of him, no reaction to the bag at all. He is sly.

He turned off the computer screen with a sigh. "An after-hours surprise? How did you get in here? You want to talk again? I thought you'd had enough by now. I know I have. That's a warning to you." He displayed a brief smile. "Let's get it over with, and then I'll escort you out." He gestured at the luxurious leather couches in the center of the room. Next to them a cedar coffee table, decorated with fresh roses in the dead of winter.

Katherine stopped herself from demanding a confession and surrender. Smarter to wait for Anthony. How soon would he get here? She'd stall until then. Shouldering the messenger bag, head held high, she sat in the middle of the couch facing the door, so she would be the first to see Anthony when he arrived. She positioned the messenger bag on the coffee table, once again in full view of the CEO. Stephen sat across from her, still showing no interest in the bright red leather elephant she'd set in the middle of the room.

He squinted. "If I'd known you were coming I'd have had a reception, with the security guard."

The tapping of a finger on his leg annoyed her even more than his caustic tone. "One of your receptions ended Donna's life? And Professor Randall's?"

The tapping stopped. "You accuse me of murder? Ridiculous. How dare you."

He made a sudden move to stand, and Katherine froze. What defensive weapons stood within reach? The roses' vase? The heavy books on the shelves, if she could get there fast enough? He paced back to the desk. She glanced at the coffee maker, full and steaming. She could scald him. Or use the mace in the messenger bag. Scissors lay on the desk. He turned with a raging glare. She met that challenge.

He broke it off first, leaning against the side of the desk and admiring the view through the window. Katherine checked the door for Anthony. A shadow moved in the hall. She focused again, ignoring Stephen. Had the light played tricks on her? Then a hand movement on the side of the door, so brief and then gone. Why would Anthony wait? Her courage surged knowing her reinforcement had arrived.

Stephen spoke again. Did his voice tremble? "Two co-workers took their own lives. You think I don't feel guilty enough that I knew them, yet had no idea they could turn suicidal? If I could have stopped them… got them help. I'm tormented. I'm a doctor. I save lives."

Katherine frowned. He puts on some act. "I've investigated—"

"Yes, I'm not the only person you've annoyed."

Katherine cleared her throat. "I've uncovered some important evidence, and it points in one direction. Not suicide. I'm in pursuit of a killer."

Stephen sat on the couch again. He hovered over the coffee table with clenched fists. "I should throw you out of here right now."

Katherine shook her head. "You won't. You want to know what I've found. You're afraid of what I know."

"You won't get away with accusing me of murder."

His bulging brown eyes squinted, and his lips formed a firm, tight, straight line.

She quickly re-inventoried the possible weapons in the room and decided on the mace as her best bet. She put a hand on top of the messenger bag, ready to reach for the protection inside. "You haven't said a word about my bag. You've chased this bag all over the place. You shot at me to steal it because of the story it hides, the story you want buried."

He gave a loud sigh and sat back on the couch. "Two people are dead and you're begging for a fashion review? I'm in the business of saving lives, not accessorizing them. Why in the world would I chase a woman's purse?"

"Not the purse, what's in it. That's what you fear. It threatens you." Katherine heard a muffled sound in the hallway. Anthony remained out of sight.

Stephen groaned. "There's nothing in that handbag I remotely care about."

"You care about your company and the billions of dollars you'll make from a new miracle depression cure you're pushing to market. Nothing else. How ironic that you staged two depression suicides for the people who stood in your way."

"Lady, you're way off."

"Donna found flaws in the testing. You wanted the drug on the market. She stood determined to stop you. The professor corroborated her, and they planned to present their findings to the board and the press. You couldn't have that."

"There's no flaws in those tests. None of your business, but I'll tell you anyway. I worked through those findings with Donna's office. Brittany gave me a preliminary report."

"Worked with Donna's office? That's what you call murder? You had a problem though. You didn't get it from the professor, then you stole the wrong messenger bag when you wrestled it from Donna. You can't safely release your drug until you've destroyed that elusive USB drive and its incriminating findings."

He laughed. "You have no evidence of any of this drivel."

"Plenty of evidence. A witness identified you at the professor's office the night he died. You didn't know that did you?"

"I went there to discuss the testing. Full of assurances he agreed with Donna and planned to attend her presentation, he rushed me out, said his date would be arriving any minute and he had a fun evening ahead. He stood very much alive when I left."

"You didn't talk with Donna about her recommendations."

"I'd already talked with Brittany, Donna's assistant."

Frustration set in, Katherine took a shot in the dark. "You showed up at Donna's favorite weekday coffee stop Tuesday morning."

"She suggested I meet her."

Rewarded, Katherine pressed on. "After you talked, you followed her, didn't you?"

"You're wrong. I drove there late and missed her. I went on to the office. She never made it to work, as you know."

"No. You followed her and killed her when she didn't give you what you wanted. She fought you hard on that trail, didn't she? She hadn't agreed to your terms, and you refused to leave it at that. She didn't give you the drive with her presentation on it. You didn't want to let her go. You killed her."

"You're off track. I didn't fight Donna. I missed seeing her that day, so I went to the office. There's nothing wrong with the drug. It will help people. I'd never launch a truly flawed drug into the marketplace."

Katherine ignored that feeble protest. "In your business how easily can you get fentanyl to poison the professor? How could you stand to watch your victims fight for their last breaths?

"Each of them committed suicide, alone. Let them rest in peace."

A sudden movement at the door brought Katherine a wave of relief, then an ominous chill. What delayed him? Come on, Anthony.

The voice oozed tension as the athletic woman crossed the threshold. "I come here to check you're not making love to that teal haired thing. Instead, this one dances around you." The intruder cackled, as she shut the door and approached her husband. She kissed him on the lips and pointed at Katherine. "You nosy busybody. No use pretending any longer. You'll never let it rest. You're right, Katherine, nothing personal. I only did the necessary. Sometimes that means murder."

Katherine gasped. They did it together.

In a slow, subtle movement, Cleo took her hand out of her coat pocket and held it low, close to her hip.

Katherine sat trapped, outnumbered, and out gunned.

Chapter Forty-Four

Stephen turned to her. "Cleo, what are you doing?"

"I heard everything." Her voice softened. "Don't worry, I'll stop her now." He took a step back.

Cleo's diamond earrings sparkled in the office light as she turned back to Katherine. She laid her black velvet clutch with the jade clasp on the back of the couch. With her free hand, she undid the top button on her fitted, plaid, full length coat "You should have left it alone. You're up against a force you'll never defeat. Meet your dead end."

Her stomach twisted with a sick ache. "Cleo, you're not responsible for what your husband did. You don't need to cover up for him. Do what's right. Help me turn him in."

"What he did? Him? Design brilliant crimes like this? The police couldn't even figure it out." She reached over and rubbed the back of her hand along her husband's cheek. "Dear Stephen. He has no understanding of our situation. He would have caved to an insolent staffer who refused to endorse the new product. We would have lost millions. I had to save Stephen from himself. We didn't grow accustomed to our glorious lifestyle to have it denied by two jealous losers."

Katherine wondered if she could keep them talking long enough for Anthony to get here. If only she could get to her phone and click on 911. Too bad she forgot her e-watch. Could she get to her mace in the pocket under the messenger bag flap?

She slowly leaned forward and put her hands palm down on the table, right next to the bag. "You? How did you make it all happen?"

Stephen broke in. "Cleo, my dear. What are you saying? You couldn't kill."

She never took her eyes off Katherine as she answered him, "I'd do anything for us, for our life together. I did it for you, your reputation, and the amazing company you built. I did it well, didn't I? Even you didn't know. You still wouldn't know, except for her."

His tensed jaw, tearing eyes, slumped shoulders, frozen stance. He stood in shock. Katherine stared. Stephen hadn't attacked Donna or Professor Randall, but would he act now to defend his wife?

Katherine confronted the killer. "You fooled almost everybody. How did you even know about the professor's involvement in the test results? You don't work here."

She motioned to indicate the office. "He doesn't work only here. He works at home. He takes calls. He has files there, and a laptop. I hear him on the phone all the time. I can easily see who he spoke with and the messages they leave. I can put two and two together." She kept the gun poised. "That woman-crazy, egotistical professor, such an easy person to fool. He'd never seen me with Stephen. I met him as a stranger. A little flattery along with my proclaimed adoration went a long way to get what I wanted."

Her husband shook his head. "You had an affair?

You killed him?" He stood unsteady.

"I came on to him, for you. I did it all to save our life together. We stayed together such a short time and never seen with each other in public. Very clandestine. He liked the secrecy, and I needed it."

Stephen staggered another step back. "No. Not again. After what you did in Boston to break that patent, you promised you'd stay out of my business. You promised no more violence."

Cleo sighed. "Don't you see? You needed help with NRML. I'm not letting you mess that up. I stayed out of your Brittany business. Nathan Randall, he's nothing, a means to an end. He wanted to play. He didn't want to talk work, especially about the consultant job. I manipulated him. I told him he could make millions if he signed off on the test." She shook her head. "Stubborn man, he wouldn't agree."

Stephen stammered, "You didn't do this. We had the new year's party, you and me."

"I told you I had a late hair appointment." She sneered at Katherine. "Such an easy excuse for a husband who's preoccupied. Remember how I met you at the party? As far as Nathan Randall thought, I'm his date for a hot night. Instead, I left early, and he dropped dead."

Katherine inched her hand closer to the back side of the messenger bag flap. How quickly could she reach into that front pocket underneath? Faster than Cleo's speeding bullet? Katherine leaned further forward, keeping full eye contact with Cleo. "You went to the professor's office?"

"I offered him one last chance to endorse the test results. I'm a reasonable person, but he had to agree before the presentation meeting. He wouldn't agree."

She pouted at her husband, and Katherine felt sweat down her spine as the gun barrel remained fixed between her eyes. "Darling Stephen, I never betrayed you. I had to get rid of Randall so I could edit the write up he did and change it to endorse the drug test."

Stephen groaned. "No."

"He kept everything on his phone, and the idiot kept all his passwords in a little book. I could access anything, but I couldn't find that phone. I searched all over the office after I left him on that hill to die. I planned to search his home, but Brittany came through and endorsed the testing, so I didn't have to."

Stephen shook his head. "Brittany conspired with you?"

Cleo re-focused on Katherine. "Donna didn't trust the cloud, and some of the people who would have access. She planned a surprise attack at that presentation, I found out from the professor. She hid her research on an old time drive. Clever woman to avoid someone hacking into it elsewhere. Once I took care of lover boy, I knew I had to find it, and I knew what I had to do next."

No sound at the door. Katherine turned that way in desperation. If only she'd kept her phone in her hand recording what they said, in case she never got out alive. She must get out alive.

Cleo laughed. "No one's coming to save you. I've got all my bases covered."

Katherine's hands trembled. Stop. Think positive. Keep talking. "So, you went to see the professor that night?"

"I hoped for plan A, but stood ready for plan B. I gave him the sexy date he'd been hoping for, but no happy ending for him. The wine I brought to share in the car by the beach packed a fentanyl punch."

Katherine urged her on. "And you murdered Donna too."

"She refused to give me the USB. I knew she had to have it with her that morning at the transit center. Then my lucky break. She slipped in the ice and broke something in her foot. She screamed in pain. She couldn't walk or stand. I grabbed her arm and dragged her in the bushes. She screamed for help."

Stephen gasped and leaned against the desk.

She patted his hand as if to reassure him, while never compromising her vigilant watch over Katherine. "No worries, darling. I came prepared. I slipped the plastic bag over her head. The tape wound secure around her neck. I pushed her face into the wet ground."

Stephen crouched over with hands on his knees. "I feel sick."

"I make sacrifices for us, Stephen. Donna fooled me though. I tore into that briefcase purse she carried, but only found kid's stuff, schoolbooks. People on the trail worried me. I had to get away before light. I ran to the truck for a tarp, climbed back and slid her onto it so I could drag her down and onto the truck. I returned that night for what I'd left behind." She shook the gun at Katherine. "Then you got in my way. You won't stay in my way."

Katherine flinched but held her ground. "You made up the rumors of a love affair between Donna and the professor. They worked together. The affair gossip spread because of you. Admit it."

"I may have suggested it. You know how people talk. I encouraged conversations. I may have manufactured clues here and there for the police to discover."

Katherine made a move to pull out the mace. The bag fell over. She stood and pulled it by the strap away from Cleo and into her arms. The harsh shriek terrified her, "Drop that bag." Katherine hugged it tight.

The gun aimed at her heart. It shook in Cleo's hands. One pull of that trigger and deadly results. She had to summon her courage for what could be her last chance.

Stephen groaned between gasps of breath, "No Cleo, stop."

Katherine kept the bag tight against her. "Your hand shakes, Cleo. You don't want to shoot me. You need me."

"Need you? No. I need that bag."

"You want Donna's drive. You broke into Tomás' house didn't you, thinking you'd find it there? You found a dear, scared pet doggy and nothing more, but you left a mess, didn't you?"

"All that trouble to find out you had it all along. You're a pest and need to be exterminated."

"You saw Julia give it to me so, you came back to steal it. You shot at me then." Katherine raised her voice louder. "You wanted to kill me then."

Cleo took a step forward, then another, and the gun barrel drew too close. "Yes. So, you know I'm serious. If Donna had given it to me, she'd be alive today. Learn from that."

"If I give it to you, I walk out of here? You won't kill me?"

Cleo squinted. "Not like I killed her. You deserve a little time away. You'll spend the weekend alone in the walk-in freezer down the hall. How does forty below sound? A wintry retreat with a dead end."

Katherine studied the table. Break the vase? Bring a jagged glass edge to a gun fight?

"Someone will find you Monday. We'll mourn the idiot who couldn't let go of a mystery that didn't exist. Won't we Stephen?" Cleo laughed. "Then we'll spend our millions."

Katherine's response muted when Cleo shouted, "The bag, or I shoot. I don't care how you die."

Stephen rushed forward and shoved Katherine. Two loud bangs. Katherine hit the floor on her side, next to the messenger bag.

Chapter Forty-Five

Every muscle in her body tensed. Cleo stepped closer. Lying flat out on the floor, Katherine reached slowly, imperceptibly for the handle on the tipped over messenger bag.

The killer's attention zeroed in on her husband's body. "Stephen. No."

An escape leaped to mind, and Katherine moved. She had to get past Cleo. With a tight grip on Donna's bag, she focused on the door.

"No, you don't" The gun stabbed into her stomach as Cleo slammed her against the wall. Running back to Stephen, Cleo's agitation grew exponentially. She swayed side to side over her husband's bloody body. She stared at Katherine and spewed hatred. "You killed my husband, all I had, all my future."

Without a word, Katherine swung Donna's bag with all her strength, knocking the gun into the air and skidding under the desk. Cleo gasped. She stumbled over her husband's body, as she ran after her loaded gun barrel of leverage. Wasting no time, Katherine raced after her and swung her bag with both hands in a mighty blow to the head. Cleo stumbled, then fell hitting her forehead on the edge of the desk on her senseless way down to the floor.

Cautious, Katherine circled around Cleo, wary of any conscious motion. Her chest barely moved with each breath. Poised with bag in hand ready to strike again, Katherine moved into position between where the gun slid and where the killer lay. "I speak softly and carry a big bag. Don't underestimate me."

The door behind her clicked and flew open. Anthony, finally. Relief washed through her like a cleansing breath. She turned, then stood stunned. "You."

He burst into the room, weapon raised, sweeping the space with sharp and practiced movements, scanning corners and shadows too for any danger. Satisfied, he holstered the gun. "Apparently you've wrapped the case." He grinned briefly.

"Jason?"

"I've been tracking Cleo. Stand back Katherine, please." As Katherine stepped aside, he moved toward the unconscious killer.

"Jason, I hit her with the bag in self-defense." She pointed to the desk. "Her gun slid under there. I had to stop her. The CEO, she shot her own husband." She pointed over the couch, in Stephen's direction.

Jason frowned. He rushed over to Stephen and checked for pulse, then clicked his radio with a request for immediate paramedics and back up.

Katherine stammered, "He's dead, isn't he?"

Jason shook his head, and Stephen groaned as he moved. "I'm not dead."

Jason applied a handkerchief to the wound. "Stay still. I called an ambulance."

Stephen lay still on the floor, facing Cleo. A tear rolled across his cheek. "Katherine, you'll give me that drive." He groaned again. "If the drug is truly flawed, I won't launch it to market."

Katherine leaned against the desk as the shock of it

all hit, and her knees went weak. "I came here to confront him. Then she came in, and I thought they schemed together. No. She did it all herself. She admitted it."

Jason tended to Stephen and then Cleo. Her words tumbled at a runaway pace as one thought immediately after the next exploded with its own message, "Jason, she's the killer. The drug test results threatened her. She wanted to stop the professor so she seduced him and when he wouldn't help her, she killed him. He wouldn't discredit Donna's test results. Then Donna wouldn't change her report, so Cleo attacked her. A new drug on the market making the company money sacrificed lives. If it had made it to store shelves, more lives would have been lost. That will stop now." Katherine had the documentation that would stop all sales.

Paramedics rushed in, and Jason directed them first to Stephen. As he stepped away to let them work, Jason's gray shirt registered with Katherine for the first time. "Where's your uniform? That's a NRML employee badge. You work here now?" She gently brushed her hand over a prominent security patch sewn to the sleeve.

"I'm moonlighting, but tonight I'm handing in my notice." He sighed.

"You left Bayside's police?"

"No, I'm quitting NRML. These closed cases needed more investigation. A security gig put me where I needed to be to follow the evidence. Tonight, that's over."

"I never knew. I thought you worked overtime shifts for the department, including working against my sons. It felt like you'd turned against us."

"Better for you not to know during my investigation. Remember your New Year's saying? When something goes wrong, everyone says someone else should do something. I'm someone, so I did something."

Jason knelt and checked Cleo's pulse. Cleo moved her arm along the floor and moaned. Jason kept an eye on her, although she made no attempt to get on her feet.

Concerned Cleo might reach for the gun, Katherine grabbed the pen on the desk, dropped to her knees, reached underneath and pulled the gun out with the pen.

When she stood up and dangled the gun from the pen to show Jason, he reached for an evidence bag. "I'm betting the same caliber as the bullet in your desk."

A voice boomed behind him, "Drop it. Hands up."

Wide eyed, Katherine slowly placed the gun on the desk and raised her trembling hands. The red faced police chief stood with gun drawn.

Jason stepped into the chief's aim of fire. "I've secured the scene, sir. The shooter lies on the floor. Katherine retrieved the weapon from under the desk."

The chief holstered his weapon and sneered, "If civilians are waving weapons around, then you haven't secured the scene. Good thing I heard the call and got down here fast." He pointed to Cleo. "She's injured?"

Katherine lowered her arms. "Yes." The chief glared as if daring her to continue, so she did. "I hit her with the messenger bag."

Jason smothered a laugh. The chief pointed. "That? What have you got in it?"

Katherine put her hands on her hips. "Remember that case you closed? I'm holding Donna Ruiz's handbag, and it knocked out her killer." She pointed at Cleo. "If you'd bothered to investigate, you'd know this greedy woman killed for money. She killed Donna and Professor Randall. Her greed would have killed who knows how many innocent people with a poisonous drug on the market."

Sirens sounded close. Cleo's groan underscored that soundtrack.

The chief confronted Jason, "What are you doing out of uniform?"

Jason's cheeks flushed red. "I've gathered evidence against Cleo. I expected her here tonight. I monitored the security cameras. When I viewed the stream for this office the three of them stood involved in a deadly face off. I rushed to get here, but the elevator never came. I switched to run up the stairs, and that's when I heard shots."

The chief addressed Jason formally. "You openly defied my orders. When you met with me about opening the case again, I told you the evidence did not warrant it."

Jason straightened and squared his shoulders. "I have the evidence now, on camera and video, ready for your review."

Katherine cocked her head sideways. "Recorded?"

"Security has cameras and audio set up in the office here, and all over the labs."

Katherine smiled. "Cleo's full confession got recorded."

Another set of paramedics rushed in. Jason directed them to Cleo and motioned to Katherine. "Let's give them room."

The chief ignored Katherine as she passed, but he stopped Jason. "Your actions will have consequences. There's a chain of command and the importance of orders…"

A familiar voice came from the doorway. "It pays to

be on the police alert band."

"Rob." Katherine backed up to stay out of the camera shot.

The chief muttered to Jason, "We'll finish our discussion first thing in the morning. I want your report on my desk and you in my office. That's an order you will follow."

"How dare you." Katherine's indignant gasp registered no reaction from the chief.

Turning to the door with a professional poker face, the chief cozied to Rob's camera. "I see the news has arrived. The public will be relieved to hear the Bayside Police have stopped a threat. No pictures as we secure the crime scene. I'll give you an official, statement outside."

"An exclusive?" Rob eagerly scanned the room. Over his shoulder he said, "Katherine, don't leave the building until you talk with me."

Katherine smiled. "Only if I'm an anonymous source."

Rob grinned. "You'll want your name on our Pulitzer interview."

Katherine gave a heavy sigh as they left. "Jason, can the chief make trouble for you at work?"

"I'll face him for the actions I took."

"He's wrong." Katherine picked up the messenger bag.

Two officers rushed into the room. Jason held up a hand to them. "I'll be back after I walk this witness out." He glanced at the bag, and Katherine tightened her grip on the strap. He turned back to the officers. "You can take pictures and secure evidence, including that gun on the desk."

He put an arm lightly on Katherine's back and guided her into the hall. "You know that bag is evidence."

"I'll hand it to you only, and I need it back. Julia trusted me to keep it for her."

Jason held a hand out. "I'll see that you get it back." She handed it to him.

He pointed at the sign. "Let's see if the elevator's working now."

Jason pressed the down button while Katherine fidgeted. "Still broken?"

Jason stared with intense interest at the closed doors. "Did you hear something? I thought I heard someone."

"I didn't." She pointed to two more officers approaching from the stairs. "You could have heard them."

Jason motioned. "You'll find them a couple more doors down the hall, that office on the right."

One of them answered. "Thanks. You'll have to take the stairs."

Katherine asked, "Why?"

"Someone cut the elevator power. Phones too. Deliberate. Some guy got stuck in there. Hey, are you Katherine? He yelled he's meeting up with someone named Katherine."

Her cheeks burned. "Anthony! I've been waiting for him." She stared at the closed doors. "I bet Cleo did it, to stop him."

A voice rose through the shaft, "Katherine? Can you hear me?"

Another voice answered in an official tone, "We should have you out soon, sir."

Jason chuckled under his breath. He leaned toward

her, showing off dancing brown eyes and signature rogue grin. He kissed her. "Let's take the stairs."

Chapter Forty-Six

The intermittent sunshine of partly cloudy skies felt warm on Katherine's shoulder as she leaned into the gift shop's display window. She straightened the colorful tie-dye cinch bag, one of the many icons of the 1960's decade Purse-onality Museum featured. She tugged on the hem of her mini skirt. She picked up her iconic purse from the decade, a leather tube with two small handles. She thought of her vegan designs and relished being part of fashion's evolution.

MJ's proclaimed month of love, February brought optimism and finally the new exhibit's grand opening and celebration. Katherine strolled through the museum for a final check before guests arrived. Sandy had arrived early in the kitchen with a tantalizing variety of bakery delights and got to work organizing her buffet.

Delectable scents drifted from the Clutch Cafe, as she approached the murmurs and laughter. The party had begun. She paused in the hall with Purrada, who stopped licking her paw with a loud meow. She lifted her pet into a hug. "Good morning, Purr. You may want to find yourself a hiding place. I'm not sure you'll find happiness at a hippie love-in." The unsuspecting cat purred and settled in Katherine's arms. David's cheerful voice drifted out of the Clutch. In a short time, he'd created a caring place for himself in the Bayside community and in her family. She'd come to enjoy his spirit.

He stood behind the bar. Small groups of friends faced him. Everyone held their barista blends high in the air. The Ladies of the Round Table joined in while seated at their usual table. He spoke in a deep, gentle voice, "Understanding, friendship, and love grow where our paths cross." Everyone cheered and sipped their drinks.

As Katherine walked in, Purrada saw the crowd and scrambled to be put down. She darted away. Katherine gave her grandmother a hug and smiled to the rest of the ladies. "You're setting the right mood, David." She scanned the room for an important, missing person. "Where's MJ?"

"She's on the patio doing final set up for our band. Our live music will revive the spirit and feed the imagination."

"And blow your mind." MJ appeared in the room followed by a gasp from the group, and then applause and cheers.

Katherine mocked her. "Who are you?"

Moonjava replied, "You don't recognize your own mother?"

"Oh no." Katherine laughed and shook her head. "I don't believe I'm related to a being in a tie-dyed t-shirt, denim jeans that swell out at the bottom so wide you barely fit through the door, long hair hanging dyed every color in the world and some colors from another universe, and what's that shoulder bag slung across your body with fringe hanging past your knees."

MJ posed sideways with one arm up and palm against her hair, and hip turned out to display the full bell bottom flare. The other hand slid down the strap of the purse. "Go with the flow mini skirt mama. We're all family."

Pam held up her right hand with a peace sign. "Peace. Time to party." The three generations of women hugged each other. More people arrived and mingled. Anthony happily accepted Peggy's invitation to join their table.

He sat between Peggy and Margaret who eagerly asked, "How goes your thriller? How much longer until you finish it?"

"I'm working on a new scene where the hero climbs up the shaft of an elevator…" He smiled and winked at Katherine, who happily welcomed back that signature sense of humor. Amber walked in with Tomás and Julia, so Katherine excused herself and hurried over.

"You won't believe who I ran into." Amber smiled.

Katherine gave Julia a hug. "Wonderful. I'm sorry I haven't stopped by to see you, with all the last minute work for the party." She stooped down to pet the dog.

Tomás put an arm gently across Julia's shoulders, with his other hand on Perro's leash. His slacks and polo shirt completed a relaxed attitude. "We're moving forward. Julia went back to classes, and I'm back at work. The pain remains sharp, but staying busy works as good medicine."

Katherine stood up again. "I respect that prescription from you, doctor." She spoke to Julia. "Your mother watches over you with great pride. She loved you so much."

Julia stood fresh and young in her light blue leggings and high school sweatshirt. "I talk to her every night, and I'm writing a song for her. She's in my heart, like you told me."

"I'm so glad you came today."

"I couldn't make up my mind, but Moonjava… when she talked with me…so nice. She had an idea …I brought my guitar." She tapped her hand on the top of the case next to her.

"I don't know what you and MJ have dreamed up, but it sounds intriguing. Tomás, will you excuse us for a minute? I have something for Julia. Please help yourself to a drink."

Tomás picked up the case. "I'll put your guitar behind the bar, honey."

Katherine guided Julia to the door. As they reached the hall, Katherine saw Tomás standing and talking to Anthony at the ladies' table. Anthony stood and faced Tomás. The move put Perro on alert, but he quickly calmed as the two men solemnly shook hands. Peace, love, and caring launched Katherine and Julia down the hall to her office.

On the design table sat Donna's refurbished messenger bag. The Beverly Hills team had skillfully restored the bag to its original style and condition. Julia never needed to know what her bag had gone through to find evidence. She told Julia how Donna's bag had given her the test report that now saved an untold number of lives, and how Donna's bag had delivered the killer's knockout blow.

The girl slowly stepped forward and rested a hand on the messenger. "When we unwrapped matching bags for Christmas I thought, how lame. Now I'll treasure it always. My mom had courage. Can I leave it here until after the party? Then I want to take it home."

Katherine nodded. "Of course. I wish we'd been able to recover your bag. Cleo isn't talking at all now that she's in jail awaiting trial. Someday we might find out what she did with it. Your mother's bag will always be special for you. Now, let's go join the party."

For those who dared to face the elements of Bayside before official spring, the portable heaters aided the sun to make the covered patio pleasant. Jackets also helped. Most of the crowd milled through the museum, Sandy's buffet, and the Clutch Cafe.

Rob took pictures and video for the news. He'd interviewed her with MJ that morning. They talked about the new exhibit and the women of the decade, their lives, struggles and dreams, all represented by their purses. She'd watch the online news tonight.

Rob's article may not win a prize, but it brilliantly described Cleo's arrest and the compelling accusations against her. Katherine had also commended Rob for the implied questions raised about the police chief's actions. The viability of NRML as a company remained in question. Although it appeared Stephen knew nothing about the crimes or the flaws in the tests, the company's credibility reeled, and stock prices had plummeted. Employees applied for other jobs. She'd heard Brittany still hoped for a promotion, but not at NRML. The police might have a place for her, one she wouldn't like, as they continued their investigation into whether she covered up the drug test results when she recommended moving the drug forward for market release.

MJ and David left the bar to Sandy's staff and ventured outside to the makeshift stage where they tuned up. Katherine thanked Sandy and headed to the shop. She signaled Amber at the busy cash register. They'd agreed to close the shop to encourage guests to enjoy the main show, and so Amber could too.

"Wow, you put on a great event, Katherine. And

what a sale." Cynthia beamed as she held up two big customer bags filled with merchandise.

"I'm so glad you could come celebrate."

"Fabulous goodies, delish food, and can't wait for the music. I walked through the new exhibit too. Nice job."

Katherine blushed. "MJ put her heart and soul into that room."

"You both did a fabulous job."

When Kevin arrived, Julia suddenly appeared and in great excitement pulled him toward the outside patio.

Cynthia's young son tugged on her skirt. "Mommy, I want to see the show."

Katherine agreed. "You don't want to miss that."

Cynthia juggled her packages. "Lead the way."

They moved out of the gift shop. Purrada surprised her by peeking out from under the floor length curtain. The last place she'd expected to find her shy cat would be the gift shop.

Charlene stepped past the cat. "You've done it again, my friend." She put her purse on the floor and hugged Katherine. Purrada and the purse dog stared at each other with mutual disdain.

"I'm glad you're enjoying yourself, Charlene."

"A great party, but also I read Rob's exciting article about catching Cleo Rider. You solved the case. Thank goodness I could provide you that critical evidence on the new year's hair appointment. I'm glad to help."

Katherine laughed, happy to share the victory. Purse dog leaped out of the bag and chased after a fleeing and hissing Purrada.

"Oh no, Dolly, come back." Charlene rushed after them.

Katherine received congratulations and happy thoughts from more friends, as she made her way to the counter. "Amber, are you ready?"

She smiled. "Go ahead. I'll be right there."

Charlene caught Dolly on the stairs and sat there now consoling her and offering treats. Katherine sympathized, "Purrada's tough to catch. Come join us outside for music." Charlene packed the pup back in the purse and followed.

The sounds from MJ, David, and their friends grooved through the museum, a tribute to the grand opening of the 1960's exhibit. Katherine stepped onto the patio. MJ played guitar, David on drums, a couple of their friends played keyboard and saxophone. Nostalgia and curiosity blended generations of guests into a magical party. The rhythms lightened hearts. The band played song after song, giving life again to the power of a decade. The love and peace of the folk music blossomed from songs with a resounding beat of rock, intermixed with a sprinkling of jazz.

Purrada stared down from the bedroom window. A drone buzzed overhead. A quick glance across the patio revealed Nicky, intent on the controller. The crew from All Man's Land had arrived. Katherine ran over and gave her sons hugs. "Did you see the purses in the new exhibit?"

Will held up a steaming mug. "We saw the drinks."

Christopher held up a loaded plate. "And the buffet."

Everyone laughed. Amber joined Michael, and they danced. Their motion became contagious as others joined in, and the patio became a dance floor. Next to the raised platform for the musicians stood Julia holding hands with Kevin. Her father walked up to them, and Katherine steeled herself, wondering if she'd need to break up a confrontation. Tomás stood directly in front of Kevin. He held out a hand, as he had with Anthony. He said something, Kevin hesitated, then shook hands with Tomás. Julia pulled them both toward her into a trio hug.

To Katherine's delight, Jason walked her way, one hand gripping leashes on both dogs and in the other hand a bouquet of gorgeous, deep red flowers. Her heart skipped a beat or two. She didn't recognize the long stemmed beauties, but she gasped at their intensity. Jason appeared relaxed and casual in jeans and a zipped up leather jacket. The dogs trudged along, tired. They approached the back of the band stand.

Katherine hurried over and they stood out of sight from the party crowd. "You made it."

Hobbs greeted her with a rub against her leg, and she scratched the favorite spot behind his ear. "The dogs had a game of fetch on the beach." Jason reached out a hand, "These are for you."

A delicate scent of citrus and clover delighted Katherine as she took the bouquet in both hands. "Oh Jason, they're beautiful. I'm speechless."

He laughed. "That's unusual."

She peered at him over the flowers and laughed. "What a beautiful gift for the celebration."

His voice softened, "Katherine, when I saw these vibrant ranunculus flowers, I saw your charm and radiant love." He paused. "Our complex relationship brings depth like the layers of petals on each of these flowers. The fire of their red reflects the passion in my heart to rekindle our romance." In an instant they embraced.

They held each other so tight Katherine felt breathless.

The dogs paced and the leashes tangled around the couple's legs. Jason rescued them and Katherine pulled his free hand. "Come on. Come enjoy the party." They walked hand-in-hand to the edge of the crowd. Jason commanded the dogs to sit. They both obeyed, but Hobbs stared at Katherine intently and panted with enthusiasm, tongue hanging out. He gave a couple of barks in competition to the music. Robby joined in.

Katherine held up her hand. "Wait a minute." She ran into the kitchen and put Jason's beautiful flowers in water, then put them on her studio desk. She raided the doggie cabinet and brought back a dog cookie shaped like a bone for each of her delighted canine guests. Jason grinned. She sneaked up to the side of the stage where Perro lay next to Tomás and gave him a dog treat too. When she turned and walked back, Hobbs watched her every move. At Jason's side, he took her hand, and they swayed to the music while the dogs crunched their treats.

MJ broke into a big grin. She strummed with fervent energy. The audience clapped to the beat, as they danced and swayed. At the end of the song, David and MJ exchanged a few sweet notes just between the two of them, no doubt a shared melody of a distant memory. He signaled to the band to take a bow. The applause continued, and they smiled and waved.

MJ invited Julia on stage. David handed her guitar over as MJ introduced her to the audience. "Julia Ruiz will now join us for a special folk song she wrote."

Julia stood beside MJ and announced to the party. "I dedicate my performance to my mother and my dad." Tomás beamed.

Katherine's heart warmed at the sweet tones of the

song, and Julia's peaceful expression. When the song ended everyone burst into applause. Julia bowed as she brushed away a tear.

Moonjava stepped forward. "Thank you everyone. In my meditation today I visualize each person as a unique note in a groovy concert. You're each contributing your own special melody to the collective song of life. Harmony arises not from uniformity but from the blending of our diverse voices and talents for something beautiful." The crowd cheered.

Moonjava strummed her guitar. "Here's a song we can sing together…"

Katherine took Jason's hand and led him, and the dogs to her studio and closed the door. Jason dropped the leashes, and the dogs walked to the snack cupboard, lay down on the floor, and stared at it. Katherine fed each dog one more treat, as Jason sighed.

She walked back to him, and they wrapped their arms around each other. The sunshine through the bay window lingered on the floral arrangement on her desk. The pretty citrus scent sweetened the moment. Katherine drew in a deep breath and sighed. "Alone at last."

"Right. You, me, and a hundred or more people right outside the door."

Katherine massaged her hands up and down his back. "So tense. Try to relax. Any better with the chief today?"

He sighed. "No, but I can handle it. I'll figure out how to fix it. You know, I can't depend on someone else. I'm someone."

Katherine smiled and leaned the side of her face against his thick shoulder. "You shouldn't have to. That man puts lives at risk. People did not elect him to put them in danger. Then he twists everything to make it sound like he spearheaded the undercover work. I'll campaign against his re-election."

The warmth of Jason's embrace deepened, enveloping her. "I wanted to tell you about the undercover, but I couldn't. That night she shot at you, I saw my worst nightmare."

She kissed him. "That's all over."

He suddenly held her away from him and spoke urgently, "I don't ever want you to be in danger again. Promise me your crime solving days are done."

Katherine slipped one hand behind her back in a pose she hoped looked sultry. "I'm a designer, not an investigator." With her other hand, she picked up the latest design for her new line. "I promise. Cross my body…"

He gently pulled her hand from behind her back and revealed her crossed fingers. "I suspect you meant to say ask me no questions, and I'll tell you no lies." They both laughed.

His tender touch warmed her heart. She dropped the crossbody bag. He moved toward her with deep passion and longing. They wrapped themselves around each other. She felt so close to him, from the stubble of the beard against her cheek, to the beat of his heart and the depth of his soul. Faint rhythms from the patio music swelled as one of the dogs breathed a heavy sigh. Katherine massaged Jason's back in rhythm to the music's beat. With one arm holding her tight against him, Jason rubbed a hand against the base of her spine and moved infused with longing all the way up her back. He held her tight, pressed against her. They kissed like their lives depended on it. Long, luxurious, breathless, and with an intensity that raised their temperatures and heated the room. Katherine melted into the moment.

Case closed.

A word about the author…

The result of Wendy Kendall's passion for purses, mystery and romance is the intriguing In Purse-Suit Mysteries Series. Kat Out of the Bag introduced Katherine Watson purse designer/sleuth. As Katherine moves from designer bags to body bags, she's uncovering clues to murder.

Wendy enjoys investigating the Pacific Northwest life, and she leaves a trail of her own clues as a blogger, YouTube podcaster, speaker, project manager, and syndicated columnist. Find out more about the author and her books at her website - WendyWritesBooks.com